"Are you listening, Will?"

"I'm listening." The porch swing beside Tessa wobbled with the weight of someone settling into the seat, and a chill breeze swept over her. In spite of the summer heat, she shivered. She was never going to get used to that—the way Will was so cold all the time. Of course, the whole situation wasn't really the sort of thing anyone ever got used to, was it? What woman expected her husband to die and come back as a ghost?

"I don't want another husband . . . I just need someone useful. Someone who knows about horses and doesn't drink too much. Someone young enough to be strong . . . but not too handsome."

"Why not handsome?" Will sounded surprised.

She shifted in the swing. If only she could *see* Will. He had been a handsome man, and he'd stolen her heart so easily. Better not take any chances. "I don't want talk in town," she said.

"They're gonna talk no matter what." The swing shook as it emptied of his weight. *"You just leave everything to me. . . ."*

A WILLING SPIRIT

CYNTHIA STERLING

JOVE BOOKS, NEW YORK

HAUNTING HEARTS is a registered trademark of Penguin Putnam Inc.

A WILLING SPIRIT

A Jove Book / published by arrangement
with the author

PRINTING HISTORY
Jove edition / July 1999

The Penguin Putnam Inc. World Wide Web site address is
http://www.penguinputnam.com

ISBN: 0-515-12530-X

A JOVE BOOK®
Jove Books are published by The Berkley Publishing Group,
a division of Penguin Putnam Inc.,
375 Hudson Street, New York, New York 10014.
JOVE and the "J" design
are trademarks belonging to Penguin Putnam Inc.

PRINTED IN THE UNITED STATES OF AMERICA

10 9 8 7 6 5 4 3 2 1

For Julie
Thanks for being the kind of friend every writer needs.

A WILLING SPIRIT

Chapter One

TEXAS, 1855

The dried peas rattled in the crockery bowl with a sound like hail on a tin roof. Tessa Bright frowned, thinking of the holes that needed patching in her own shelter and the hundred other chores that were more than one woman alone could see to, especially a woman with one arm in a cast. She balanced the bowl awkwardly on her knees and began sorting through the peas for rocks and dirt. "If you really want to help me out, Will, could you see about finding me a hired man?" She raised her head and addressed the empty air. "Are you listening, Will?"

"I'm listening." The porch swing beside her wobbled with the weight of someone settling into the seat, and a chill breeze swept over her. In spite of the summer heat, she shivered. She was never going to get used to that— the way Will was so cold all the time now. Of course, the whole situation wasn't really the sort of thing anyone ever got used to, was it? What woman expected her husband to die and come back as a ghost?

"Well? Can you do anything to help?" She glanced down the long drive that led to the road. Not that she got a lot of visitors out this way, but if anyone were to come by and see her having a conversation with thin air, they'd likely want to send her off to the madhouse.

"I'm working on it." Though she couldn't see him, Will's voice was as familiar to her as his face had ever been. He had a beautiful voice—low, with a hint of gravel in the throat. Hearing it now, without the comfort of his physical presence, brought a hollow ache to her chest, a different kind of hole that couldn't be mended with mere tarpaper and tin. *"I don't want just any man to take my place,"* he said.

She shifted the bowl, trying to get a better grip. "I don't want another husband, Will." She was just getting used to looking out for herself. Why complicate matters by trying to start over with another man? "I just need someone temporary, until my arm heals." She scowled at the plaster cast on her left forearm, as if it were personally responsible for all her troubles. Maybe if she'd had help to doctor that gelding, she wouldn't be in such a fix now.

"You need someone to look after you and this place, the way I did," Will said. *"Someone upstanding and respectable, who can help you make friends in town."*

"I just need someone useful." She nodded. "Someone who knows about horses and doesn't drink too much. Someone young enough to be strong . . . but not too handsome."

"Why not handsome?" Will sounded surprised.

She shifted in the swing. If only she could *see* Will. He had been a handsome man, and he'd stolen her heart so easily. Better not to take any chances. "I don't want talk in town," she said.

Will made a noise like a horse snorting. *"They're gonna talk no matter what."* The swing shook as it emptied of his weight. *"You just leave everything to me."*

She sighed and turned her attention once more to the peas, stifling a rush of irritation. Will had done such a good job of looking after her when he was alive that she supposed it was only natural he'd want to continue now that he'd passed on. But wasn't it about time he realized she could look after herself?

"What's this?"

His question made her look up. She squinted into the bright sunlight. A man was walking down the drive toward the house. A tall man in a dirty brown hat, carrying a saddle. "I wonder what happened to the horse that went with that saddle?" she mused.

Will was silent, retreating as he always did whenever anyone else was around. She stood, cradling the bowl of peas, and walked to the edge of the porch, squinting into the bright June sun at the stranger. The broad brim of his hat cast a shadow across his face, but his quick and steady gait identified him as a young man. The saddle, though heavy with tooled leather and silver conchos, seemed hardly to burden him as he carried it on his shoulder. The blue of his flannel shirt had faded to a soft pewter, and his trousers were clumsily patched above one knee. Instead of a gun, he wore a long-bladed knife at his side.

He stopped at the wooden gate in the low picket fence that surrounded the yard and nodded politely before lowering the saddle to the ground. "Morning, ma'am," he said. "Is your man at home?"

She resisted the urge to smile. In Will's present condition, he couldn't exactly be said to be anywhere. "I'm afraid my husband passed on last year."

He paused for a moment, as if considering his next move. She wondered if she should have gotten the gun from the house. She forgot sometimes how vulnerable she was, a woman alone.

"Then I guess you're the one I need to talk to," the stranger said. He nodded toward the corral beside the house. "I saw your horses. Wondered if you'd be interested in buying this saddle."

She relaxed a little. Nothing about this man seemed threatening. He was just a traveler, passing through. She studied the firm set of his chin, the only part of his face she could see clearly in the shadow of the hat. "I've got saddles."

"This is a good saddle. Hand-tooled leather and finest Mexican silver." His voice was soft, barely accented, like one who hadn't been born speaking English, though he spoke it well enough now.

She followed his gaze to the saddle. "If it's so wonderfully fine, why do you want to sell it?"

He tilted his head, and she thought she detected a hint of a smile at the corners of his lips, but she couldn't be sure. "A saddle like this isn't much good without a horse."

"Then you've come to the right place." She stepped down off the porch, into the yard. "Those horses you see are for sale. One of them might be perfect for your saddle."

He turned his head toward the half dozen horses that had gathered along the corral fence, like spectators at a sporting exhibition. Necks stretched over the top rail, ears arched forward in curiosity. Tails flicked at flies and hooves stamped as if to demonstrate the vitality of all her stock. In truth, it hurt her each time she had to part with one of her dears, but there were bills to be paid, and she couldn't let sentimentality get in the way of eating.

The stranger turned back to her. "Fine animals. Expensive?"

She nodded. "Of course."

He looked down at the saddle and nudged it with the worn toe of one knee-high boot. "Which brings me to the second reason the saddle is for sale. I don't have the price of a beer on me, much less the gold to buy one of your horses."

She wondered how far he'd walked, carrying that saddle. She'd assumed he'd come from town, but anyone there would have given him a good price for his burden. Now she thought he must have been traveling through and turned into her drive because it was the first place he'd come to. "So I can't sell you a horse and I don't want to buy your saddle." She took a deep breath, her heart fluttering in her chest as she searched for the right words. She'd never offered anyone a job before. What if he turned her down? Or worse, what if he saw through her pretense at boldness and laughed at her timidity? "But maybe we can still do business."

He was silent, his gaze fixed on the saddle.

"I need a man to help me around the place," she continued. "Just a couple of months, until my arm mends." She nodded toward the cast. "I can pay you fifty cents a day, plus room and board."

He looked past her, to the house. She wondered if he saw the fine place it had been or only the disrepair into which it had fallen this last year. Then he nodded. "All right, ma'am. I'll take the job." He swept off his hat and held his hand over the fence.

A tremor ran through her as the stranger's eyes met her own. She gasped and fumbled with the bowl, but the cast made her awkward, and the crockery slipped through her fingers. The bowl shattered on the hard dirt, and peas rolled and bounced across the yard. "Oh, no!" she cried as she knelt and attempted to scoop up the fragments.

"Here, let me help you." He opened the gate and knelt across from her. She couldn't take her eyes off him, realizing that her first impression of him was true.

He was one of the handsomest men she had ever seen, with sharply chiseled features that melded strength and beauty. The sight of him made her insides go all quivery and her thoughts tumble over themselves in a panic.

Not only that, but he was an Indian. How could she have missed that before? She had mistaken the brown of his hands for the effects of the summer sun, until she'd seen the coppery tan of his face. Out of the shadow of his hat, his sculpted cheekbones and chiseled nose betrayed his heritage, as did the ink-black hair tied at the base of his neck with a leather thong. Only his eyes seemed foreign to his features, eyes the deep green of Mississippi pines.

He was a half-breed, then. The realization did nothing to slow the rapid drumbeat of her heart as they continued to stare at one another, motionless.

"Is something wrong?" He was the first to break the spell between them.

She shook her head, trying to hide the shaking in her hands as she gathered broken bits of pottery. Why was this happening to her? This man could only mean trouble.

Of course, she could always send him away. She raised her eyes to look at him once more, at the smooth blackness of his hair and the deep brown of his skin. His broad shoulders strained at the fabric of his shirt as he reached out to capture a rolling pea. Here was a man who could work hard. A man familiar enough with horses to own a custom-made saddle. He was everything she'd hoped for, and who was to say when she would come across another one like him out here on the edge of the wilderness?

She gathered her apron to hold the errant peas and pottery and stood. "What's your name?" she asked.

He rose also and replaced the hat on his head. "Fox," he said. "Micah Fox."

She forced a businesslike expression to her face and extended her hand. "Pleased to meet you, Mr. Fox. My name's Tessa Bright."

He hesitated only a moment before taking her hand. His grasp was gentle but firm, sending a wave of warmth through her. Once more his eyes captured and held her gaze, and her knees began to tremble beneath her long skirts. "Why don't you put your things in the barn, and I'll go fix you something to eat," she said, looking away.

He shouldered the saddle once more, and she turned toward the house, forcing herself to walk slowly, when inside, all she wanted to do was run. When she reached the privacy of her kitchen, she sagged against the doorway. "So, Will, what do you think of that one?" she whispered.

But the only answer that came to her was silence.

• • •

The ornate iron gate first caught Micah's attention as he trudged through the dusty ruts that cut across the Texas plains. Shaded by a single scrub oak, it marked the entrance to a long drive. Instead of simple bars or rails, this gate was formed of pictures: trees and deer and horses and people, and the slanting rays of a sun beaming down from behind a mountain, like the fancy work of a silhouette artist he'd seen once at a fair. Iron, strong yet delicate as lace, formed the branched antlers of deer, the curved outline of a woman, and the muscular figure of a man.

Micah stood and stared at the gate for a long time, the saddle weighing heavy on his shoulder and hunger gnawing at his belly. A little while before, a passing drover had told him it was four miles to the nearest town, four miles on top of the fourteen he'd already walked, the saddle biting into his shoulder, his steps growing heavier with each mile away from the coffee he'd had for breakfast.

He'd opened the gate and walked down that long drive because he wanted to meet a person who would hang a work of art in the middle of the prairie. He hadn't expected a woman, certainly not that frail-looking figure with the bandaged arm. Her brown hair hung in a simple braid down her back, and the dress she wore was faded the same brown color from sun and many washings. She was like a little wren standing in front of her house. But when she spoke, she had all the cockiness of a jay, challenging him to buy her horses. And her brown eyes flashed with humor.

He liked her even before she asked him to stay, and he was glad enough to do so, to get to know her better. But her friendliness had vanished the moment he removed his hat, and she drew away, as others had before.

She'd recovered well, but he hadn't missed the fear. He'd seen it before, the turning away at the sight of his black hair and brown skin. Would she send him away, as others had, or was she so desperate for help she'd take it from a half-breed?

He bit back his anger and carried the saddle to the barn. The woman was not the only one who could put aside her true feelings for the moment. He'd stay for a while, long enough to fill his belly and put aside some cash. Let her think what she liked about him.

He shoved open the door to the barn and the familiar scent of hay and manure and leather filled his nostrils. As his eyes adjusted to the dimness, he made out a row of horse boxes on one side, feed bins and saddle racks arranged on the other side of the room. He found a place for his own saddle, then went in search of somewhere to bed down. One thing for sure, he'd need to borrow a couple blankets. The barn was cold as creek water in January.

"Nice saddle you got there."

Instinctively reaching for the knife at his waist, he whirled and stared at the man who stood before him. He wasn't accustomed to people sneaking up on him. The kind of life he'd led, letting a stranger get the drop on you might be your last mistake. But the man before him now didn't appear to pose much of a threat. For one thing, he was at least twenty years older than Micah, deep furrows plowed on either side of his mouth. Everything about him was pale, from his long silver hair to his round, fleshy face. "Who are you?" Micah demanded as his heartbeat slowed to normal.

"A friend of Tessa's." The old man leaned against an empty stall and folded his arms over his barrel chest. He didn't look very strong now, but judging from his build, at one time he must have been. "What brings you to this part of the country?" he asked.

Hiding his annoyance, Micah shrugged. "Just passing through."

The old man grunted. "You running from the law?"

Micah bristled. "Who are you, anyway? What makes you think any of this is your business?"

The old man straightened and unfolded his arms. "It's

my business to see that Tessa isn't taken in by some no-account drifter ready to steal her blind the first time her back is turned." His face wasn't exactly flushed, but it did look . . . brighter?

Micah curled his hands into fists at his sides. "And of course Indians will take anything that isn't nailed down. Isn't that right?"

To his surprise, the old man laughed. "Sure, I know all about Indians." His expression quickly sobered. "You just give me your word you don't mean Tessa any harm. That'll be enough for me."

Micah felt the tension go out of his shoulders. He didn't like the old man much, but he guessed he couldn't blame the fellow for wanting to protect his friend. A woman alone couldn't be too careful. He put his hand over his heart, the sign for a promise or pledge. "I don't mean to do anything but help her out with her ranch until her arm heals. Then I'll be moving on."

The old man nodded. "There's a tackroom at the end of the barn. You can clean it out and bunk in there."

Micah nodded his thanks and made his way to the single door at the end of the barn. One corner had been walled off to form a box room, filled with trunks and old tack and farm implements. "I'll need to borrow a couple of blankets." He glanced over his shoulder to address the old man, but the barn was empty. He scratched his head. How had the old guy left without him even hearing the door open?

He decided to leave the storeroom for later and walk back up to the house. Tessa Bright had promised him a meal, and it wasn't an offer he intended to pass up.

The smell of frying bacon that hit him when he stepped into the kitchen was better than the aroma of the most expensive perfume. Tessa, tending the pan on the big iron cookstove, looked over her shoulder at him, a nervous smile on her lips. "I'll have you a plate fixed in a minute," she said. "You can pour yourself a cup of coffee and have a seat."

The coffee was fresh and hot; he couldn't remember

tasting better. He sat at the scrubbed wooden table and watched Tessa as she cooked. She'd put on a clean apron and smoothed her hair, and the heat of the stove—or maybe his presence?—flushed her cheeks a becoming pink. She was young, he guessed, twenty-five or so. So what was a young, pretty woman doing here, in the middle of nowhere, alone? Of course, she wasn't really alone, was she? "Who was the old man I met in the barn?" he asked.

The spatula slipped from her hand and clattered loudly against the skillet. "Wh . . . what old man?"

"Short, silver hair, broad shoulders. Wanted to know what I was doing here and where I came from and just what were my intentions." He chuckled. "You'd have thought I was here to court you and he was your father."

"He's not my father." She picked up the spatula and resumed turning the eggs.

"Who is he, then?"

"Just . . . a friend." She hefted the skillet, handling it awkwardly because of the cast, but managing to transfer its contents to a plate. "I didn't have time to make biscuits. But I've got cornbread from last night."

"Cornbread is fine." He glanced toward the back door. "Is your friend going to be eating with us?"

She shook her head. "No. He . . . he went on home."

"I didn't know you had close neighbors. Yours was the only drive I passed in quite a while."

"Not too close. He . . . he's sort of a hermit." She waved the spatula vaguely in the air. "You know—lives off in the wilderness, keeps to himself."

Micah nodded. He'd met the type once or twice in his travels—old trappers or hunters who preferred solitude to the hustle and bustle of humanity. Some of them went months, or even years, without saying two words to another human being. He watched Tessa balance the plate of food on the cast while she plucked a knife and fork from a crock on the counter. "What happened to your arm?" he asked.

She made a face at the cast. "There's a gelding out

there who cut his leg on some wire. He didn't appreciate my efforts to doctor it, and he knocked me into a cocked hat.''

"Broken?"

She nodded. ''The doctor in town says it'll be another five or six weeks before the cast comes off. In the meantime, I'm not good for much of anything.'' She slid a plate in front of him. ''You showed up just in time, Mr. Fox.''

The bacon-and-egg smell rose to him in sweet waves, and his hands trembled as he picked up his fork. She buttered a slab of cornbread and set it beside his plate, then poured a cup of coffee and took the chair across from him.

For several minutes, the only sound in the room was his fork scraping against the plate. ''Looks as if it's been a while since you had a decent meal,'' she said softly after a moment.

He swallowed before he answered. ''Got a rabbit day before yesterday.''

"Game's scarce this time of year."

"Have you lived out here long?'' His questions bordered on rudeness, but he couldn't stop asking them. Tessa Bright sparked his curiosity as no one had in a long time.

In any case, she seemed willing enough to answer him. ''Seven years. My husband and I came out here right after we married.''

He used the last of the cornbread to wipe his plate clean. ''How long have you been here alone?''

"My husband died last spring. One of the horses threw him, and he hit his head.''

"I'm sorry."

"He made that gate.'' She nodded toward the road. ''That fancy one up front.''

"That's some gate. Never saw one like it before."

"Folks thought it was crazy to put something like that way out here, but it brought us more customers than anything. My husband was a blacksmith. Besides shoeing horses and fixing wagons, he made candlesticks and firedogs and lampstands. Anything out of iron, he could do." She gave him a long, measured look. "Tell me the truth now. The gate brought you here, didn't it?"

He blinked. "Why do you say that?"

She stood and took his empty plate. "You strike me as a curious man, Mr. Fox."

He watched as she carried the plate to a basin of soapy water on the table by the door. She moved with an easy grace despite her bandaged arm, unself-conscious, though she must have known his gaze was fixed on her. "You're right," he said. "I came here because I was curious about your gate. But I stayed because I'm curious about you."

She looked up, eyes betraying her surprise—and was that a flicker of fear again? "There's nothing very curious about me, Mr. Fox. I'm a very ordinary woman."

He hid his smile. He liked knowing he could ruffle that cool exterior. "No ordinary woman would be out here on her own, raising horses without a husband, with one arm in a cast. And doing fairly well, from what I see." He stood and drained the last of the coffee from his cup.

She looked away and began scrubbing furiously at the plate. "I expect to do better with your help. You might as well get to work right away. There's a gate in the south corner of the corral that needs re-hanging and stalls that need cleaning."

He had to pass very close to her on his way out the door, and it seemed the most natural thing in the world to steady himself with a hand on her shoulder as he squeezed past. He could feel the delicate bones beneath his fingers and the tremble that shot through her at his touch. He carried the feeling with him out to the barn, like the memory of a wild bird held in the palm of his hand, or the feel of a skittish colt beneath his legs.

Chapter Two

"He's not the right one."

Tessa looked up from the bucket she was filling at the well. She didn't have to ask who Will was talking about. She'd known the minute she laid eyes on Micah Fox's handsome face that he wasn't the sort of man Will had in mind for her. He wasn't the sort of man she had in mind for herself either, but Will couldn't care less about that. He'd certainly taken his time about showing up to express his opinion. Mr. Fox had been working for her almost a day now, already accomplishing more than she'd thought possible.

"Will, he's the *only* one who's even offered to help me. Don't you dare run him off." She shoved the pump handle down with more force than was necessary. That was the trouble with arguing with a ghost—you couldn't see him to know for sure he was getting your point. "I can't believe you actually showed yourself to him yesterday! I'm lucky he didn't pick up his saddle and leave right then."

Will grunted. *"He wouldn't have left before he ate."*

"I almost fell over when he asked me about you."

She began fastening the filled bucket to one end of a wooden yoke.

"What did you tell him?"

"What was I supposed to tell him? I pretended you were some crazy old hermit who lived around here."

Will laughed, a deep chuckle that vibrated the air around her. *"That's good. I think I'll enjoy pretending to be a hermit."*

She faced the direction she thought he'd been speaking from. "Don't you do any such thing. I don't want you talking to him again."

"I'm behind you now."

She whirled around. "Stop moving and listen to me! I need Micah Fox's help until my arm heals. Don't run him off."

"You need a husband to take over the burden of running the ranch permanently." Will sounded annoyed. *"Someone respectable and well-thought-of in town. A half-breed from nowhere isn't the right man."*

"And just what respectable, well-thought-of man from town is going to want to have anything to do with me?" She shook her head and crouched down to settle the yoke on her shoulders. "I don't want to get married again, Will. I can run things fine with a hand like Mr. Fox."

"I won't try to make him leave as long as you need his help. But I intend to keep an eye on him all the same."

She straightened, struggling to balance the yoke and the water buckets hanging from either end. "Things will work out fine. You'll see."

"I'll see because I'll be watching."

The chill in the air gradually gave way to the heat of midmorning, and she knew he was gone. Frowning, she started toward the garden. She was perfectly capable of looking after herself. She didn't need Will interfering. But she might as well try to argue with a fence post, for all the satisfaction she'd get from trying to reason with him.

• • •

Micah watched over the top of the roof as Tessa hauled water to the vegetable garden behind the house. It was an arduous chore, working the hand pump to fill buckets with water, attaching the buckets to a wooden yoke, then lugging the heavy pails to the rows, all made more difficult by the cast on her forearm. But she'd refused his offer of help.

"You'd better see to the roof," she said. "That's one job I can't handle."

Despite her stubborn toughness, it was obvious to Micah that there were quite a few chores around the ranch she'd been unable to handle. In fact, he was pretty sure if he hadn't come along when he did, she wouldn't have held out another winter. The corral fence needed mending in several places. Both the house and the barn leaked, and a busted axle rendered the largest wagon useless. Her supply of firewood was low, and the smokehouse was empty.

The horses were the one thing she had not neglected. The quality of the small herd impressed him. There were several sturdy wagon horses, a pair of Morgans, and half a dozen crossbred saddle horses. Their coats gleamed with good health, and their manes and tails flowed like silk from frequent currying. Tessa had put all her efforts into the animals, at the expense of the rest of the ranch.

He moved a few feet over on the roof and began hammering a sheet of tin in place. Just as well he had plenty of work to do here. Chores made it easier for him to stay out of Tessa's way. She'd been civil enough to him at supper last night and at breakfast this morning, but tension hummed in the air around them like a busy telegraph wire. The message came through to him loud and clear: Tessa Bright regretted hiring him, but now that he was here, she couldn't afford to let him go. And now that he'd accepted the job, he couldn't bring himself to leave her in the lurch.

He stopped hammering and looked down on her again as she carried more water to the garden. The wooden yoke seemed too heavy for her frail figure, but she made steady progress down the rows. Only the way she rubbed her back when she set down her burden betrayed the difficulty of her task.

She tipped the buckets into the irrigation ditches she'd dug between the rows. Water and mud slopped over her bare feet and ankles. She'd tied her skirt up to her knees to keep it dry, revealing shapely calves.

He smiled approvingly. She had said her husband had been dead over a year now. He couldn't believe she didn't have a line of men waiting at that fancy gate to court her. Here was a beautiful young woman, free of husband and children, who owned her own property, was good with livestock, and undeterred by hard work. The perfect western wife. Yet so far not a single visitor had appeared—outside of the old hermit who had questioned him in the barn. And no mention had been made of any expected callers.

She stooped to pull a weed from a row of beans, then picked up her empty yoke and buckets and made her way back to the pump. Yoke and buckets once more neatly in their places, she surprised him by working the pump again and raising her leg to wash away the mud under the streaming water.

It was an unconscious gesture, the action of a woman who either is sure no one can see her or sees no shame in washing the dirt from her legs. He kept his eyes on her, unable to tear himself away from the innocent, yet intimate, scene. Familiar stirrings of desire swept through him, making his heart beat faster, his blood run hotter. He shifted to accommodate the swelling in his trousers and quickly averted his eyes.

"Lay one hand on her, and I'll cut it off."

For a fleeting second, he thought his conscience was talking to him, but at the same moment he realized the voice was real enough and coming from the old man, who was perched on the peak of the roof a few feet down from where he was working. Micah stared. This was the second time the old hermit had slipped up on him. Had he been so engrossed in watching Tessa that he hadn't heard the old man climb the ladder and walk across the roof? "I don't know what you're talking about," he snapped.

"Don't you?" The old man looked pointedly at the crotch of Micah's trousers.

He hefted his hammer and began pounding in a nail. "I don't have time to talk," he shouted over the racket. "I've got work to do."

As he reached into his pocket for another nail, an icy hand gripped his wrist. Will, much closer now, froze him with an angry stare. "Tessa's a beautiful woman, but she's also respectable."

"And I'm not—is that it?" He wrenched his hand away from Will's grasp. He resisted the urge to rub the wrist, which was so cold it almost burned. "You don't have to worry, old man. I'm not saying I'd turn her down if she invited me into her bed, but that's about as likely to happen as a hound dog being elected president."

Will sat back. "What makes you so sure of that?"

Micah hazarded another look at Tessa. She'd finished pumping and was drying her legs with an old feed sack. "It's just like you said. She's respectable. I'm not. The minute she realized I was a breed, she was sorry she'd asked me to stay. She'll let me work for her, but you can bet your last dollar she'd never risk her reputation by socializing with the likes of me."

Will began to laugh, holding his stomach and rocking back and forth. Micah frowned. "What's so funny?"

"Never mind, son." He shook his head. "You just get back to work and remember what I said."

The old hermit is obviously crazy as a loon, Micah thought as he turned his attention to the tin patch once more. *I ought to be worried* he'll *hurt Tessa. He seems almost obsessed with her.* He looked down at Tessa again. She'd untied her skirts and was smoothing them down. Just then, she raised her head, and for a brief moment their eyes met. He caught his breath, struck by her beauty and by the turmoil he read in her eyes. He would have done anything in that moment to erase that haunted look from her face—slain dragons, fought wars, or gathered her into his arms to kiss away the pain.

She ducked her head, breaking the spell, and ran across the yard to the house. The sound of the back door slamming echoed in the air around him.

"See. I told you she doesn't want anything to do with me." He turned to address the old man, but the rooftop was empty, the air ringing with silence.

Tessa ran into the house, the memory of Micah's heated gaze pursuing her up the stairs and down the hall to her bedroom. Safely behind closed doors, she sank onto her bed and covered her face with her hands, trying to cool cheeks that burned with shame. What had she been thinking, bathing under the pump like that when she knew good and well Micah Fox was working on the roof?

She took her hands from her face and sighed, shoulders slumped in defeat. There was no sense lying to herself. She'd pulled up her skirts and let him see her legs on purpose. Not because she was a loose woman, or so desperate for a man's attention she would throw herself at him. No, she'd done it because her conversation with Will had left her feeling frustrated and angry.

Why couldn't Will understand that she needed to start making her own decisions about the ranch and her life? She was the one who had to bear the consequences of whatever choices she made.

She'd been so moved when he first came back to her, relieved that he loved her so much. But lately she'd begun to wonder how much of what he'd done was done out of love and how much was motivated by the need to keep control of all that he'd held so tightly here on earth. When would he be able to let go—of the ranch and of her?

She'd seen Will sitting up on the rooftop, putting no telling what ideas into Micah's head. So she'd raised her skirts and offered Micah Fox a glimpse of her legs, to prove to Will and to herself that she could still act without needing his approval. She'd wanted, too, to make Micah think twice before he allowed Will to talk him into leaving.

Only when his eyes met hers had she felt shame— shame that she'd let this wildness in her override her common sense. And beyond that, she was ashamed that she had disregarded his feelings altogether in her petty war of wills with her husband's ghost. She wouldn't blame him if he lost all respect for her now.

She stood and went to the washstand in the corner and splashed the tepid water on her face. She'd made a mistake in teasing Micah that way. Now she'd have to work doubly hard to repair her reputation and to rein in that part of her nature that compelled her to think and do such irresponsible things. She would keep him at a distance, let him know she had no intention of throwing herself at him. He was her employee. He could never be anything more.

Micah found a plate of sausage and beans and cornbread waiting for him on the kitchen table when he came in for supper. He helped himself to a cup of coffee and listened for Tessa's approach, but there was no sound in the house except the ruffling of curtains stirred by a vagrant breeze.

He stared at the cooling food, anger rising in his throat. Was she condemning him to eat alone because he had watched her at the well? Would he find his meals on the back porch next, as befitting a slave or a dog?

Agitation drove him to his feet and into the parlor. A horsehair sofa and wing chair sat empty. Framed photographs of people he didn't know stared back at him. He left the room and paused at the bottom of the stairs, looking up toward the part of the house where he had never been and had never thought to go. He grasped the newel post, unconsciously rubbing his palm across its slick coolness. Damn propriety! He wouldn't let her hide from him.

His boots echoed on the wood as he took the steps two at a time. A window at the end of the hall looked out over the fields. Twin doors on either side of the hallway confronted him; he chose the one from under which yellow lamplight glowed.

No answer came to his knock. "Tessa." Not "Mrs. Bright." He would not call her that again. "I want to talk to you."

The door opened slowly. A worried frown creased her pale brow. "Is something wrong with one of the horses?" she asked, avoiding his eyes.

She was afraid of him. The thought cut him to the marrow. He grabbed hold of the doorframe to keep himself from turning around and leaving her alone. He hadn't meant to frighten her or to confirm her worst fears—that he was a savage, unmannered and unschooled. But he couldn't leave yet. "No. There's something we need to get straight between us right now."

She stepped into the hallway, shutting the door to her room firmly behind her, shutting out the brief glimpse he'd had of this personal side of her life. The gesture galled him, though of course he had no right to enter her bedroom. He stepped back, making room for her, but she refused to look at him, focusing instead on a picture on the wall behind him. "What is this about, Mr. Fox?"

"Call me Micah."

She shook her head. "I don't think—"

He wished she would look at him. "You don't want to call me by my given name. You don't want to eat at the same table with me." He struggled to keep his voice from rising in anger. "Is it because I was watching you this afternoon while you were at the well?"

She jerked her head up, a red flush sweeping over her face. "You had no right—"

"I'm not some tobacco store prop!" He swallowed hard, reining in his feelings, forcing his voice down to a normal level. "I'm a man like any other man, and I'm going to watch a beautiful woman every chance I get, especially if she chooses to display herself in my full view."

The blush deepened and she looked away. "I'm sorry." Her whisper barely reached his ears. "I shouldn't have . . ."

He took a step toward her, fighting the urge to gather her to him. She looked so frail and wounded, so utterly alone. "There was nothing wrong in what you did, nothing shameful or sinful about it."

She nodded, but still refused to meet his gaze. Her face held a feverish flush, and her full lips were slightly parted. More than anything at this moment he wanted to kiss those lips, to taste their sweetness and feel their warmth. She was close enough to touch, but he dared not lay a hand on her. "I want to know why you're afraid of me," he asked.

"What makes you think I'm afraid of you?"

Her averted eyes confirmed his own worst fears. "You've been avoiding me. Are you worried I'll scalp you in your sleep?"

"No!" Her response was sharp and immediate. She met his gaze at last. Her eyes held an unexpected look of surprise. "I've never thought anything like that."

He believed her, and now it was his turn to be startled. He hadn't expected her to be that different from other women he'd met. "Then stop avoiding me," he said. "We're working together here. We can at least be friends."

When she didn't answer, he turned away, a gnawing emptiness in his stomach. Tessa Bright was different, but not different enough. "I'll just pack my things and go, then. There's no use in my staying where I'm not wanted."

"No, Micah. Wait."

At the sound of his name on her lips, some tension

inside of him eased. Some cold place deep within began to warm.

"Please stay."

He glanced over his shoulder and saw her silhouetted in the light streaming from the window at the end of the hall, her hands clasped in front of her in an unconscious gesture of pleading. "I didn't mean to offend you," she said. "From now on, I'll remember to treat you just as I would want to be treated."

He nodded. "That's fair enough." He made his voice purposely light, not wanting her to know how much she'd affected him. "Now come down and eat. Tomorrow morning I want to take a look at that hurt gelding. I noticed him limping again today."

She hesitated, then hurried past him. He followed at a slower pace, her last words running through his mind. Exactly how *did* Tessa Bright want to be treated? What did she want from him? She needed a man to help her with the ranch, but when he looked into her eyes, he saw a yearning for something more. Maybe more than he was prepared to give.

I should make it into town more often, Will thought as he drifted down the one main street of Pony Springs, Texas. *Keep abreast of what's going on.* He crossed the street and moved past Wilkins's Mercantile. Old Man Thornton and Milo Adamson drowsed on the whittler's bench out front the way they'd done every day for the last seven years. Milo's old hound raised up and bared his teeth at Will as he passed, but the two men snored on.

Inside the store, Bob Wilkins carved a wedge from a wheel of yellow cheese for pretty Mamie Tucker while her oldest boy, Donnie, filched crackers from the barrel by the door. Will studied the cheese for a moment, trying to conjure up the taste and smell and feel of it in his mouth. He sighed. There were definite drawbacks to lacking a physical body.

Outside again, he moved on. He paused in front of Jackie Babcock's smithy and debated going in and putting a damper on the fire in his forge, or bending some of the fresh horseshoe nails that lay cooling on the rock windowsill. *Babcock, I could make a better nail than those on my worst day,* he thought. He hovered near the door for a while, half hoping someone would come in and bemoan the loss of the county's best blacksmith, but no one showed.

Where is everybody? Will wondered as he moved on down the street. Pony Springs wasn't a big town, but it was usually busier than this. How was he supposed to choose the right man for Tessa if they'd all disappeared?

Pretty soon, however, he noticed more traffic on the street. Sour-faced Trudy Babcock drove by in her one-horse cart, head held as high as if she were trying to keep a crown from falling off. Will scowled at the back of her head. You'd have thought she was married to some foreign royalty instead of a poor excuse for a blacksmith. Will could have forgiven her for being homely and snooty, but he couldn't overlook the fact that she'd snubbed Tessa every chance she got. If he hadn't had more important things on his mind right then, he would have made it a point to spook her horse.

More vehicles passed, filled with the town's most up-standing citizens. Wes Drake and his wife, Ada, drove by in a piano box buggy, and Will hopped in back, making himself comfortable between a plate of deviled eggs and a twenty-pound sack of flour. He amused himself blowing the feathers on Ada Drake's new black straw hat, until she pulled her shawl up around her neck and complained to her husband about the unseasonably cold wind.

Before long, the buggy fetched up in front of the Pony Springs church. A dozen other vehicles huddled in the shade of a lone cottonwood, while most of the town's more respectable population gathered on the steps of the whitewashed chapel.

Will grinned to himself. Perfect. Everyone here in one place so he could look them over good. Somewhere in this bunch had to be the right man for Tessa.

He went down the row and considered each bachelor in turn. Woody Monroe was first. He was respectable enough, a deacon in the church and head of the board of education. That was important. He wanted someone who could give Tessa instant status. Town folk like Trudy Babcock had looked down their noses at her long enough.

Only problem was, Woody Monroe was so thin he looked as if a stiff breeze would bend him over. He had a nagging cough that hinted at consumption and a tendency to the sniffles all winter. Will needed a strong man to work the ranch.

Gabe Emerson was the next single man, a widower and stout as an ox. Will had once seen him wipe out an entire saloon with his bare hands. Nope, he wouldn't do. Gabe was entirely too fond of liquor to make a good husband for Tessa or a good manager for the ranch.

One by one, he surveyed the assembled men and found them lacking. Pete Trask had too many children. Bryan Ritter was good with horses, but every time he had to so much as speak to a woman he turned beet red and stuttered. Allen Knox was young, childless, strong, respectable—and too handsome by half. After all, Tessa wouldn't want a man other women were always trailing after.

Isn't there one suitable man in this entire town? Will thought. He turned away in disgust and almost ran smack into an approaching rider. The man's horse, a fine-looking bay, went white-eyed and bucked like a green bronc as it felt Will's presence. The man held on, giving the animal its head and talking in a calming voice. By the time he brought the horse under control, he'd lost his hat and his trim black suit was in disarray, but he'd won the admiration of everyone in the crowd, including Will, who decided to stay around for the introductions.

"Reverend Deering, we're so pleased to welcome you to Pony Springs." Woody Monroe stepped up and pumped the new arrival's hand.

Deering leaned down to shake hands, then dismounted, one hand keeping firm hold of the bridle of the still-skittish horse. "I'm happy to be here," he said in a rich baritone voice. "Though I didn't mean to make quite such a spectacular entrance."

A preacher. What could be more respectable? Will moved closer. *The man obviously had an eye for horseflesh, too. The bay was no nag.*

"We've prepared a little welcome reception for you, so you can eat and get to know some of your congregation." Wes Drake handed the preacher his hat, retrieved from the street.

"That sounds mighty fine," Deering said. "But if you don't mind, I'd like to see to my horse first. We've had a long ride."

"I'll take care of him for you." Allen Knox stepped up. "The stable is nearby."

"I'd like to get him settled myself," Deering said. "If you'll just show me the way, I won't be long."

Will followed Knox and Deering to the stable, excitement building within him. *Yes, this is the one*, he thought. *Not too young, not too old. He looks strong and healthy enough. His character is beyond reproach, and he knows how to handle horses. He's perfect.*

"Would you like me to help you with anything?" Knox asked as Deering bent to loosen the girth on his saddle.

"No, thank you. You go on back to the church. I'll join you shortly."

Will waited until Knox was out of sight, then moved in closer. *"Reverend Deering, I'd like a word with you."*

Deering froze in the act of lifting the saddle off the gelding. "Who's there?" He turned his head, searching the empty stable.

"That's not really important. What's important is that I have a job for you."

To Will's amazement, Deering dropped the saddle and fell to his knees on the dirt floor of the stall. "Lord, I came here to do your will, whatever it is."

Will hesitated. Usually when he spoke to people, they mistook him for the voice of their conscience, or the effects of too much liquor. Some even recognized they were being haunted. Nobody had ever mistaken him for God before.

He cleared his throat. *"I . . ."*

"I just want to say, Lord, what a privilege it is to be visited by you this way. Me, a lowly sinner, not fit to touch the hem of your garment. That you would choose me—"

"Hush a minute and let me speak!"

Deering blanched and fell silent.

Will sighed. Might as well work with what he'd been given. *"As soon as you can see your way to it, I want you to pay a call on a woman who lives near here, a young widow name of Tessa Bright."*

"I'll go right now, Lord." Deering started to rise.

"Not now. You don't want to ruin the town's plans for you." He looked the preacher up and down. *"Besides, you might want to get a little spruced up before you go calling."*

Deering glanced down at his travel-stained garments. "What do you want me to do for this widow?" he asked.

"She's fallen on hard times, and she's in need of, uh . . . spiritual guidance." That ought to do for a start. Once Deering met Tessa, he was bound to appreciate her charms. If not, well, the "Lord" could always steer him in the right direction.

"Yes, Lord. I'll go first thing tomorrow, then—if that's all right with you."

"That's fine." He started to leave it at that, then added, *"Now get up out of the dirt and see to your horse. Then get back to the party before Monroe and his bunch come looking for you."*

"Yes, Lord. Hallelujah."

"One more thing."

"Anything, Lord."

"Don't go telling anyone about our little, uh, con-

versation. This is just between you and me."

"Yes, Lord. And may I say again what a privilege—"

"Amen, Reverend. That means 'the end,' right?"

When Will left the barn, Deering was scooping oats into a bucket for the gelding, humming a hymn under his breath. Will only hoped that when he came to call on Tessa, he could bring his mind down to a more earthly level.

Chapter Three

Tessa watched as Micah snubbed the injured gelding to a post in the barn and wondered how she had managed this long without him. He tackled the most grueling chores without complaint, handling saw and shovel, hammer and harness with equal ease. The horses quickly grew to trust him; even the most high-spirited of them obeyed his gentle commands.

But his effect on the ranch, and on Tessa herself, went beyond skill and brute strength. As the days passed, the ever-present knot of worry in her stomach began to loosen. The list of repairs shortened, and the roster of future improvements that now seemed possible expanded. She recognized an almost-forgotten emotion swelling within her; because of Micah, she was beginning to hope again.

She alternated these days between an almost giddy happiness and a trembling wariness. It didn't seem right to be so dependent on a man who was, after all, virtually a stranger. The same quiet strength that drew her might in the end prove to be nothing but a trap to lure her into behavior she'd regret later. She told herself she was being wise to keep her distance from him, but then there were times like these, when they were forced to work together, that made her doubt the strength of her resolve to remain unaffected by him.

She watched now as he slipped a pair of hobbles around the horse's hind legs. As he straightened once more, he stroked his hand down the animal's broad flank. Against the horse's dark coat, the light tan of his fingers contrasted sharply. They were long and square-tipped, disconcerting in their masculinity.

"You go around and stand in front of him where he can see you," he instructed Tessa. "Scratch his ears or whatever you think will help keep him calm."

She welcomed the opportunity to concentrate on something besides Micah and his overwhelming nearness. "I didn't do a very good job of calming him down the first time," she said as she took her place at the gelding's head. She smoothed the whorls of hair between the animal's ears. Her own fingers were red and work-roughened. She curled them under to hide the broken nails, wondering if Micah had noticed.

"Well, this is really a job for two people." He bent and reached for the gelding's injured foot. The horse lowered its ears and did its best to step away, but Micah captured the foreleg firmly in his hands and examined the swelling on the left front pastern.

Tessa winced. She couldn't stand to see an animal in pain, especially one of her animals. "I was trying to lance it the day I broke my arm. I thought I'd taken care of it, but now I see it's much worse."

"The infection doesn't look to have spread too far yet." Micah held the injured leg firmly with one hand. With the other, he reached up and stroked the horse's neck, speaking in low tones. "It's all right, fella. You're going to be just fine."

The soft murmuring soothed her as well as the horse. The words seemed meant for her.

He slipped the knife out of the sheath at his side, and Tessa looked away. The horse jerked and let out a plaintive squeal as Micah opened the wound, and the foul smell of infection filled the air.

"That's a nasty one all right," Micah observed. He braced against the struggling animal and held the leg firm, carefully cleaning the wound with the tip of the knife. Then he reached into his shirt pocket and pulled out a tobacco tin he had earlier instructed Tessa to fill with a mixture of powdered sulfur and lard. "You brought the bandages?" he asked as he packed the wound with the thick salve.

"Right here." She pulled the strips of linen from her skirt pocket and held them out to him. He wound the bandage around and around the fetlock, weaving a neat covering. His hands moved swiftly, the fingers deft, with no wasted motion. She watched, mesmerized by the juxtaposition of such strength and gentleness. This hardly seemed the same man who had faced her outside her bedroom the other afternoon, frightening her with his barely controlled fury.

Or was it only his overwhelming maleness that frightened her—the power he had to distract her attention from everyday duties and send her thoughts spinning off into foolish fantasy? What good could come of allowing her mind to wander so? Yet even now, in the close confines of the barn, his presence overwhelmed her. As he bent to doctor the horse, his shoulder brushed against her skirts, and a corresponding tremble shot through her. Beneath the mixed odors of medicine and manure, his own musky scent teased her senses, and she was unable to tear her gaze away from him, as if she felt obligated to memorize the part of his hair and the solid line of his spine.

"There. That ought to do it." He released the gelding's foot and straightened, meeting her gaze head-on.

She felt a hot blush wash over her face, as if she were a child caught in some forbidden act. Half afraid he would read the longing in her eyes, she turned away. "Thank you for taking care of that for me," she said. "Have you had a chance to look over the other animals?

Is there one in particular you'd like to ride? Feel free to do so.''

She started down the row of horse boxes and felt him fall into step behind her. At the end she stopped and looked through an open box into the corral beyond, at the horses milling there. "The sorrel gelding is a good mount," she said. Will's favorite, in fact. She worried her lower lip between her teeth. What did it mean that she was so willing to give Will's horse to this man? "Or maybe you'd prefer one of the Morgans."

He stopped beside her, arms resting on the top of the half-door leading into the stall, almost but not quite touching her. "What about that strawberry roan over there? She's a nice animal."

Tessa didn't try to hide her dismay at his choice. "That's Pigeon. You don't want her."

"Why not?"

"She's a runaway." She shook her head. "As soon as she gets her head, she runs—usually back to the barn here. I've tried everything I know to break her of the habit, but it's no use." She sighed. "I can't sell her and I can't ride her. I don't know what I'm going to do."

"Then why do you keep her around?"

She hesitated. Would he dismiss her feelings as feminine foolishness? Well, what if he did? She lifted her chin. "Because I like her. In spite of everything, she has a sweet personality. And she's beautiful. Maybe I'll use her as a brood mare."

Micah clicked his tongue and held out his hand, coaxing the mare over to him. He rubbed the horse's nose and smoothed his hand along her jaw. "Why don't you let me work with her? See what I can do?"

"I doubt if it will do any good. I've tried everything. I'm beginning to think she's ruined."

"Oh, I don't know . . . a lady like this . . . maybe she just needs a man's touch."

His eyes met hers, and a bolt of heat shimmered through her. She flinched, fumbling for composure.

"F-feel free to work with her if you like. I'm grateful for your help."

"Then why do you resist it so?"

His hand on her shoulder robbed her of speech and thought. Her breath caught. Even to her ears it was a pitiful, desperate sound.

"What do I have to do to convince you I mean you no harm?" he asked.

No physical harm, perhaps. But he could so easily upset the delicate equilibrium she'd established in her life, this balance between passion and pain she'd struggled to obtain. Some part of her longed for those dizzy heights of happiness that were part and parcel of the business of falling in love. But the rest of her cringed at the thought of the searing pain that always came along sooner or later. Better to ignore the tug of attraction she felt for Micah and avoid hurting them both.

Then why couldn't she bring herself to pull away from him now? Instead, she all but leaned into him, savoring the weight of his hand on her and the heat of his skin through the thin calico of her dress.

"Hello! Anyone home?"

The shout jolted her out of her reverie. She jerked away from Micah and hurried to the door of the barn. A man on a dark bay was approaching them. "Who is that?" Micah asked, close behind her.

She shook her head. "I've never seen him before." Still shaken by what had passed between them in the barn, she brushed the dirt from her hands and walked out to meet the visitor.

"Good morning, ma'am." He pulled the horse up short at the picket fence and swept a broad-brimmed black hat from his head. Sunlight glinted on his brown-gold hair. He was a tall man, wearing a starched white shirt and a black broadcloth suit. Tessa pegged him as either a preacher or a gambler. No one else in these parts dressed so fine.

"I'm Reverend Jonathan Deering, the new Methodist minister in Pony Springs." He smiled, an expression full of warmth. "I'm looking for a woman called Tessa Bright."

"I'm Tessa Bright." Now why was a preacher looking for her? "Won't you get down? Come in and have some refreshment."

He replaced the hat on his head and swung down out of the saddle. "I'd like to water my horse first."

"You can turn him loose in the corral." She went to open the gate for him, but Micah was there first, regarding the preacher with a less than friendly expression. "This is Micah Fox," she said. "He helps me around the ranch."

Deering offered his hand, and Micah shook it, his gaze sweeping over the preacher, taking his measure.

"Pleasure to meet you, Mr. Fox." Deering openly stared at Micah, his smile broadening, then he leaned forward, excitement in his voice. "I hope you won't think I'm impertinent, but you're an Indian, aren't you?"

Micah stiffened. "Half."

"Ah. Well, I've not met many Indians before. None, actually. I've seen pictures, of course, and done some reading . . ." He glanced at Tessa. "From the beginning of my ministry, I've felt a strong calling to minister to this nation's native peoples."

Micah frowned. "No offense, Reverend, but most Indians I know have had about all the ministering to by white people that they can stand."

Deering's smile didn't dim. "Then it's time for a new approach—don't you agree?"

Tessa wasn't sure what any of this had to do with her. Had the preacher ridden all the way from town just to meet his first Indian? "What brings you out here today, Reverend?"

At once, he assumed the dignified posture of a man in the pulpit—sober expression, hands clutching his lapels. "I've been instructed to pay you a call."

She caught her breath. So the town busybodies had decided to send the new preacher to make her see the error of her ways, had they? "Sent by whom?"

His face paled, and he let his hands fall to his sides. "Well, uh . . . I'm not at liberty to say."

Tessa stared. The good reverend looked decidedly . . . guilty? What was going on here?

Deering cleared his throat. "Actually, I plan to visit all my flock. You're the first."

All this time, Micah had never taken his eyes from them. He stood beside the corral gate, his gaze fixed on her as if he could read every thought behind her words. The scrutiny made her uneasy, as if he, too, like those in town, might weigh her and find her wanting.

"Come into the house, Reverend," she said, turning away. "I'll fix you a glass of cool water."

"This is a lovely place you have here, Mrs. Bright," Deering said as he fell into step beside her.

Tessa glanced up at the house. Though the unpainted wood had weathered to silver over the years, and the roof was pocked with patches, she still loved the home she and Will had built together. "My husband and I built the house and barn five years ago," she said. "Before that, we lived in a dugout on the prairie."

The preacher opened the gate in the picket fence and held it aside for her to pass in front of him. "I understand you're a widow."

So he had been talking to people in town. What else had they told him? "Yes, my husband passed on a little more than a year ago." What would the good reverend think if she told him Will was now a ghost? She crossed the porch and went into the house, and he followed her to the kitchen, his boot heels ringing on the plank floors. The smell of beans simmering with bacon and onions— dinner cooking in a pot on the back of the stove—perfumed the air.

"My sympathies. It must have been difficult for you, managing alone."

"It was." She took a cup from a hook under the cabinet and filled it from the bucket by the door. "After I broke my arm, I hired Mr. Fox to help. Things have been easier since then.''

"You have no children?"

"No. Will and I never did.'' She braced herself against the pity that came to his eyes. It was always this way, though she'd long since stopped feeling sorry for herself.

"I'm very sorry to hear that.'' He cleared his throat. "So is it just you and Mr. Fox here now?"

She froze, the dipper halfway out of the water pail. Of course, she might have expected this. The townspeople would read the worst possible scenario into the most innocent actions. But she hadn't seen any of them racing out here with offers to help her since Will's death. Flushed with anger, she turned to face the preacher. "I assure you, there is nothing the least bit improper about my relationship with Mr. Fox. He is my employee. He sleeps in the barn.''

Reverend Deering paled and tugged at his collar. "Of course not, Mrs. Bright. I never meant to imply—''

She handed him the cup of water. "Now that you've done your duty and paid your call, is there anything else you need to say?"

He took a long drink. "I'll be preaching my first sermon in Pony Springs tomorrow. I hope I'll see you there.''

She held herself still, wary of showing too much interest in the invitation, though a little flare of hope shot up within her. "It's been a long time since I've been to church,'' she said.

He focused kind blue eyes on her. "Why is that?"

Chin up, she tried not to let the hurt creep into her voice. "I wasn't made to feel welcome the first few times I attended, so I quit coming.''

His face sagged downward, a picture of distress. "Now I understand the importance of my visit today.''

What an odd thing to say. "What do you mean?"

He shook his head. "Only that it's clear that there are many here the church must reach out to.'' He handed her the empty cup. "I hope you won't let your past experiences keep you from attending worship tomorrow. I mean to make a difference here."

His earnestness moved her. "I . . . I'll give it some thought," she said. "Thank you for stopping by."

"Until tomorrow, then." He reached out and clasped both her hands in his, a gesture filled with encouragement and comfort. She followed him out onto the porch and watched while he fetched the bay and mounted up again. When he was on his way once more, she returned to the kitchen, feeling unnerved by the encounter. Preacher Deering had been kind, in spite of her less-than-welcoming attitude. Maybe she *would* go to hear him preach tomorrow.

"So what did you think of Pony Springs's new pulpit pounder?" Will's voice came from near the stove, where a wooden spoon was tracing figure eights in the pot of simmering beans.

She went and took the spoon from him, flinching only a little at his icy touch. "Were you listening to us the whole time?"

"Someone had to make sure dinner didn't burn."

"Since when are you so interested in cooking?"

An empty chair moved back from the table. *"I like the smell. Since I can't eat anymore, I have to be content with savoring the aroma of food. So, tell me, did you like Reverend Deering?"*

She shrugged. "He seems like a nice enough man."

"He really knows horses, too. You saw the bay he was riding? Fine animal, that. I spotted him yesterday when he came into town."

She tasted the beans and added a little salt. She hadn't thought before about what Will did when he wasn't with her. "What were you doing in town yesterday?"

"Oh, just looking around. Deering came alone—no mention of a wife. And, of course, you can't get any more respectable than a preacher. The minute I laid eyes on him, I knew you'd like him."

Almost choking on her own breath, she whirled to

face the chair, the spoon in her hand dripping onto the floor. "No, Will! You can't be serious!"

"Why not? He's the perfect man to look after you and the ranch."

She shook her head. "I'm sure Reverend Deering isn't interested in me that way."

"Why not? This is a prosperous ranch. You're a pretty woman. What's not to interest a man?"

She turned back to the stove and began stirring the beans so furiously she was in danger of turning them into soup. "I'm sure the reverend is more concerned about his ministry here."

"He'd be concerned about you and the ranch, too, if he received a 'calling' to do so. He seems very big on callings."

She gasped. "You wouldn't!" The spoon slid into the pot as she clenched both hands into fists. "I told you before, I'm not interested in remarrying. Now that Micah is here, I'm managing just fine."

The chair scraped against the floor and a sudden chill cloaked her back. *"Micah Fox is only a temporary solution. You need someone who can take care of the ranch like an owner. And someone who can take care of you like a husband."*

She stiffened. "So what I want doesn't matter at all? You'd marry me off to a man I don't even know?"

"All I'm asking is for you to give him a chance. He's everything you could want in a second husband. Trust me."

The coldness at her back melted away, and she knew he was gone—too obstinate to entertain any further argument from her. She slumped against the dry sink, feeling angry and defeated. *How do you know what's best for me?* she wanted to ask him. *You were married to me, but that doesn't mean you could know what's really in my heart.*

How could you, when I'm not even sure what's there myself?

• • •

Micah turned the doctored gelding loose in an empty stall, then busied himself with odd jobs around the barn. He had no desire to join Tessa and the preacher in the house and endure more of Tessa's uneasiness and the preacher's questions about Indians.

Maybe he'd been wrong to touch her, back there when she tried to turn away from him. He'd thought he'd seen something in her eyes, some longing that echoed his own empty feelings, and he hadn't been able to stop himself from reaching out to her. But he must have been wrong. She wanted nothing to do with him.

He waited until the preacher left before he washed up at the pump and went in for supper. Tessa turned from the stove as he came through the back door and greeted him with a smile that halted him in his tracks, like a man surprised by unexpected beauty. He'd known prettier women in his time, but none with this combination of delicateness and strength that moved him so. She was like some wildflower that had been trampled and bruised but continued to bloom, unbowed.

"That gelding looks like he's coming along real well," she said, placing a cup of water at his place at the table.

He nodded and moved to his chair. "He'll do."

She slid a plate of beans in front of him and another of cornbread, steam curling up from its surface. Then she filled her own plate and sat across from him. "I'll need you to hitch the wagon for me in the morning," she said. "I've decided to go into town. To church." She glanced at him, her eyes asking his opinion or approval, he wasn't sure which.

"Reverend Deering's church?" His stomach tightened as he said the man's name.

She nodded, and crumbled a piece of cornbread atop her beans. "He seems very nice. Very sincere."

Micah shrugged off this praise. "Doesn't know much about Indians."

She nodded. "But he struck me as the type who would be willing to learn."

"You've taken a shine to him mighty fast." As soon as the words were out of his mouth, he regretted them. Who was he to judge her choice of friends?

"I do like him." Her voice trembled. "He's the first person from town who's had two nice words to say to me since Will's passing."

Of all the things she might have said, this shocked him most. He stared at her, at the pale part separating the strands of her thick brown hair. She looked very young to him, too young to know such grief. "I don't understand. What did you ever do to anybody in that town?"

She shook her head and studied her plate, her fork making roads between hills of beans and cornbread. "More what I didn't do, I guess. I didn't conform to their idea of what was right and proper."

Her words were like sparks that started a burning in his chest, spreading warmth throughout his body. "You didn't fit in."

"No." She shrugged, and he could almost see the thought behind the gesture. She was shrugging off self-pity, refusing to dwell on the past. How many times had he done the same? "Maybe Reverend Deering will help to change all that," she added. "He said he was sent to talk to me. Seems like I ought not pass up the chance to make peace, so to speak."

He clenched his jaw to keep back the ugly words that matched his ugly feelings. He had little charity in his heart for any people who would shun this young woman who hardly seemed capable of harming a flea. He'd spent too many years on the receiving end of wounding words and stinging looks from folks like them. A few kind words from a preacher couldn't wipe all that away.

"Will you hitch up the wagon for me?" she asked.

He nodded. "Of course." He looked across at her bowed head, at her fingers smoothing the edge of the tablecloth. She looked so forlorn, and alone. "I'll drive you into town if you like."

"No!" She looked up, eyes wide, and covered her

mouth with two fingers, as if she wished she could take back that sudden denial. "I mean . . . well, it's nice of you to offer . . . but . . ."

He gripped the fork so hard it was in danger of bending. *Fool!* he cursed himself. Of course she wouldn't want to be seen in town with the likes of him. "I understand." He shoveled a forkful of beans into his mouth, though now they tasted like so much sawdust.

The silence around them had the heavy quality of the air before an impending thunderstorm, thick and hard to breathe. "Of . . . of course you may come to church with me tomorrow," she said after a long moment, her voice thin and wavery. "I would never deny you the opportunity of Christian worship."

The stilted speech grated on his nerves. "Don't worry yourself over my soul," he snapped. "I've been baptized proper enough, in Peach Creek on my fourteenth birthday." He broke a wedge of hot cornbread in half. The steam rose before his face, reminding him of the mist that had hung heavy on the water that long-ago day. Without much effort, he could still feel the stinging cold of the creek water closing over his head as the preacher bent him backward and dunked him under. He'd come up sputtering, hoping for a new beginning and some kind of acceptance from those around him.

But all the river water in the world couldn't change the color of his skin or bleach out the black of his hair. "You go on by yourself tomorrow. Make your peace. I've got plenty to do around here as it is."

They ate in silence for a while. He hardly tasted his food, his senses overwhelmed by an awareness of her and the sadness that hung like a veil around her. Was she thinking about past hurts or regrets? Was she fretting over the future and what people would say when they learned she'd hired a half-breed to come work for her?

"You're welcome to a bath tonight." The soft words startled him as he was scraping the last of his meal from the plate.

He glanced up and saw her eyes fixed on him, meek

and apologetic. "I think I have some clothes packed away that will fit you."

He wanted to harden his feelings against her, to fix a safe distance between them. Instead, the words he spoke were gruff, half joking. "You think after a week of shoveling manure I need a bath?"

A half-smile danced to her lips, shy and flirtatious. "I wasn't trying to be rude, but now that you mention it . . ."

He didn't think she meant to tease him, but the look sent a spasm to his groin, a shock of desire made stronger by the knowledge that it could never be satisfied. He'd have to content himself with moments like this, when he could imagine they were close. He nodded. "Sounds like a good idea."

"I'll leave the water in the tub for you," she said. "When I'm done, I'll put a lamp in the window. You'll have the kitchen all to yourself."

He started to tell her he'd spent too much of his life all to himself, but he rejected the idea before it was fully formed. Tessa was extending him a kindness, not an invitation. He'd do well not to forget it.

Micah waited that night until he saw the lamp in the window, then slipped into the kitchen. The door creaked loudly as he closed it behind him, announcing his entrance. He flinched at the sound. No matter that he was here at Tessa's request; he still felt like an intruder. He'd never ventured closer than the well pump after dark, though more than once he'd stood out by the corral and watched until the light in her bedroom window blinked out.

A zinc hip bath sat near the table, half filled with water. A kettle steamed on the stove. A man's shirt, trousers, and summer drawers were folded neatly on the table. He unfolded the shirt and held it up to his chest. Tessa's husband had been a broad man, thick through the shoulders and arms. He tried the pants and found them too short, but tucked into his boots, they would do. The garments were clean and ordinary. They told him nothing he wanted to know: What had Tessa's husband been like? How did she feel about him? Did she grieve for him still?

He laid aside the clothing and turned to the fresh towel and soap that rested on a chair beside the tub. The towel was worn soft, and the soap smelled like lavender. Like Tessa. He glanced overhead. Was she still awake, listening to him moving around down here? Did his presence in her house disturb her? Or was she already asleep, her drying hair spread out across her pillow?

He forced the image from his thoughts and turned back to the bath. Working quickly, he added fresh water from the kettle, then stripped off his own worn-out garments and sank into the tub.

A sigh escaped him as the warm water flowed over him, teasing knots from muscles and aches from joints. When he'd first come as a boy of twelve to live with his white relatives, he'd thought they meant to boil him alive in the hot baths. But he'd soon learned to look on a good soak in a tub as one of the advantages of living a white life, along with fried chicken every Sunday and thrilling stories revealed in their printed books.

He'd have to ask Tessa if she had any books she could lend him. It had been a while since he'd had a new one. He sank further into the bath, letting the hot water flow over his torso. The water was milky from where Tessa had bathed before him, and lightly scented with her perfume. He breathed in deeply and relaxed further, his imagination wandering to thoughts of how she must have looked, seated in this same tub, her hair undone and hanging damp past her full breasts . . .

He bit back a groan and sat up straighter. Such thoughts were dangerous and best put behind him. It wouldn't do him, or Tessa, any good to pursue such fantasies. Hadn't he learned a lesson from the last time he'd dared to think of a white woman in less than distant terms?

True, he'd done little to encourage that woman, Margery Watkins. But when a handsome woman forces herself upon you, going so far as to visit your tent at night, what is a normal, healthy man to do but return her attentions? He smiled at the memory. Ahh, Margery! They'd spent some pleasant hours together, though in the end he'd barely escaped being run through by a jealous colonel.

Fortunately he'd come to his senses in time to avoid such a fate. He'd resigned his commission as Army guide and headed north. He'd outrun one brand of trouble only to meet up with another.

Clearly the attraction in this case was all one-sided. Tessa Bright wasn't an Army-raised adventuress like Margery. Tessa was too respectable by half to think of getting involved with someone like him: a despised half-breed, penniless and homeless to boot. She might talk about not fitting in with people in town, but she had no idea what it meant to be a true outcast. Associating with him would damn her forever in the eyes of the respectable people in town—even that "sincere" preacher who professed such an interest in Indians. Reverend Deering's friendliness would likely fade when confronted with a breed who made the mistake of trying to be one of them.

Still, even a lady like Tessa might get lonely and make a mistake she'd come to regret. Sometimes, like this afternoon in the barn, he imagined he could feel the longing in her, a need for comfort that matched his own. He'd have to take care not to encourage her, to ward off disaster for both of them.

Chapter Four

Tessa gripped the wagon reins so tightly her fingers ached. Yesterday's excitement over Reverend Deering's invitation to church had given way to a paralyzing fear. She'd scarcely slept last night, her dreams haunted by scenes in which the good people of Pony Springs shunned her once more.

They'd certainly turned their noses up at her when she and Will had first come to town, seven years ago. She would never forget the cold stares that greeted them when they walked into the mercantile that first day. Will's skill as a blacksmith had eventually silenced most of his critics, but they'd continued to regard her with disapproval. After a while, she'd stopped trying to win them over.

She stared out over the landscape around her, forcing herself to think of something, anything, besides what lay ahead. Dust rose in powdery clouds around the horses' hooves and coated the grass on the side of the road so that the whole landscape seemed covered in a sifting of flour. She watched dust drift onto the sleeve of her black bombazine dress and wrinkled her nose in distaste. Maybe it was time she put away these widow's weeds.

Will had been dead more than a year now, though of course he wasn't really gone.

The wagon rocked as it crossed a rough spot in the road, and she adjusted the reins in her good hand. "Will?" The steady cadence of the horses' hooves on the hard-packed dirt road was her only answer. Even her ghostly husband had abandoned her this morning.

She almost wished now she'd taken Micah up on his offer to come with her. Almost, but not quite. The memory of the hard look in his eyes when she'd rejected him left a bitter taste in her mouth. She knew she'd been wrong to refuse him, certainly un-Christian. But she also knew what people would say if she rode into their midst beside him. They'd shut her out before they'd even given her a chance. She didn't think she was strong enough to bear that.

Within the hour, the town of Pony Springs came into view. A double row of weathered wood storefronts lined the town's main street, with the Red Dog Saloon at one end and the white steepled church at the other. Already a crowd of wagons and buggies shared the shade of a tall cottonwood beside the house of worship.

She found space for her wagon, set the brake, and climbed carefully down, trying to avoid looking too awkward as she did the job one-handed. The horses began cropping grass. Smoothing the glove on her good hand, she surveyed the scene from beneath the shadowing brim of her sunbonnet.

Families and couples were making their way toward the church house. The women all wore brightly colored calico dresses, with softly gathered skirts and fitted basques. Tessa looked down at the full sleeves and full skirt of her own Sunday best and felt awkward and out of fashion. Keeping to herself so much, she was unaware of the latest styles.

Maybe she should just turn around and go home. She didn't belong here. They wouldn't like her any more now than they had seven years ago. She pushed away the discouraging thoughts and took a deep breath. She wasn't the same person she had been seven years ago. With effort, she could fit in again. She could make them like her. Either that, or she'd spend the rest of her life alone, and that was no choice at all.

She raised her head, adjusted her out-of-fashion bonnet, and started toward the church house.

Milo Adamson was the first to notice her approach. Tessa recognized him from seeing him parked on a bench in front of Wilkins's Mercantile. Adamson squinted from beneath the brim of his hat, then nudged Bill Thornton next to him. The two stood with a group of men just outside the door, like a receiving line, inspecting each new arrival. 'Mornin', Miz Bright,'' Adamson said. He tugged at his hat brim and grinned, revealing a missing front tooth.

With as much dignity as she could muster, Tessa nodded. "Good morning, Mr. Adamson."

"M-mornin', m-m-ma'am." Bryan Ritter had lost a considerable amount of his hair over the years, but apparently none of his shyness. When she nodded to him, he blushed clear up to his bald spot.

The other men mumbled greetings as Tessa moved past. Legs wobbling, heart pounding, she made it up the steps and into the sanctuary. Her boots echoed on the wood floor, causing the cluster of women near the front of the room to turn and watch her approach. Tessa wished she were back home in her kitchen, or in her barn tending the horses, or cutting hay with Micah— anywhere but here under the judging eyes of all these people.

"Why, I declare, if it isn't Tessa Bright!" An older woman detached herself from the group and started down the aisle toward Tessa. She wore a green-and-black-figured calico dress and an elegant paisley shawl. She looked vaguely familiar, but Tessa couldn't put a name to the face.

"We're glad to have you with us this morning," the woman said, grasping Tessa's hand firmly in both her own.

Enveloped in the warmth of the woman's grasp, and the equal warmth of her smile, Tessa felt some of her nervousness ease. "I'm glad to be here," she said, and the words were now only half a lie.

"Have you met Mamie Tucker?" Her hostess led Tessa over to a plump, pretty blond woman who cradled a baby.

"How do you do?" The woman smiled and nodded, and Tessa returned the greeting.

"Of course, you know Trudy Babcock." Tessa turned to the next woman in the group, struggling to keep her smile in place. She wasn't likely to forget Mrs. Babcock—and the wife of the man who had been Will's chief competition didn't look any more pleased to see Tessa than she'd ever been. She gave a curt nod and looked away.

"And you probably haven't met Ambrosia Smith. She's our new schoolteacher."

A tall black-haired woman offered her hand. "Ada, let go so she can greet all of us," Miss Smith teased.

Ada Drake! The name came back to Tessa in a rush of memory. Her smile brightened with relief.

"Please, call me Ammie," the young teacher said to Tessa.

"It's nice to meet you, Ammie," Tessa said, hoping she'd remember all the names and faces. She was sorely out of practice at this sort of thing.

"My goodness, what happened to your arm?" Mamie Tucker inclined her head toward the cast.

Tessa rubbed the rough plaster. "I was trying to doctor a horse, and it kicked me. The doctor says it will be healed in a few more weeks."

"You poor dear." Ada shook her head. "You must have your hands full trying to take care of that big place of yours by yourself."

"I was so very sorry to hear about your husband's passing," Mamie said. The other women murmured their own sympathies.

"Thank you," Tessa said.

"I would have come to call afterward, but, well, I thought you preferred to be alone." Ada looked apologetic and . . . was she actually as nervous as Tessa felt?

"We were surprised to hear you'd decided to stay on after your husband's passing." Trudy Babcock sounded disapproving, but perhaps that was just Tessa's imagination. "We assumed you'd want to go back east to be with your family."

"Oh, I could never leave the ranch and Will." She flushed, realizing what she'd said. "I mean . . . his gravesite."

The women made more sounds of sympathy, then an awkward silence hung in the air between them. Tessa avoided looking at the others, fearing the disapproval or suspicion she expected to see in their eyes. Instead, she focused on the room around them. The simple wooden pews, narrow pulpit, and unadorned wooden cross hadn't changed since her last visit. The scent of candle wax and lemon-oil polish hung heavy in the air, along with an unfamiliar, flowery scent that seemed out of place.

"What is that smell?" Ammie Smith asked, wrinkling her nose. "Is something blooming nearby?"

"You must mean my new perfume." Trudy flashed a self-satisfied smile. "It's called Jasmine Nights. Imported all the way from France."

Ammie didn't seem impressed. "It's quite . . . strong, isn't it?"

Tessa hid her smile behind her hand. Poor Trudy was always trying, and failing, to impress people.

"We were just discussing the need this town has for a library." Ada Drake diplomatically changed the subject. "Don't you think it would benefit everyone, especially our schoolchildren, if we instituted a lending library?"

Tessa stared at her. Was Mrs. Drake actually asking her opinion? "Oh, yes. That sounds like a wonderful idea," she replied. "I've always loved to read."

"We're forming a committee to spearhead a drive to

establish a library in Pony Springs," Ammie said.
"Would you like to be on it?"

"Yes. Yes, I think I would." Tessa hoped she didn't
sound too pathetically eager. To think that they would
include her . . .

"I'm sure running your ranch occupies all your
time." Trudy's words were like a dart aimed at her in-
flating spirits.

There had been a time when Tessa would have retreated at such a remark, but today she met the challenge
head-on. She gave Trudy her most winning smile. "I'm
sure I can make time for such a worthy cause."

If the other women noticed Trudy's irritated expression, they ignored it. They showered Tessa with words
of thanks and news of their plans for the Library Society.

"The men are coming in. It's time to start." Trudy's
announcement broke through the women's happy chat-
ter. She nodded toward the back of the church, where
the men were indeed filing in. The women scattered to
take their places in the pews. As if it were the most
natural thing in the world, Tessa found herself beside
Ammie, who, as a teacher, was of course unmarried.
When the piano player struck up the first hymn, Ammie
even offered to share her songbook with Tessa.

It was as easy as that, then? Ten minutes after arriving
here, she'd been accepted as one of them, even invited
to join their library group. What had happened? What
had she done to dissolve the animosity of years past?

At the last chorus of "O, for a Thousand Tongues to
Sing," Reverend Deering stood and walked to the pulpit.
He wore the same black suit she'd seen him in the day
before, his hair neatly slicked down, a fresh collar on
his shirt.

"Our new minister is certainly a handsome man,"
Ammie whispered.

Tessa glanced at the schoolteacher. A pink flush
across her cheeks made her look quite lovely. Tessa
looked down at her lap, fighting back a smile. Of course,
every single woman in the congregation would set her

cap for the good-looking preacher. The question was, would Tessa be one of them?

"I take my text today from Hebrews 13:1 and 2. 'Let brotherly love continue. Be not forgetful to entertain strangers; for thereby some have entertained angels unawares.' "

Tessa smiled. Whether or not she decided to go along with Will's scheme to match her with the preacher, she admired his choice of a sermon topic. If this was a declaration of the focus his ministry here would take, she could see nothing but good to come for the church and the town.

Micah watched Tessa leave, an uncomfortable emptiness expanding in his chest as the buggy grew smaller and smaller in his vision, until all that was left to mark its passing was a cloud of dust hovering in the still air over the road. He whirled, turning his back on the forlorn image, and stalked to the corral, where he saddled the strawberry roan mare, Pigeon, and rode her toward a field east of the house. They hadn't gone far before he felt the mare straining to turn toward home. She tossed her head and fought the bit, risking damage to her mouth and trying his already thin patience.

"So you want to go back, do you?" He reined the mare to a stop, still keeping her facing away from the barn. "Fine. We'll go back. But you'll do it my way." He pulled on the reins and nudged her with his heels, forcing her to back up. She tossed her head and protested, but he kept it up, one awkward step at a time. He turned in the saddle to make sure the path was clear and kept the horse backing, all the way to the corral fence. The mare snorted and rolled her eyes at him, a hateful expression if he'd ever seen one. "Are you ready to go back and do it right this time?" he asked.

He let her rest a moment, then nudged her forward again. Halfway to the field, she threatened to turn again, but the minute he nudged her backward, she appeared to change her mind and straightened out her course. The minor victory dispelled some of his earlier gloominess. Once in the field, he tied the mare in the shade and began to cut hay.

It was work he enjoyed, feeling his muscles bunch with each swing of the scythe, seeing the grass fall away in sweeping arcs. The sun warmed his back, and the sky above was the blue of turquoise stones.

He felt the visitor before he saw him, the hairs on the back of his neck prickling with the sensation that someone was watching him. Scythe in hand, he turned slowly and saw an Indian on a spotted pony some fifty yards away. The two men faced each other, unmoving, the only sound a mockingbird caroling in the tree where Pigeon was tied.

The Indian looked to be close to Micah's own age. He wore only a breechclout and low moccasins, his dark hair hanging loose almost to his waist. He had a bow and quiver of arrows slung across his back, the hindquarter of a deer tied across the rump of the pony. *Comanche,* Micah thought. Was he a scout for a raiding party, or simply out hunting a little meat?

Though he'd had plenty of encounters with members of various Indian tribes in his years with the Army, every confrontation left Micah feeling at odds with himself and the world. He stared at the man before him now with the unnerving sensation of looking into a trick mirror. The image he saw was more like himself than any white man could be. And yet to Micah, it remained an unfathomable mystery, a dim reminder of a past he'd struggled to leave behind.

He waited, perfectly still, with a firm grip on the scythe. After a long moment, the Indian kneed the pony and moved closer until he was in front of Micah, no more than a yard away.

"Who are you?" the man asked in Comanche, signing the words as he spoke.

"Fox," Micah said, using the Comanche term for the animal. He'd become fairly fluent in the language during his years as an Army scout.

The Indian's eyes swept over Micah, taking his measure.

"Who are you?" Micah asked in turn.

The Indian squared his shoulders. "Esahiwi."

Drinking Wolf, Micah translated in his head.

"Where are you from?" Drinking Wolf asked.

He might have been asking about Micah's origins, but Micah chose to answer the question more superficially. He nodded in the direction of the ranch house. "I live on the ranch here."

The Indian looked puzzled. "You know Tes-Sah?"

Micah took firmer hold of the scythe and nodded. What did this Comanche know about Tessa?

Drinking Wolf turned and unfastened the haunch of venison. "This is for Tes-Sah," he said.

Micah stared at the man, then at the meat. "Why?"

Drinking Wolf grinned and dropped the meat at Micah's feet. "You will have to ask Tes-Sah." Then he whirled and kicked his horse into a gallop.

Micah dropped the scythe and ran to the mare, intending to follow. But the Indian and the pony were out of sight before he could even untie the reins. He stared at the empty horizon. What was that all about?

He retrieved the venison and tied it to his saddle horn, then headed back toward the house. He'd gather the hay later. Tessa would be home soon.

After church, the congregation spilled out into the sunshine; children first, anxious to be free of their confinement, boys divesting themselves of jackets and even shoes as they raced toward the trees, girls following more sedately, the bolder ones untying bonnets or stripping off gloves. Next came the men, some filling pipes or cutting off plugs of tobacco. The women filtered out last, in pairs and small groups. Some of them, including Tessa, lingered around Reverend Deering in the church doorway.

"An excellent sermon, Reverend," Trudy pronounced with a regal smile.

"Thank you, Mrs. Babcock." He nodded amiably and turned to shake the next well-wisher's hand.

"My husband and I will have you over for luncheon soon," Trudy continued.

"That's very kind of you, Mrs. Babcock. I hope to visit all my congregation as time permits." He spotted Tessa in line and beamed at her. "I'm so pleased you decided to join us today," he said, leaning forward to take her hand.

"I'm very glad to be here," she said, returning his smile. "I particularly enjoyed your message."

"It's one I intend to put into daily practice," he said. "There is entirely too much strife and petty differences in the world. In fact, I hope you'll persuade Mr. Fox to accompany you to services one day soon."

Tessa's smile faded, as she remembered how she'd rebuffed Micah's offer to accompany her. How could she have behaved so shamefully?

"Who is Mr. Fox?" Ada Drake asked pleasantly.

"Micah Fox is Mrs. Bright's hired hand," Reverend Deering answered.

"Do you mean to say you are living alone on your ranch with a single man?" Trudy's severe tone of voice and raised eyebrows conveyed her disapproval.

Tessa would have given anything to hold back the blush that warmed her cheeks. She brushed nonexistent lint from the sleeve of her dress and wished she could as easily have brushed away Trudy's censorious words. "Mr. Fox lives in the barn," she said crisply. "Our relationship is perfectly proper."

Trudy sniffed, as if she doubted this was so. Tessa fought the urge to tell the old biddy just what she could do with her narrow-minded opinions.

"I've visited with Mr. Fox, and he seems quite respectable." Reverend Deering's attempt to defend her was destroyed by his next words: "He's a fascinating man—half Indian."

An audible gasp sounded sharply just behind Tessa's elbow. She turned and met Mamie Tucker's shocked look. "Aren't you afraid of being scalped in your sleep with a man like that around?" Mrs. Tucker asked.

"Afraid? Of course not." She'd never thought to be afraid of Micah. Besides, Will would never allow anything to happen to her. "Mr. Fox has been very helpful. I couldn't have kept the ranch going without his help."

"Couldn't you have hired a white man to work for you?" Trudy's scolding words attracted attention from across the churchyard. "Instead of bringing another savage to live among us?"

"I assure you, Mrs. Babcock, Mr. Fox is no savage," Reverend Deering said. "He appears completely adapted to the white way of life."

Trudy looked no less disapproving. "Still, there are plenty of white men in need of work. I'm sure one of them would help Mrs. Bright."

"Except none of them ever did." Barely containing her anger, Tessa nodded a curt good-bye, then whirled and rushed down the steps.

"Good-bye, Mrs. Bright. I hope to see you again soon," Reverend Deering called after her.

She didn't pause to acknowledge his words, just gathered her skirts and walked as quickly as possible toward her wagon, fighting the urge to break into a run. All she wanted was to be away from this place and these people who judged her so harshly by the company she kept. How could she have supposed things would be different this time?

She climbed into the wagon, released the brake, and slapped the reins across the rumps of the drowsing horses. "Get up," she called. The sooner she was out of sight of this town, the better.

Of course, a quick departure was out of the question in the crush of other buggies and wagons. She had to sit and wait while Wes Drake backed his buggy out from the space in front of her. She tapped her toe against the footboard, fretting.

"You should have stayed and visited, been more sociable."

She glanced around to see if anyone else had heard the words, but no one paid her any attention. "Will, what are you doing here?" she muttered through clenched teeth.

"I came to see how you were getting along," he answered. The seat beside her creaked as he took his place. *"And it's a good thing I did, too. What did you mean, rushing off in a huff like that?"*

"Did you hear what that old biddy said?" She spoke softly, glad now of the sunbonnet that concealed her face. "Of all the hateful . . ."

"Trudy Babcock's never forgiven me for taking away the lion's share of her husband's business. Besides, she's just one person," Will said. *"You can't expect everyone to welcome you with open arms right away. If you want to fit in, you've got to earn their approval."*

"What difference does it make? They've already judged me because of Micah."

"I told you not to hire him. I warned you he'd make trouble."

"I couldn't very well go on with things the way they had been." The Drakes' buggy out of the way, she guided her rig forward. "You can't say he hasn't done a good job."

"He's done a good job all right. But not as good as the ranch owner would do. As a husband *would do."* His icy breath stirred the bavolet of her sunbonnet as he leaned toward her. *"Micah Fox hasn't done as good a job as Reverend Deering would do. And no one would dare say a word against the preacher's wife. At least, not that anyone would listen to."*

"You leave Reverend Deering out of this!" She gave the reins an angry shake, sending the horses plunging forward.

"Watch out!" Will shouted, as a heavy Army ambulance lumbered into her path.

Her horses screamed and reared. Heart in her throat, Tessa stood and struggled to control the frightened animals with one hand. The leather burned through her glove, and pain shot through her arm and shoulder as she strained against four thousand pounds of frightened horseflesh. She stared across at the wide-eyed young soldier driving the ambulance and saw the door of his vehicle pop open and a figure in blue leap toward her.

The man vaulted into her buggy and took the reins from her shaking hands. The heavy broadcloth of his officer's uniform scraped against the stiff bombazine of her dress as he stood beside her, hauling on the lines, forcing her horses to calm and turn the buggy, somehow avoiding the wreck that seconds before had seemed inevitable.

As her knees turned to jelly, Tessa sank onto the seat, her hand over her mouth to stifle a moan of relief and terror.

The officer, a major by the insignia on his shoulder boards, sank down beside her, keeping firm hold on the reins. "Are you all right?" he asked.

She nodded. "I . . . I'm so sorry." Her voice had an appalling vibrato, and she struggled to bring it under control. "I . . . I wasn't watching where I was going. I don't know what I was thinking."

He waved aside her apology and pulled a handkerchief from his pocket and offered it to her. She took it, aware for the first time of the tears sliding down her cheeks. The handkerchief was of fine white linen, with the initials "A.L.F." embroidered in the corner in neat stitches. She dabbed her cheeks and extended it to him. "Thank you so much, Major . . . ?"

"Alan Finch, at your service." He tucked away the handkerchief and extended a leather-gauntleted hand to her.

She touched her fingertips to his briefly. "I'm Tessa Bright."

A drooping blond moustache hid his upper lip, but his lower lip curved in a pleasant smile. "You seem somewhat shaken still, Mrs. Bright. I was on my way to the stage stop. Why not allow me to drive you that far?"

She nodded her head. "I'd be much obliged."

Major Finch maneuvered the wagon through town at a sedate walk, the Army ambulance following behind. Tessa studied him out of the corner of her eye. She judged him to be about forty years old. His hair, the same sunny shade as his moustache though silvering at the temples, curled up at the collar of his flag-blue tunic. His eyes, a somewhat lighter shade of blue, fixed in the perpetual squint of a man accustomed to spending hours on patrol, searching the horizon for unknown dangers. "Are you stationed at Fort Belknap?" she asked as they neared the stage station.

He nodded. "I've recently been appointed commander there." He glanced at her. "My wife is coming in on the stage today. At first we thought it would be best for her to remain back east while I was posted here." He smiled. "But I must confess I've missed her too much. When she pleaded to join me here, I couldn't refuse her, though I worry about her living in such rough conditions."

There was something wistful and boyish in his expression. Tessa couldn't keep from smiling. "Any woman with a taste for adventure would enjoy this country, especially with a loving husband to share it with her."

His smiled expanded. "You've said it exactly, Mrs. Bright. My Margery definitely has a taste for adventure. I've no doubt she'll soon have the whole country tamed to her satisfaction."

"I'll look forward to meeting her," Tessa said. Of course, it was the polite thing to say, but she discovered she actually meant it. Margery Finch, a stranger to town almost as much as Tessa was, might be easier to make friends with than those who knew Tessa's past.

Major Finch parked the buggy just down from the stage station and turned to her. "What does your husband do, Mrs. Bright?"

"When he was alive, he was a blacksmith and raised horses. He died over a year ago. Now I run our ranch, a few miles out of town."

"I'm sorry to hear about your husband. It must be difficult for you alone."

"I have a man who helps me with the work." She tensed, waiting for the questions that would follow. How would she explain Micah to this man who made his living quelling Indian disturbances?

But instead of questions, Finch turned the conversation back to his own pressing concerns. "I'm new at this business of marriage myself. Never thought it was for me until I met Margery. Then . . . well, I can't say I can really explain what happened. I always thought it was foolish poetry when people talked about someone stealing their heart."

Tessa smiled. She couldn't recall seeing a man as smitten as Major Finch. "I'm sure your wife has missed you as much as you've missed her."

He nodded. "I expect you're right. This isn't the most glamorous job in the world. My duties generally hold more boredom than excitement. I'm here to protect the settlers and the stage line, but with most of the Indians on the reservations, things have been pretty quiet. Of course, that could change at any moment. And this post can be a stepping-stone to something better. Margery says she doesn't care where we are, but I want her to have the finer things in life."

"If you love her, that's all she needs," Tessa said, her throat tight with emotion. She could remember feeling that way about Will. Would she ever be able to risk such a powerful passion again?

The major nodded. A cloud of dust on the horizon signaled the approaching stage. He turned to Tessa. "Will you come to dinner with us soon? I'd like Margery to make friends in the area."

"I'd be delighted."

He offered his hand once more. "It was a pleasure meeting you, Mrs. Bright. I'll extend an invitation as soon as Margery is settled."

"I'm glad I met you, too, Major. Though I hope next time you see me, I won't be trying to run you down."

He grinned and handed over the reins, then leapt agilely to the ground and hurried toward the approaching stagecoach. He had hold of the door before the wheels even stopped turning. The first passenger to emerge was a tall, buxom woman in a dress of sky-blue organdy, her face and hair swathed in white veiling. She put her arms on the major's shoulders, and he swung her down, then paused to push back the veiling, revealing porcelain skin and a tumble of red curls.

Margery Finch laughed and planted a kiss on her husband's cheek, a kiss that held the promise of greater intimacy later. The major ordered Private Thompson to collect his wife's baggage, then led her away to the waiting ambulance.

Tessa smiled and turned her buggy toward home. As she drove, she replayed the morning's events in her mind. Margery Finch would certainly add color to the captain's boring existence at the fort. Her arrival had given Tessa something to look forward to as well—the possibility of new friendship and another guard against the loneliness that had weighed too heavily on her these last few months.

The major's friendliness had also taken some of the sting out of the town women's reaction to news of Micah's presence on the ranch. Maybe Reverend Deering's acceptance of her situation would make the women think twice about rejecting her again. In any case, they hadn't rescinded their invitation to join their Library Society, had they?

I'll just go to the meeting and pretend nothing ever happened, she thought, snapping the reins to send the horses into a trot. *I'll give those women, and myself, one more chance to get off on the right foot.*

A short while later, she rounded a curve in the road and saw the entrance to her drive up ahead. The ornate iron gate stood out against the stark surroundings, drawing the eye of all who passed. Will had worked on the gate in secret and surprised her with it the first summer after the house was completed. While he claimed to have made it as a way to attract business, she always felt in her heart that he'd created it to please her.

A rider moved out from the shade of a live oak, just outside the gate, a tall man astride a roan horse, an oddly shaped burden tied to his saddle horn. Even from this distance, she recognized Micah, riding the runaway mare, Pigeon. Her heartbeat quickened, and she leaned forward, caught unawares by such girlish eagerness. The sight of him there, waiting for her return home, answered a deep longing she hadn't known existed until now, a yearning to have her homecoming matter to someone else.

She slowed the horses to meet him, and he flashed the briefest of smiles. Then she knew the breathlessness she felt had less to do with the fact of his welcome than with the man himself. Something in this proud, reserved man spoke to her heart. When she looked in his eyes sometimes, she thought she glimpsed an understanding she'd never known before. Then the moment would pass, and she'd wonder if she'd imagined the kinship between them. Now, watching him lean down to unfasten the gate, instinct told her what sense would not. If she wasn't very careful, she might find herself falling in love with Micah Fox.

Chapter Five

Micah closed the gate and rode down the drive alongside Tessa's wagon. "You're riding Pigeon," she said. "How did you manage that?"

"I think we've come to an understanding." He reached down and stroked the mare's neck.

"But how?" Goodness knows, she'd spent plenty of hours working with the stubborn animal, with little results.

"Like this." He flashed the briefest of smiles and turned the mare around until she faced the wagon. With a nudge of his heels, he forced her to back up. Pigeon tossed her head and tried to turn, but he kept her in line. *Now, why didn't I think of that?* Tessa mused. Horses hate to back up. Pigeon would probably do anything, including heading *away* from her beloved barn, to keep from being forced into this unnatural position.

The sight of the two of them, backing down the drive, struck her as the funniest thing she'd seen in ages. Laughter bubbled out of her, straining the lacings of her corset. Micah turned the horse and fell in beside the wagon once more. "What's so funny?" he asked, grinning at her.

"You are." She fanned her face. "Oh, I can't remember the last time I laughed so hard."

"Then I'd say you haven't laughed nearly enough. Glad I could oblige." He lowered his head in a mocking bow and from beneath the shadowing brim of his hat slanted her a look that made her catch her breath. When had she ever felt such a mix of emotions—joy and abandon and even fear—from being around one person? Micah Fox had a peculiar effect on her, as intoxicating as wine, and probably just as dangerous.

She looked away and searched for a safe topic of conversation. The deer haunch hanging from his saddle horn caught her eye. "Where did you get the venison?"

He frowned. "A friend of yours brought it by." He didn't look very pleased with the gift.

She knit her brow in thought. "Who was that?" *Surely no one from town* . . .

"He said his name was Esahiwi—Drinking Wolf."

"Of course." She relaxed against the seat of the wagon and smiled. She hadn't seen Drinking Wolf and his people for a while. Apparently they were back on the reservation after what must have been a successful hunt, if they had venison to share.

The deer haunch bounced awkwardly against Pigeon's neck, making the mare skittish. "How do you come to know a Comanche brave?" Micah sounded irritated, though whether at her or the horse she couldn't be sure.

"He was my husband's friend, really," she said. "Sometimes he brings me meat."

"Why?"

She frowned. Why was Micah in such a surly mood all of a sudden? Was he angry because she'd gone to town without him? "I suppose because he knows I live alone."

She drew the wagon to a stop beside the corral. Micah swung down off his horse and came around to help her alight. "I thought the tribes were confined to the reservations." His grip on her hand was firmer than usual, and instead of releasing her right away once she was on the ground, he continued to hold her. Was he concerned about her association with the Indians? She didn't know whether to be touched or annoyed.

"Most of the Comanches aren't," she said. "Or they wander off and on as it suits them. They leave to hunt and trade."

"And to raid into Mexico."

She nodded. "That, too." She'd heard plenty of stories about the atrocities the Indians perpetrated, but when she was face-to-face with her friends, she had a difficult time reconciling those reports with the reality she knew. Drinking Wolf and his people had been nothing but friendly toward her.

"I don't imagine the townspeople have anything good to say about that."

She eased herself out of Micah's grasp. "Some of them don't have anything good to say about anything, so I can't see how it makes much difference."

He turned away and busied himself unhitching the wagon. "How did it go this morning at church?"

"All right. Better than I expected. Some women asked me to join a group that's working to establish a lending library in town."

"Ah, well, you're on your way to becoming a society matron, then." He began unfastening the traces.

She laughed, and the tight expression on his face eased somewhat, as did the tension between them. "I did make one new friend."

He glanced up from his work. "Who was that?"

"The new commander at Fort Belknap. Major Alan Finch. I almost ran into the Army ambulance he was riding in as I was leaving the church."

He looked away, his expression hidden. "Not exactly an auspicious beginning to a friendship."

"Not exactly. But then he offered to drive me to the stage stop, where he was going to meet his wife coming in on the afternoon stage." She brushed the powdery dust of the road from her arm. Yes, it was definitely time she added some color to her wardrobe. Next time

she was in town, she'd look for a pattern. "Did you meet
the major's wife, too?"

"No. But I hope to soon. The major said he would
have me to dinner to properly introduce me. Her name
is Margery."

The coupling chains clanged as they slipped from his
hand and hit the ground. He fumbled twice as he retrieved them. Tessa was startled to see that his face had
blanched two shades paler. "What's wrong?" she asked,
rushing to his side.

"Nothing." He turned away from her. "Just over-
heated, maybe. Was the major's wife a pretty woman?"

"Oh, yes. Lovely red hair and that kind of flawless
skin redheads sometimes have." She smiled, remembering. "They make a handsome couple."

"I imagine they do."

She peered at him. "Are you sure you're all right?
You look very pale."

"I'm fine!" he snapped. He took a deep breath and
spoke again in a softer tone. "Why don't you go into
the house and change? I'll cut up some of this venison
for dinner and hang the rest in the smokehouse."

"All right." She turned toward the house but paused
on the porch to look back at him. Why was Micah acting
so curiously all of a sudden? Had Drinking Wolf said
something to upset him? Or was Tessa herself to blame?

A week passed, and the subject of Drinking Wolf and
the Indians did not come up again. Micah finished bringing in the hay, and Tessa dried a bushel of green beans
from the garden, stringing them together to hang under
the eaves in the attic. In the evenings, she sat on the
front porch and sewed until the last light faded. Sometimes Micah sat with her, mending harness or whittling
clothespins from scraps of wood. The hours passed in
companionable silence, though sometimes Tessa found
herself watching him, wondering what secrets he kept
locked inside of him, what hurts she had only glimpsed

in the stubborn set of his mouth or the shadows that sometimes haunted his eyes.

Those shadows loomed dark as he stood with Tessa on the front porch the next Saturday afternoon, waiting for the Army ambulance that would take her to dinner with Major Finch and his wife. "Have you ever been to Fort Belknap before?" he asked.

She arranged the skirts of her new dress around her. Made of lavender calico sprigged with a design of green leaves, it featured the full gathered back, called a Watteau pleat, that she had seen on the fashionable town women last Sunday. "My husband went sometimes, delivering items he'd made for the Army, but I never went. I'm looking forward to it."

"Don't expect much." As he stared toward the approaching dust cloud that signaled the arrival of her coach, the corners of his mouth turned down in an expression of disapproval. "Every fort I've ever been in was little better than a bunch of thrown-together huts around a barren parade ground."

She glanced at him in surprise. "What were you doing that caused you to be in forts?"

"I was an Army scout."

The Army often hired Indians to serve as trackers and interpreters, so this news shouldn't have surprised her. But why hadn't he bothered to mention it to her before? Maybe it was because his experience hadn't been a pleasant one. He certainly didn't look too happy now. "Why did you decide to leave the job?" she asked.

His lips formed a narrow line. "It was time to move on."

There was more to the story than that, she was sure, but apparently he had shared all he was willing to. The knowledge stung. Would she ever really know the man beside her or would she have to learn to settle for crumbs of information like this?

Why did it matter to her, anyway? Micah had his life to lead; she had hers. She adjusted her shawl around her shoulders. "I left your dinner in the pie safe. I don't imagine I'll be home terribly late, but in any case, you needn't wait up.'' She felt foolish as soon as the words were out of her mouth. She sounded like a mother or a wife. Why should Micah, her hired hand, care to wait up for her?

The approach of the Army ambulance saved her from further conversation. They waited in silence until it rolled to a stop before her. A corporal stepped down to wish her a good evening and open the door. She turned to say good-bye to Micah, but he was gone. The thought that he hadn't waited to see her off disturbed her, though that, too, was as much foolishness as her telling him not to wait up.

Such unsettling thoughts vanished by the time the ambulance rolled through the picketed gates at Fort Belknap two hours later. True to Micah's prediction, the compound had little to recommend it. All the buildings were constructed of unpeeled logs chinked with mud. Some of the poorer quarters had only blankets for door and window coverings. Rows of canvas tents stretched out behind the wooden structures, their guy ropes festooned with drying laundry. The palisade itself was an unimposing fence of sticks and brush that served more as boundary marker than defense. But the major's simple house was freshly whitewashed, and inside, the rooms were festive with candles and vases of wildflowers arranged on tables and windowsills.

"Mrs. Bright, how wonderful of you to come." Major Finch greeted her at the door and bowed low over her hand. "Allow me to introduce my wife, Margery."

Margery Finch had the porcelain skin and sapphire eyes of a French fashion doll. Even in a new dress, Tessa suddenly felt very drab next to her hostess. But the major's wife welcomed her with a warm smile. "I'm delighted to meet you, Mrs. Bright. I understand you swept my husband off his feet when he met you."

"Rather, I almost ran him down," Tessa said as a private took her shawl.

"Let me send one of the boys for a glass of wine for you," Mrs. Finch said.

"I'll get it, ma'am!" A young corporal sprinted from her side. As Tessa followed her hostess into the parlor, she noticed a group of young men following them, like a bevy of courtiers in service to a queen.

Though in residence scarcely a week, Margery Finch had obviously made herself at home. She introduced Tessa to various captains and lieutenants and the handful of military wives and daughters in attendance, never fumbling for a name. Everyone was quite cordial, though the men in particular barely glanced at Tessa. Margery garnered all the attention in the room, like an exotic bird set down in the midst of sparrows. "You seem to be settling in nicely," Tessa observed when they had completed a circuit of the room.

Her hostess smiled. "I've lived on Army posts most of my life. Did Alan mention that?"

Tessa tried to hide her surprise. "No, he didn't say."

"My father was a career Army man. My mother died young, so Daddy took me with him wherever he was posted, except for brief periods of schooling." She surveyed the room, a half-smile on her full red lips. "I feel at home here."

Tessa sipped the wine the corporal brought her and thought how Margery Finch was truly in her element. The major had nothing to worry about.

"Military posts always have such a number of good-looking men, don't you think?" Mrs. Finch said suddenly.

The abrupt turn in the conversation startled Tessa. "Y-yes, I suppose so," she murmured.

Mrs. Finch gave her a beatific smile. "I understand you're a widow. Perhaps I could arrange an introduction . . ."

"Oh, no. Thank you, Mrs. Finch, but—"

"Mrs. Finch, I—" A portly lieutenant with a thick black moustache approached them.

"Please, call me Margery." She smiled at the man,

and Tessa wasn't sure if the instruction was for him or herself. The lieutenant apparently had no such doubts. "Margery, then—may I refill your glass?"

While Margery dealt with the crowd of men vying for her attention, Tessa sought out a quiet alcove in the hallway. She was aware that her movements did not go completely unnoticed. As her hostess had observed, there were a number of handsome men in the room and few women, so that with the least encouragement she could have attracted an entourage of her own.

She stood in her corner and sipped her wine more rapidly than was perhaps gracious, and avoided making eye contact with anyone. The thought of being "on the market" unnerved her, though underneath the nervousness ran a current of anticipation. What would it be like to have a man court her again—to have that power to please and persuade, and to be pleased and persuaded in turn . . .

"How nice to see you again, Mrs. Bright."

The wine sloshed in her glass as she looked up and found herself face-to-face with Reverend Deering. "I hope you are doing well," he said, smiling.

"Quite well, Reverend." She set her glass aside on a table. "And you?"

"Quite well. Major and Mrs. Finch are a charming couple." He leaned closer. "I've been meaning to come visit with you again soon. I have some questions to ask Mr. Fox."

She eyed him warily. "What kind of questions?"

"I'm trying to learn more about Indians. I have an idea for a ministry . . ."

She bit back her smile. Of course. The reverend was passionate about Indians. Why had Will ever thought to turn those passions toward her? As the reverend sailed into an explanation of his plans for Christianizing the reservation tribes, Tessa studied him. He was undoubtedly a handsome man, intelligent, kind, and respectful. As Will had said, perfect for a husband, except that absolutely nothing about him stirred her blood, made her think of him as a man and not just a minister.

Perhaps it wasn't right to think such things, especially about a man of God. "Mrs. Bright, are you all right?" Deering stopped his monologue and peered at her. "You seem rather flushed."

She was saved from having to answer by the appearance in the doorway of a private announcing dinner was served.

Will watched the Army ambulance pull away, carrying Tessa with it. He'd started to go with her, to meet the new major and his wife, so to speak, and to look up a few old friends. But then he'd noticed Micah Fox scowling over by the corral, and determined he had other work to do. He'd promised Tessa he wouldn't run Fox off, but that didn't mean he couldn't do a little something to discourage the man's feelings for her. It didn't take a ghost to know Fox was starting to think of her in ways that would come to no good end if not stopped immediately.

He concentrated on materializing, working up a strong mental picture of his former physical self. It seemed to take longer these days, as if the image of the old Will was fading. Haunting somebody as a bodiless voice was a lot easier, but it wouldn't do for what he had in mind for Micah Fox.

At last he had everything in place, and he strolled over to where Fox was working a grindstone, sharpening a scythe. "I see she left you here to do the work while she went off to the festivities," he shouted over the whir of the grindstone.

The scythe skidded against the stone, nicking the tip of Fox's finger. He sucked at the cut and glared at Will. "Did anyone ever tell you it's not polite to sneak up on people?"

Will shrugged. "What do hermits care for manners?"

Fox wrapped a handkerchief around the bleeding finger. "What do you want?"

"I had a hankering to go into town and I came to see if you wanted to go with me."

Fox's expression didn't lighten any. "What are you going to do in town?"

"It's Saturday night. Thought I might get drunk." He leaned toward Fox, a fellow conspirator. "When's the last time you got drunk?"

Fox shook his head. "Thanks for asking, but I'm not interested."

"Why not?" He looked down the road, in the direction Tessa had traveled. "She's been working you mighty hard. You deserve a night off. She's sure going to be having her own fun tonight."

Fox looked up. Will could almost read his thoughts. He was thinking Tessa wouldn't like it if she came home and found him drunk. "Hey, she pays your wages, she don't run your life," Will said. "Every man's entitled to blow off steam, go on a spree now and then."

He followed Fox into the barn and watched him hang the scythe on a nail on the wall. He knew by the set of the man's shoulders that he had him now, so he wasn't surprised when Fox turned to him and said, "All right. I'll go with you." He headed toward the horse stalls. "You know how to ride?"

Hmmm. Here was a problem he hadn't anticipated. No horse on earth was going to let his icy self on its back. "I can ride well enough, but I can't stay in the saddle when I'm drunk," he said. "I think I'll just walk."

Fox shrugged. "Suit yourself." He went into the corral and caught the strawberry roan mare.

"That horse is a runaway," Will observed. "Better choose another."

"This one'll do."

Will melted into the shadows and let him get the saddle on and the girth tightened before he showed himself again. Fox didn't know it, but he was going to be in for a rough ride to town, with a ghost walking along beside him.

• • •

The damask-covered dining table filled the room, china and silver gleaming in the lamplight. Margery Finch presided at one end of the table, the major at the other, their gazes frequently flitting to one another between smiles at their arrayed guests.

Tessa was seated at Margery's end of the table, with Reverend Deering on one side and a balding gentleman introduced to her as Sergeant Peterson on the other.

"The man across from you is Lieutenant Hamilton," Peterson explained in low tones as the first course was served. "He has his eye on Carmen Miller, the young woman to his left. She's the daughter of the red-headed lieutenant at the end of the table." His eyes twinkled as he helped himself to soup. "Her mother is on Hamilton's right, just to keep an eye on the young couple. Next to *her* is Hamilton's father, *Major* Hamilton, who would like nothing better than to strike up an alliance with Mrs. Lieutenant Miller."

Tessa fought back a smile and accepted a dinner roll from a silver tray. "My goodness, how do you know so much, Sergeant?"

He gave her a sly smile. "Didn't anyone tell you? I'm a terrible gossip!"

She laughed. "Then I shall listen very closely to everything you have to say and be careful not to give you any reason to talk about me."

"Ah, but even then, all sorts of stories will be circulating about such a lovely young widow before evening's end." Peterson waggled his eyebrows, and she realized with a start that he was flirting with her. She took a sip of wine. It had been a long time since she'd felt this giddy. The attention of the assembled men was proving as intoxicating as the liquor.

"Reverend Deering, I understand you yourself are newly arrived to the area," Margery said.

Deering sliced into his beefsteak and nodded. "I've been here only a few days longer than yourself. It appears to be fertile ground for doing the Lord's work."

Margery looked amused. "I've no doubt you could say the same for any Army post in Texas and the surrounding town. There's something about the isolation and hard work that inclines one toward sin."

Margery spoke as if she had firsthand knowledge, and Deering had the grace to flush. "I wasn't speaking of sin in general, Mrs. Finch," he said. "Rather, I was referring to my own calling to work among this country's native peoples. The nearby reservations are convenient for that work."

"You want to be a missionary to the Indians?" Lieutenant Hamilton spoke from across the table. "No offense, Reverend, but do you have any idea what you're getting into?"

Deering smiled. "No, sir, and I've a feeling this is one case where ignorance really is bliss. But I'm certain the Lord is going to bless my work. Why, the very first day I was here, he sent a message directing me to visit Mrs. Bright here. And what do you think the first thing was that I saw when I arrived at her house?"

The preacher had the attention of almost everyone in the room by now. Tessa wanted to disappear under the table. She knew good and well God hadn't been the one speaking to Deering that day, and the message he'd received hadn't been intended as anything to do with his supposed ministry to Indians.

"What did you see?" Margery leaned toward him, her eyes dancing with amusement.

"An Indian!" Deering looked triumphant. "I knew right then and there that it was a sign my work would be blessed."

Margery turned a curious gaze on Tessa. "You have an Indian at your ranch?"

Tessa raised her chin, wishing she could will away the bright blush she knew stained her cheeks. "I have a half-breed who works for me."

"How interesting," Margery mused.

"Mr. Fox is interesting." Deering dug into his steak once more. "And a hard worker, from what I've seen."

"We had a tracker named Fox out at Fort Inge," Lieutenant Hamilton said. "Not very trustworthy. He up and disappeared in the middle of the night."

Margery paused with her soup spoon halfway to her lips. "Is your Mr. Fox a tall, quite handsome man with green eyes?"

Tessa caught her breath. "Why, yes, how—" She was saved by the bell, or rather, by a crystalline ringing from the opposite end of the table.

"Quiet, everyone." Major Finch tapped his water goblet, commanding everyone's attention. He held his wineglass aloft and smiled down the table at Margery. "I'd like to propose a toast to my wife, who has made me a very happy man indeed by agreeing to join me here."

"To Mrs. Major Finch," chorused around the table.

Tessa turned her attention back to her meal, but more than once during the remaining courses, she felt Margery Finch's gaze on her.

No one looked up when Micah and Will entered the saloon. They ordered beer, and the bartender served them without comment. Micah sipped his drink slowly and looked around the place. A rickety piano sat at one end of the room, the thick coating of dust on its keys suggesting it served more for decoration than entertainment. A trio of scarred tables surrounded by mismatched chairs filled the needs of card-playing clientele, while everyone else was obliged to stand at the bar. That carved mahogany behemoth ran the length of the building. Brass-railed and equipped with cigar lighters that sent foot-high tongues of flame into the air when struck, the bar held pride of place second only to the polished gilt-framed mirror behind it.

Micah watched in the mirror now as a young woman in a stained purple dress detached herself from a card game and wandered over to him. "Hello," she purred, leaning against the bar beside him. "You're new in town, aren't you?"

He nodded, scarcely looking at her. Out of the corner of his eye, it looked as if her breasts were in danger of spilling out of the top of her dress. The smell of sweat and cheap perfume filled his head. "My name's Tina," she said. "What's yours?"

"You can call me Mike." It was the name he used when he wanted to avoid long explanations. He glanced at Will, but the old man seemed intent on watching a trio of cardplayers.

"Buy me a drink?" Tina asked.

He nodded and signaled the bartender, who bought him another beer and some dark liquor for the woman. He scarcely listened as she talked to him, letting her words flow over him with the same soothing effect as the beer. He felt some of the tension ease out of him. Coming here had been a good idea. He deserved a night out, after all the hard work he'd been doing. After all, Tessa was out enjoying herself. He certainly didn't intend to sit up waiting for her. Tessa Bright didn't own him.

"Silent type, aren't you?" Tina placed her hand on his thigh. She squeezed, sending a jolt to his groin. "I like the strong, silent type."

It had been a long time since a woman had touched him that way. Too long. He saw that knowledge reflected in her eyes. "We could have a good time together," she said. She slid her fingers between the buttons on his shirt. His heart pounded against the warmth of her hand.

He was about to tell her yes, he would go with her, when he felt a rough hand on his shoulder. "Who do you think you are, comin' in here like you got the right?"

Every muscle tensed as he turned to face the drunk, a beefy man with graying hair and a road map of broken red lines across his bulbous nose.

Tina took her hands off him and melted away into the shadows. Micah made a point of taking another sip from his beer mug, slowly.

"Didn't you hear me, injun? We don't want your kind around here." The slap of a single card on the table sounded like a gunshot in the room, and then everything was so silent, Micah could hear the drunk's heavy breathing. Out of the corner of his eye, he searched for Will, his only ally in the room. The old man had either taken off or was hiding, leaving Micah to fend for himself. It wouldn't be the first time.

He sighed and set the beer mug aside. "If this is about the lady, you'll just have to wait your turn," he said.

"I ain't talkin' about no whore. I'm talking about a worthless polecat of an injun thinkin' he can stand up at a white man's bar like he owns the place." The drunk puffed out his chest, as if trying to make his body as big as his own picture of himself.

Micah fixed the drunk with an icy glare. "I don't recall asking your permission," he said softly.

The drunk's face turned flannel red, and the veins in his temples throbbed. The man looked as if he wanted to tear Micah limb from limb, but Micah had sobriety and youth on his side, which ought to count for something.

"I'll show you permission!" The drunk opened his coat and pulled out a blue steel revolver. Micah swallowed hard. So much for the odds. He stared at the opening at the end of the gun barrel. He'd never been shot before. He didn't relish finding out what it felt like now.

Chapter Six

After dinner, a group of enlisted men cleared the furniture from the parlor and rolled out a large square of heavily waxed canvas to serve as a dance floor. A tall private tuned up a fiddle and began to play a quadrille. "Will you do me the honor, Mrs. Bright?" Sergeant Peterson asked, bowing low.

"I haven't danced in years," she said. Will had never been a dancer.

"All the more reason to dance now." Peterson grinned and offered his hand.

She took it, and he swept her into the complicated steps of the dance. "Mrs. Major Finch is a curious woman," he observed after a moment.

"She . . . she seems very nice," Tessa said, determined to make only bland comments to a self-professed gossip. "And very lovely."

"Yes, very lovely. I wager she'll bring our poor major plenty of grief."

"Why do you say that?"

"When Finch had her back east, he didn't care for some of the rumors that made their way to him about how she spent her time. At least out here he can keep an eye on her, and the threat of court-martial hangs over any man who'd take a chance on conduct unbecoming an officer.''

''I'm sure you're wrong. I believe she loves him very much.''

Peterson shrugged. ''Maybe so. But a woman like her, so beautiful and full of life, needs attention, like some exotic flower. An Army officer has precious little time for that, so it's understandable if she were to choose to . . . amuse herself in other ways. It happens all the time, I assure you.''

''I . . . I really don't think we should discuss our hostess this way,'' Tessa said primly.

''All right,'' he said pleasantly. ''We could talk about you. What made you decide to hire a breed to work for you?''

She faltered in the steps of the dance. Peterson grasped her hand more firmly, steadying her. ''Has my question upset you, then? I apologize.''

''Of course not,'' she protested, even as she felt a heated blush race up her neck. She turned her eyes from the sergeant's searching gaze. ''I needed help. He was available. I didn't set out to hire him. He was just there.''

''Just a word of caution.'' Peterson squeezed her hand, drawing her gaze to him again. ''I'd be careful if I were you.''

She gave him a withering look. ''Afraid he might scalp me in my bed one night? Really, Sergeant Peterson!''

He laughed. ''More likely you'll simply wake up one morning and he'll have left. His kind are wanderers. It's bred in them. They're undependable. You heard what Hamilton said about that tracker he knew—Fox. He left in the middle of the night. Your Fox is likely to do the same. And no telling what valuable things he'll take with him when he goes.''

''I don't believe Mr. Fox is like that.''

Peterson shrugged and released her as the last strains

of the quadrille died. "Suit yourself. Just trying to be friendly."

A young lieutenant was waiting for the next dance, but Tessa pleaded a need for air and fled to the front porch. She leaned her head against the post and closed her eyes. What had ever made her think she wanted to be a part of this group of gossiping busybodies?

"The parlor is terribly stuffy, don't you think—not to mention some of the guests." She turned and saw Margery Finch seated on the porch swing at the end of the gallery. Margery wafted an ostrich feather fan in front of her face. "Come down here with me, and we can visit."

Tessa walked to the end of the porch and leaned against the railing.

"Please, sit down." Margery patted the space beside her in the swing.

"Thank you, but I prefer to stand." She felt too restless to sit still. Instead, she half turned to look out across the empty parade ground. A single lantern glowed in the guardhouse across the way, while more lights showed from the enlisted men's tents in the distance, like a cluster of overgrown fireflies. The faint scent of tobacco smoke drifted on the warm breeze, and the lilting strains of "My Old Kentucky Home" filtered from inside the house. Tessa sighed and felt some of the tension ease from her shoulders.

"Tell me more about this helper of yours, Mrs. Bright. This half-breed." Margery's voice broke through the evening stillness.

Tessa flinched, remembering Peterson's words. "He's just a hired hand," she said. "I don't know a lot about him. He hasn't worked for me very long."

Margery smiled, the fan tracing a lazy path in the air. "I shall have to come and visit one day, to see your ranch. And perhaps you can introduce me."

Tessa tried not to show her shock at this odd request. Certainly none of the town women she knew would have dreamed of asking for an introduction to a half-breed ranch hand. She was beginning to believe Margery Finch enjoyed flaunting convention. And though she knew the proper reaction to such behavior should be disapproval, she found herself admiring her hostess's ability to carry it off.

"Oh, there you are, dear." Major Finch walked out on the porch. Tessa thought he looked relieved to see them. She wondered if he'd thought his wife had become *too* occupied with one of the young men.

"Mrs. Bright and I needed some fresh air." She reached up and caressed the major's neck. A soft look came into his eyes. It was an intimate gesture, but Tessa thought it calculated to reassure the nervous newlywed of his wife's loyalties.

Finch glanced at Tessa. "I'm so glad you could come tonight, Mrs. Bright. There aren't very many women here for Margery to make friends with."

"The other wives have been polite, of course, but less than welcoming," Margery said, though she did not look very regretful.

"They're just jealous of your beauty," Finch said. "They'll love you as much as I do when they know you better."

"I don't care if they love me, as long as you do," she said in a throaty voice.

Tessa excused herself, though she doubted if they heard her. Once inside again, she located Sergeant Peterson. "I'd like to go home now," she told him. "Would you find someone to drive me?"

"Not up to post politics, dear?" He shook his head sympathetically. "You know they'll all talk about you after you leave, don't you?"

She glanced over at the small crowd. Many of the men and several of the women were already quite drunk. "Let them talk. I'm a subject easily exhausted, I'm afraid."

Peterson nodded. "Wait here. I'll see what I can do."

A short time later, he escorted her out the door to a waiting ambulance. She sank back against the leather cushions and closed her eyes. She'd been so anxious to come here tonight and now all she could think of was getting back home, to her safe little world and her own familiar things. And to Micah. She smiled and drew her shawl more closely around her shoulders. She'd told him not to wait up, but now she hoped he had. She wanted to tell him about everything that had happened tonight and hear his opinion. He'd help her somehow make sense of all this, she was sure.

Things are getting a little out of hand, Will thought as Gabe Emerson pulled a gun on Fox. He'd brought the young man into town tonight to give him a taste of the kind of reception he could expect from the rank-and-file citizens. He really hadn't expected anything more than rudeness and stone-faced silence—just enough to make Fox see that he wasn't welcome here, and if he cared two cents for Tessa, he wouldn't sully her name with any association with him.

But violence—violence was going a little too far. And how would he ever rest in peace with another man's death on his hands? He moved out of the shadows, over next to Emerson. "No need to trouble yourself, sir. We were just leaving."

Emerson scowled at him, no inkling of recognition on his face. Funny how you could see a man a hundred times in life, but once you died, and he knew you'd died, your ghost was a stranger to him. As if the knowledge of your death canceled out the evidence right before his eyes.

"You stay out of this, old man," Emerson growled.

"What's the matter, injun? Are you yellow?" Old man Thornton moved down from the other end of the bar, apparently not wanting to miss out on the fun. "A yellow-livered polecat, that's what you are!"

Will winced. Thornton always did have a talent for cussing, but Will wouldn't have called his worst enemy a yellow-livered polecat. Even Fox didn't deserve that.

He had to hand it to Fox, though. He wasn't backing

down. He hadn't even flinched when Emerson pulled out that hogleg of his.

"Put that thing away, Gabe," the bartender, Emmett Hardy, barked. He moved down to that end of the bar. "It took two weeks to replace the mirror last time you started something."

"What's the big idea, servin' a redskin?" Emerson asked.

Hardy peered at Micah. "I ain't never seen a redskin with green eyes."

"He's still a redskin." Emerson leaned closer, pressing the gun into Fox's chest. "Like the redskins that murdered my wife."

"Now, you know I'm sorry about your wife, Gabe," Hardy said, "but this ain't the one who killed her."

"Don't matter if it is or not," Emerson said. "They're all the same to me. None of 'em deserve to live."

"I reckon he's a breed." Jackie Babcock, one of the cardplayers, shoved back his chair and joined the group at the bar. Will rolled his eyes. Everybody had an opinion. Micah regarded them all with a grim look on his face, trapped, but maybe watching for his chance to break.

"I heard old Will Bright's widow hired a breed to help out on her place," Thornton said.

Babcock laughed. "Yeah. That figures."

Will stiffened at the mention of Tessa. So did Micah. Anger flashed in those green eyes, and his fingers curled into fists at his sides. Emerson pressed the gun against Micah's chest. "You ought to know better than to be messin' with a white woman," he slurred. "Even an injun lover like Tessa Bright."

"Take it outside," Hardy ordered.

"Damn it, Emmett, quit interruptin' me!" Emerson swiveled toward the bartender.

Will saw his opportunity. He crowned Emerson with a beer bottle at the same time Fox landed a solid punch in the man's gut. Babcock hit Fox, his fist slamming against the half-breed's eye with a smacking sound that made Will wince. Will beaned Babcock with a chair, sending him staggering backward into a table of cardplayers. By the time Emmett Hardy waded in and started breaking up things with a broom handle, Will grabbed Fox's elbow and dragged him to the door.

"Let go of me!" Fox struggled to free himself. "I'm not finished with them yet."

"Yes, you are," Will said, keeping a firm hold of Fox's arm. "You'll never come out ahead in a fight with that bunch. Even if you win, you lose. They'd as soon shoot you as look at you, and the law wouldn't even blink."

Fox glared at him, chest heaving, but he stopped struggling. He was young and hotheaded, but he wasn't stupid. He recognized truth when he heard it. Will let him go.

"Thanks for evening the odds a little," Fox said, rubbing his elbow, which Will knew had to be half frozen.

"I didn't do it for you. I did it for Tessa." He followed Fox to the hitching post and watched him mount up. "She'd be up a creek without you to help out around the place," he added grudgingly.

Fox turned the horse toward home, and Will fell in beside him. The moon was almost full, shining high in the sky like a Spanish silver piece. The horse cast a long shadow as it plodded along, and Will moved over to walk in the shadow so that Fox wouldn't see that Will himself didn't cast one. The mare sidestepped and rolled her eyes, trying to distance herself from him. "I don't know what's gotten into her," Fox said, struggling to keep control of the horse. "She was giving me fits on the way over here, too."

Will smiled to himself. "I reckon you'd best keep a low profile for a few days," he said. "Give Emerson and Babcock a chance to cool down."

"Hmmmph," Fox snorted. "Do you really think a few days will make that much difference? It won't change the fact that I'm half Indian."

"No, it won't." He fell silent for a while, letting that knowledge sink in. Fox's eye had swollen almost shut; it looked like it probably hurt. For a few days or a week he wouldn't be able to look in the mirror without remembering tonight and the bar patrons' opinion of him.

Fox didn't say anything else until they were in sight of the ranch gate. "Did you know Tessa's husband?" he asked.

The question startled Will so much he almost disappeared. As it was, he had to concentrate to bring himself up to sufficient brightness. "Yes, I knew him," he said when he'd recovered. He grinned. "A fine man. One of the finest men I've had the pleasure to know."

Was he imagining things, or did Fox slump a little lower in the saddle at this news? "I wondered why anybody would make a gate like that and set it out here in the middle of nowhere."

Ahead of them, the lacy ironwork of the gate had a satiny sheen in the moonlight. The figures of the man and woman and animals looked real enough to come to life any moment. Will's chest swelled with pride. That gate was his masterpiece. He'd spent hours laboring over it, not only because he wanted everyone to see his skill but because he knew it would please Tessa. He couldn't give her diamonds or a fancy house, but he could give her something no one else had: this gate.

"That gate brought in more business than a red light at a whorehouse," Will said. "After they saw it, half the women in the county wanted some fancy ironwork for their house, even if it was just a lampstand or firedogs." He chuckled. "Trudy Babcock, the wife of the other blacksmith in town, was madder than a wet hen when she heard about it. She nagged at her husband, Jackie, until he made his own fancy gate. But it was a pitiful sight."

"I stopped here that day because of this." Fox waited while Will raised the latch and swung the gate wide. "I couldn't pass by without finding out about it."

Will frowned to himself. He certainly hadn't made the

thing to attract drifters like Fox. "It's a fine gate, all right," he said as he fastened the latch. "And a fine reminder for Tessa of her husband. She was absolutely devoted to the man," he added pointedly.

Fox fell silent. Will followed him down the long drive. "I wonder if Tessa is back from her party yet," he said.

Fox grunted. "If it was anything like the post parties I've seen, she'll wish she hadn't gone."

"Oh, so you've attended Army dinner parties, have you?" Will let his disbelief show in every word.

"I said I'd seen them, not attended. Trackers aren't welcome among the officers any more than Indians are welcome in your saloon."

"And if Tessa was with you, she wouldn't be welcome, either." He drove his point home, the reason for the whole evening's exercise.

To his dismay, Fox laughed, a brittle, bitter sound. "As if Tessa Bright would ever take up with the likes of me." He glanced down at Will, his face all shadows in the moonlight. "You don't have to worry, old man. Tessa's reputation is safe from me."

"Glad to hear it," Will mumbled, confused. Was Fox saying he didn't want Tessa? Was the man addled? "I just assumed a pretty young woman like her would attract your attention."

"I never said I wasn't interested in *her*. And she's woman enough to feel an attraction to me. But her pride won't let her stoop so low, no matter what her urges."

Will swallowed hard. He had half a mind to drag Fox down off his horse and punch him in the other eye as punishment for talking about Tessa in such a vulgar way. After all, she was so young and innocent, almost as innocent as she had been at seventeen when they met. She needed a man who was older and wiser, a protector, not some randy young wanderer who talked about her "urges" but didn't have sense enough to stay out of saloon fights.

He nodded to himself. Yes, he'd been right to eliminate Micah Fox from the running for Tessa's next husband. The sooner Reverend Deering took his place on the ranch, the better.

Tessa came awake as the ambulance jolted to a stop in front of her house. She rubbed sleep from her eyes and waited for the driver to open the door. "You're home, ma'am," the private said, leaning in to offer her his hand.

Home. Was there a more comforting word? She looked up at the house, its weathered boards gleaming in the moonlight. Over in the corral, one of her horses stamped and whinnied, and an Army mule neighed a reply. She thanked the young private and watched while he piloted the ambulance down her drive, then she started for the house and bed.

But before she reached the porch, she turned toward the barn. Her head was too full of images and news and excitement to sleep. If Micah was awake, she'd talk to him a while.

She pulled open the barn door and called softly in the darkness, "Micah?"

A horse stuck its head over the stall and whiffled an answer. Something small scurried in the straw on the floor. Then all fell silent.

She gathered her skirts close around her and stepped into the barn. *He's probably asleep,* she thought. Feeling foolish, but compelled to know, she started toward the box room at the end of the barn. She'd just listen at the door. If she didn't hear him moving about, she'd go back to the house.

She found the lantern by the door and lit it, casting a circle of yellow light in the blackness. Her skirts rustled loudly with every step, and her slippers scraped against the dirt floor. Halfway across the barn, she bumped against something—an empty saddle rack. She glanced along the wall, and her heart sank as she realized Micah's saddle was missing.

Maybe he put it in his room, she told herself, *to . . . to work on it.*

Likely you'll simply wake up one morning and he'll have left. His kind are wanderers. It's bred in them. Sergeant Peterson's words echoed in her mind. She knocked at the door of the box room. Once, twice, then a rapid tattoo, a frantic summons to be answered. When no response came, she pressed her cheek to the rough wood and listened. Only an empty, rushing sound greeted her, the murmur of her own blood pulsing in her veins. Choking back a cry, she wrenched open the door and held the lantern aloft.

The single bunk was neatly made, his few belongings arranged around the room—an extra blanket, a winter coat, some books she had lent him. He would not have left without those, would he?

She crossed to the bed and sank down on it, absently stroking the worn woolen blanket. What would she do if Micah was gone? How would she manage, not just the ranch, but being alone again? In such a short time, she'd grown accustomed to his presence in her life.

The echo of a horse's hooves on the drive pulled her to her feet. Grabbing up the lantern, she hurried to the barn door. Relief filled her as she saw Micah riding toward her. "Where have you been?" she asked as he swung down off the mare.

He glanced at her, then busied himself loosening the saddle girth. "You didn't have to wait up for me."

"I just got in," she said. "I decided to check on the horses before I went to bed and I noticed your saddle was missing."

"I went to town with the recluse."

Will? She glanced behind him but saw no sign of her husband. Of course not. Will was never around when he might be in trouble. "W-what did you do there at this time of night?" she asked, struggling to keep her voice light.

"We went to get drunk."

All the breath went out of her at the words. She

looked at him more closely. Micah didn't appear to be drunk, or at least not very. "I . . . I didn't know he drank." Ghosts couldn't drink, could they?

"I imagine there's a lot of things about him you don't know."

She frowned. That was probably true. Like what the devil he thought he was doing taking Micah into town with him. "So, did you have a good time?"

"Not really." He led the mare past her into the barn. "How was the party?"

She followed him inside. "I met some interesting people there. I saw Reverend Deering. We had a nice meal, and afterward there was some dancing."

"Did you enjoy yourself?"

She opened her mouth to tell him yes, that while he'd been out enjoying himself in town, she'd had a very good time, thank you. But the lie died in her throat. "Not really. There was too much drinking and gossip. I felt . . . out of place."

He nodded. "I didn't think you'd like it. Fort life is very . . . closed."

She looked at him, trying to read his expression, but he stood with his head down, his face concealed from her by the shadowing hat. "Mrs. Finch is very lovely, though," she said. "She wants to meet you."

He stiffened. "How does she know about me?"

"I believe Reverend Deering mentioned you. There was a Lieutenant Hamilton there who thought he remembered you from Fort Inge. Were you ever stationed there?"

He nodded, slowly this time. "I can't say I remember him, though."

"He said you left in the middle of the night for no reason."

He pulled the saddle from the mare. "I had my reasons. I don't care to talk about them now."

She looked down at the sputtering wick of the lantern in her hands. She told herself she should turn and go back into the house, but the desperation she'd been feeling swelled inside her, seeking relief in words that tumbled out of her mouth. "I was afraid, when I came in and you weren't here, that you'd decided to leave *me*."

He settled the saddle on the rack. "I promised I'd stay until your arm is healed."

Was that all that kept him here, then? A sense of obligation? "People break promises."

His hand rested on her shoulder, heavy and warm. "I don't."

She suddenly felt foolish, standing here arguing with him this way, when she should have been safely tucked in bed, leaving them both free to live their own lives. A drugging weariness settled over her with the force of a blow, and she reached out, intending to steady herself for just a moment. But when her hand touched his arm, she gave in to the urge to cling to him, to savor the warmth and strength he offered. She raised her eyes to his, her lips parted to apologize for her momentary weakness. He bent his head, and his shadow covered her, then he erased all pleading or protest with his kiss.

His lips were warm, their heat seeping into her, warming some cold space deep within that had been chilled too long. She felt the tingling roughness of his beard scrape her skin and tasted the malty sweetness of beer that lingered in his mouth. She leaned into him, desperate to prolong this exquisite pleasure. His hand tightened on her shoulder, then slipped down her arm, caressing her, urging her closer still. Her skirts crushed against him, her starched petticoats scratching her legs.

He cradled her injured arm in his hand, caressing the cast as he caressed the rest of her. He kissed her eyelids, her nose, her cheeks, always coming back to her mouth. He teased and suckled, tracing the delicate inside of her mouth and stroking her with his tongue until she felt dizzy with arousal. She could have gone on kissing him forever, yet her body trembled with the need for more.

He took the lantern from her—the lantern she'd forgotten she was holding—and hung it on a nail overhead. They stood in the circle of its yellow light, their skin burnished amber. Only now, in the light, could she see the purpling bruise around his eye.

The sight shocked her into speech at last. "What happened?" She reached up to feather a touch along the edge of the wound.

He captured her wrist in his hand. "I had a little disagreement with a drunk in a bar."

"A disagreement? Over what?"

"He objected to the bartender serving an Indian."

The words were like a blow to her stomach. Will had done this, had purposely led Micah where he knew he wouldn't be wanted. How dare he!

"There's no sense getting upset over it," Micah said. "I should have known better than to go in there. Just as I should know better than to be standing here with you now." He took a step back. "Go on to the house, Tessa. If you want me to stay here, we'd both best pretend this never happened."

She stared at him, her lips still burning from his kisses, her body still aching for his touch. The lantern cast harsh shadows on his face, etching his cheekbones, outlining his nose. He looked like an artist's painting of an Indian chief, all pride and anger and honor melded on his face.

Choking back a cry, she whirled and ran toward the house, stumbling across the yard and up the steps, running from temptation and from the truth: Micah was exactly the kind of man she *didn't* need in her life. And right now he was the only man she wanted.

Will watched his wife kissing Fox and fought back a murderous rage. He'd saved Micah Fox's life tonight, and this was the thanks he got. He'd half a mind to take up a pitchfork and— Truth, cold as ice and valid in any realm, stayed his hand. Tessa wasn't his wife anymore. Not really. And Micah Fox wasn't doing anything Will himself wouldn't have done if given half a chance.

He'd given up a lot to come back to look after Tessa—a physical form and all that went with it, such as eating, sleeping, and having sex. But Tessa wasn't a ghost, and though he hated to admit it, she wasn't a girl anymore. He studied her as he might have looked at a stranger. The full-skirted dress made her look very elegant, and her high-piled hair elongated her neck. She seemed more buxom, too. And the way she pressed her body against Fox's was definitely not the movement of an inexperienced girl.

Hadn't Will himself taught her everything she knew, and then up and died, leaving her alone? Could he really blame her if she still wanted what he could no longer give her?

Feeling lower than a snake, he turned away. Let her take Micah Fox as her lover if she insisted. It would only be for a little while. She could still marry Reverend Deering and maybe make him a better wife for it.

He was drifting across the yard toward the house when he heard her footsteps behind him. Across the yard and up the steps, he followed her into the house. Tears streaked her face. If Fox had hurt her, by Jupiter, he'd—

No. This was for the best. He settled into the woodwork outside her bedroom door, trying to stop his ears to the sound of her crying. Of all the things about being a ghost, this was the hardest. He'd never be able to do anything about her tears.

Chapter Seven

Tessa overslept the next morning and awoke feeling foggy and heavy-headed. As she lay staring up at the ceiling, the memory of last night's events came rushing back—Margery Finch and the party, and most especially the kiss she'd shared with Micah in the barn.

What had she been thinking, to throw herself at him that way? She'd been so relieved to discover he hadn't abandoned her that she might very well have driven him off altogether.

She rolled over and hugged the pillow to her chest, as if she could somehow contain and control her turbulent emotions. How could she separate the physical desire she felt for Micah as a man from the certain knowledge that a relationship with him would be utter foolishness?

He recognized the folly in pursuing her, at least. She owed him a debt of thanks for that. How many other men would have taken advantage of her in her weakness and never looked back?

"Tessa?"

His voice outside her bedroom door startled her. She

grew still, scarcely breathing. What did he want from her here—now?

"Tessa?" He knocked, and his voice grew louder. "Tessa, you'd better get up. Someone's coming up the drive."

Thoughts of a visitor finding her in disarray propelled her out of bed. She dressed hurriedly and raked a comb through her hair, then twisted it into a loose knot and pinned it in place. She thrust her feet into shoes as she tied her apron in back, and hurtled down the stairs two at a time, arriving breathless on the front porch in time to see an Army ambulance lurching up the road, escorted by a soldier on horseback.

"Who is it?" Micah asked. He stood at the end of the porch, keeping his distance from her.

She felt awkward, unable to meet his eyes, grateful for the distraction of a visitor. She glanced back at the coach and the soldier, whom she now recognized as Lieutenant Hamilton. "I believe Mrs. Finch has come to call," she said.

She knew she looked a mess, her clothes wrinkled, her hair half undone. But then, even dressed up, she looked like a dowdy sage hen next to Margery's peacock plumage. Nothing to do but smile and make the best of it.

Lieutenant Hamilton dismounted and helped Margery out of the carriage. Was the handsome lieutenant acting on orders, or had he, too, been lured into Margery's retinue of admirers?

Margery rewarded her escort with a radiant smile and a gentle squeeze from her gloved fingers. "Tessa, dear. I thought we'd never get here," she said, fanning herself with the familiar ostrich feathers. She was dressed all in pink today, a frosty shade that brought out the roses in her cheeks.

"I'm glad to see you again," Tessa said. "Please come in, and I'll make tea."

"Oh, but I want to look around first," Margery said,

her eyes searching over Tessa's shoulder. "And I'm anxious to meet your Mr. Fox."

Tessa stifled a twinge of irritation. Weren't there enough men at the fort so that Margery didn't have to travel cross-country to find another one? She looked over her shoulder to the porch, but Micah was nowhere in sight.

"I'd be happy to introduce you," she said, turning back to her guests, "but he seems to have disappeared."

"Then we'll just have to look for him," Margery said. She set off toward the barn, Lieutenant Hamilton trailing obediently.

Tessa hurried to keep up with the two of them. "Perhaps if we went into the house and waited—" she began.

"Mr. Fox!" Margery called, stepping through the corral gate. "Hello! Mr. Fox?" She started across the corral, but her progress was blocked by a pony. She glared at the horse. "Shoo!" she ordered, waving her fan. "Get out of my way."

The pony rolled its eyes and backed away. Tessa bit her tongue to keep from laughing. Margery Finch was obviously a woman who was used to getting her own way, be it from man or beast.

Tessa followed Margery and Lieutenant Hamilton into the barn. "Mr. Fox!" Margery called.

"He must have ridden out on an errand," Tessa offered. "Come in and have some tea and perhaps you'll have a chance to meet him later."

Margery's eyes searched the barn. "That's a fine saddle," she said, spotting Micah's silver-studded rig. "Is it yours?"

"It belongs to Mr. Fox," she confessed.

Margery smiled in triumph. "Then he's not likely to have ridden off without it." She moved through the barn, poking her head into the stalls.

Tessa stood in the doorway, hands on her hips. "Mrs. Finch, if I didn't know better, I'd swear you never came to visit me at all," she said after a moment.

Margery turned and hurried back to Tessa's side. "Of course I came here to see you." She put her arm around Tessa's shoulders. "But I have a confession to make."

"A confession?" Tessa regarded her warily.

She nodded. "Do you know I've been out here on the frontier three whole weeks and I haven't seen a single Indian? It's true! My husband is an Indian fighter, and I've never even seen one! How can I be a good military wife if I don't even know what the enemy looks like?"

Tessa stared at her, unsure whether to laugh or to applaud this performance. "What does Mr. Fox have to do with that?"

"He's half-Indian, isn't he? He's the best chance I've had so far." She stepped back and began to fan herself. "Truly, I thought if I met your Mr. Fox, I wouldn't be so—so *terrified* of the very thought of Indians. I almost didn't come out to the fort because I was so afraid of being scalped in my sleep."

There was that phrase again. Tessa was getting awfully tired of hearing it. She eyed Margery Finch warily. The major's wife did not appear to be a woman who was afraid of anything. "In a fort full of soldiers, I think that would be unlikely," she said dryly.

"I know it's illogical, but believe me, I have nightmares." Margery's fan beat double-time. "When I heard you had Mr. Fox out here, gentle and peaceable as you please, I thought to myself, 'Now that's what you need to be able to sleep soundly at night. You need to meet one of these fellows and see that they're men like anyone else, not two-headed monsters.'" She smiled. "So I rushed out here as soon as I could. I have to meet Mr. Fox if I'm ever to sleep soundly again."

It was quite a performance, Tessa had to admit, complete with dramatic sighs and heaving bosom. If Micah was within earshot, she hoped he didn't hurt himself laughing.

"Mr. Fox doesn't appear to be around here anywhere," Lieutenant Hamilton said.

Margery looked around the barn. "Perhaps he's fallen

and hurt himself. He could even be in trouble. We'd better split up and look for him. Derek, you and Mrs. Bright can search the house and the area behind it. I'll take the barn and corral and the front of the house.''

The next thing Tessa knew, she was being pushed out the door with Lieutenant Hamilton. ''We'd better do as she says, ma'am,'' Hamilton said. ''There's no reasoning with her when she gets like this.'' He walked with her toward the house. ''Besides, it's a long ride out here. I'd be much obliged for that tea.''

Tessa glanced over her shoulder at Margery, who was looking behind haystacks and wheelbarrows as if she expected to find Micah shrunk to the size of a chicken. She laughed. ''I could use a cup of tea myself.''

Micah recognized Margery Watkins as soon as she descended from the Army ambulance. She was more luxuriously dressed than she had been the last time he'd seen her, and she seemed more voluptuous than ever, but he'd have known that voice, and that red hair, anywhere.

He crouched in the hayloft, listening to the search below. He had to pinch himself to keep from laughing at her preposterous story. Margery had always been a great actress. She was so beautiful, and men wanted to believe whatever story she told them.

He didn't think Tessa would fall for the act, but who could fight the whirlwind force that was Margery?

He leaned back against the hay and closed his eyes. So she'd married a major, had she? An older man, no doubt, with plenty of family money to buy her fancy hats and pretty clothes. And one so smitten that she'd be able to carry on with all manner of young officers, all the while convincing him he was the only man for her.

''Sleeping, Micah? How can you sleep when I'm so near?'' Margery's head poked up through the opening leading to the loft, followed by her voluptuous body.

She leaned over and planted a kiss full on his mouth, but he pulled away.

She pouted. "Is that any way to say hello to an old friend?"

He sat up. "Hello, Margery. What are you doing here?"

"Haven't you heard? I came to see a real live Indian. You." She gently touched his blackened eye. "What happened here?"

He pushed her hand away. "A little disagreement with some men in town."

She grinned. "Well, I'm sure they got the worst of it." She looked around the loft. "This brings back memories, doesn't it? We used to make love in a hayloft like this." She moved closer to him. "I've never forgotten those afternoons we spent together," she said in a throaty voice. "It's never been the same with anyone else."

"Surely some have come close," he said. "The major, maybe?"

She smiled. "Well, yes, Alan is a dear. But he's always so *busy.*" She reached out and put her hand on his thigh. "You don't know how thrilled I was to hear you were so near. I thought I would *die* before I could get to see you." The hand moved up toward his crotch, and her perfume filled his nostrils.

He moved over, freeing himself from her grasp. "We'd better join the others for tea."

She frowned. "Don't worry about them. Derek will keep little Miss Tessa occupied as long as I like." She reached out and unfastened the top button of his shirt. "We have plenty of time."

He captured her wrist. "I'm not interested in a married woman, Margery. Sorry."

She sat back, rubbing her wrist. "Since when are you so moral?"

"Since I understood how dangerous it was to steal anything marked 'Property, U.S. Army.'"

"I'm no one's property, Micah Fox!"

"Tell that to the major." He moved past her toward the opening.

She clutched his arm. "It's that Bright woman, isn't it? Micah, you've fallen in love with her!"

He shook his head. What did fickle Margery know about love? As if what he felt for Tessa could be so easily defined. "It was good to see you again," he said. "Come have some tea."

She leaned forward and kissed him on the cheek. "I was only hoping for a fling, you know. I won't stand in the way of true love—if there is such a thing!" She moved past him and started down the ladder. "But if you ever get to missing me, you know where I'll be."

He laughed and followed her down into the barn. "Look who I found!" she called, hurrying toward the house. "Derek! Mrs. Bright! Come see!"

Tessa had to cover her mouth with her hand to hide her amusement at the sight of a glowering Micah being towed across the yard by a gleeful Margery. From the expression on his face, one would have thought the man was being dragged to torture, instead of tea with an undeniably beautiful woman. "He was taking a nap in the hayloft," Margery announced as she and Micah reached the porch.

Tessa shot Micah a questioning look. What had made him hide from Margery that way?

"Mr. Fox, we meet again." Lieutenant Hamilton stepped forward, his handsome face marred by a stern frown. "We were at Fort Inge together, do you remember?"

"Hello, Lieutenant Hamilton." Micah's expression was unrevealing, but Tessa heard the coldness in his voice. That was it! Micah had been avoiding the lieutenant, not Margery.

Fearing a confrontation, she stepped between the two men. "Shall we go inside and pour the tea?" She forced a wide smile to her lips and nodded to her guests. "Perhaps Mrs. Finch will tell us more about her stay back east.''

''That's a splendid idea.'' Margery, who still clung to Micah's arm as if she feared he might flee at any moment, led the way up the steps and across the porch. Only when they were all inside did she release her hold on Micah, who immediately moved away from her.

Lieutenant Hamilton had already helped Tessa carry the tea things into the parlor. She took her station by the tray, and Margery settled next to her on the sofa. The lieutenant and Micah sat in chairs pulled up before the little tea table, glowering at each other like two bulldogs spoiling for a fight.

''What have you been doing with yourself since you left the fort?'' Lieutenant Hamilton asked as he accepted a cup of tea from Tessa.

Micah glared at him. ''Are you addressing that question to me?''

''Yes, I was, *Mr.* Fox.'' Lieutenant Hamilton clenched his jaw, as if the polite form of address taxed him.

''I've been working.'' Micah added two lumps of sugar to his own cup.

''Working where?''

''Around.''

Tessa glared at the men, wishing polite convention and concern for her carpet didn't prevent her from dumping the rest of the tea over them. Margery Finch came to her rescue.

''Remember where you are, gentlemen,'' she chided. ''We ladies refuse to be bored with talk of the Army or past events we ourselves weren't involved in.'' She turned toward Tessa. ''I'm anxious to hear all about the activities of the townspeople. Alan so wants me to make friends here.''

Tessa gave her a grateful smile. ''I'm afraid I haven't been involved much in the goings-on in town of late.''

''But why ever not? You're so pretty and sweet. Just

the type of person I imagine as having dozens of friends. Not at all like me.''

Tessa's mouth fell open. She had to take a gulp of tea in an attempt to wash down her confusion. Margery Finch, friendless? The woman had more personality than half a dozen ordinary women. "Well, uh, I've been . . . sort of keeping to myself lately," she stammered.

Margery's expression was just as lovely in sorrow as in delight. "Of course. How thoughtless of me. You're a young widow. Of course you haven't been very active socially." She set aside her teacup and picked up her fan. "Forgive me, dear. You'll learn soon enough that I often speak without thinking. And often live to regret it.''

"Hah!''

Alarmed, Tessa stared at Micah. He began coughing, pounding his chest. "Something . . . caught in my throat,'' he gasped.

"For a real live Indian, Mr. Fox seems harmless enough to me,'' Margery said. She helped herself to another cookie. "Or perhaps it's just you who has tamed him, Mrs. Bright.''

The words were innocent enough, but Tessa found herself blushing. She smoothed her apron across her knees and searched for another topic of conversation. A shelf of books caught her eye. "Actually I have just started getting involved in some things in town,'' she said. "For instance, some women from church are forming a group to raise money to build a library in Pony Springs.''

"What a marvelous idea.'' Margery turned to the men. "Do you like to read, gentlemen?''

Micah nodded. Lieutenant Hamilton shifted in his chair. "I'm quite a fan of Shakespeare myself,'' he said.

"He's that British playwright, isn't he?'' Margery shook her head. "A bit too stuffy for me.'' She wafted her fan in front of her. "But give me a good novel, and I'm lost for hours. Do you think your library ladies would allow me to join in the fun?''

Tessa had a feeling Margery would be the most fun in any group. She tried to imagine the flamboyant Mrs. Finch and Trudy Babcock in the same room. The picture was quite appealing. "I'm certain they would," she said. "In fact, we're having a meeting tomorrow. Why don't you come with me?"

"I'd love to. How sweet of you to offer."

"I'd be happy to escort you to the meeting, Mrs. Finch." Lieutenant Hamilton sat up straighter.

Margery waved away the offer. "Never mind, Derek. I prefer to keep this a ladies' outing." She beamed at Tessa. "Something I haven't done much of before."

The next afternoon, Tessa found herself ensconced once more in an Army ambulance, with Margery across from her. The major's wife looked only slightly more demure today in a dress of dark blue, with a tight-fitting jacket and a feather-trimmed hat. "I hope this is all right," she said, tugging at the jacket and smoothing the lapels. "I feel so . . . plain."

Tessa smiled, charmed by this unexpected nervousness in a woman who seemed so confident most of the time. "You couldn't be plain in an old feed sack."

"Oh, you're sweet to say so. But I did try to tone down just a little. I want these ladies to like me."

"Why wouldn't they like you?" Despite Margery's flamboyance and flirtatiousness, she had an underlying sweetness Tessa found irresistible.

Margery leaned back against the coach cushions and picked up her fan. "Some people dislike me just because I'm beautiful. Or because I'm vain and loud and I adore being the center of attention." She pursed her lips in a rueful expression. "I know I'm all those things, but that doesn't mean I don't have a good heart. I can care about other people, but no one seems to believe me when I do."

This frank confession touched Tessa. On impulse, she leaned forward and covered Margery's hand with her own. "I'm sure the ladies of Pony Springs will be charmed to meet you," she said.

"I hope you're right." She smiled, and Tessa returned the expression.

When the coach drew up before Ada Drake's home, where the meeting was to take place, Margery leaned forward and embraced Tessa in a quick hug. "Thanks for listening to me prattle on. I feel better just knowing you're walking in at my side."

They did walk in side by side, and the ladies seemed genuinely delighted to welcome the major's wife to their committee. "It's good to see young women taking an interest in the community," Mrs. Drake said as she poured tea. She sat across from Tessa and Margery in the ornately furnished parlor of her home just off the town's main street. The room was crammed with all manner of gilt-edged knickknacks and dark, velvet-upholstered furniture. Tessa sat next to Margery on an overstuffed settee, her feet braced against the floor to keep from slipping off.

"I want to do what I can to help." Margery helped herself to several cookies and passed the tray to Tessa.

"And we're glad you've decided to join us, Mrs. Bright." Mrs. Drake smiled at her over her teacup.

"I'd given up on ever getting to really know you." Mamie Tucker perched on a footstool, her skirts making a graceful swirl around her. "You seemed so intent on keeping to yourself all the time. But I suppose now that it was more your husband's doing."

Tessa stared at her, stunned into silence. Was Mrs. Tucker saying she thought Tessa's isolation was her own fault? She had never associated with people in town because they had made it clear in the beginning that she was not welcome.

Could she have had it wrong all this time?

"Speaking of husbands, I heard there was a little ruckus over at the Red Dog Saloon last night." Ammie Smith, at one end of a fainting couch against the back wall, dunked a cookie in her teacup, and then ate it with relish. "Word is, Gabe Emerson owes Emmett Hardy for *another* mirror."

"Only because he was provoked." Trudy Babcock gave the schoolteacher a frosty glare, then turned her cold gaze on Tessa. "I heard that half-breed you hired, Mr. Fox, got into a disagreement with Mr. Emerson and several other men."

Tessa felt as if she'd swallowed rocks. She'd never thought to ask Micah exactly what had sparked the fight that led to his black eye.

"What were they fighting about?" Mrs. Tucker asked.

"Mr. Emerson asked Fox to leave the saloon." Trudy glanced at Tessa. "Everybody knows they don't serve Indians there. But Mr. Fox had the nerve to tell my husband and some others that he didn't have to have their permission to drink there. Then Mr. Emerson said the crazy redskin came at him with a knife. Of course he had to defend himself."

In the shocked silence that followed, Tessa thought Trudy looked pleased with her success in garnering everyone's attention. She searched her mind for some sharp retort, some defense of Micah that wouldn't be misinterpreted and turned against her.

"These cookies are delicious, Mrs. Drake." Margery leaned forward and helped herself to another. "I must have the recipe."

Tessa gave her friend a grateful look. "Yes, I'd love to have it, too. What do you do to make it so light?"

"It's the cream of tartar," Ada Drake said. "I'll be happy to give you the recipe. It's really very easy."

"I manage to burn even easy recipes," Margery said, laughing. "But I'd like to give it to our striker. *He* can work wonders in the kitchen."

"I'll write it down for you before you leave," Mrs. Drake answered with a friendly smile.

"Ladies—quiet, please." Trudy tapped her water glass with a teaspoon, then rose to address the group. "It is time to begin our official meeting." She walked to the front of the room. "As you know, we're here to discuss our community's need for a library. I feel, if we all work together, we can make our vision a reality. A lending library will improve the literacy of all our citizens and provide an invaluable resource for the education of our children."

Everyone applauded, and within short order, officers were elected and duties assigned. Ada Drake was selected to serve as president, while Trudy headed up the building committee. To her surprise, Tessa found herself appointed to a fund-raising committee with Margery. "I'm sure Alan will make a donation to get us started," Margery said. "And we could ask some of the businessmen in town."

Mamie Tucker smiled. "I'm sure you'll be the perfect person to persuade them to contribute," she said.

"No man would turn her down," someone observed, and they all laughed. But it was a gentle laughter, among friends.

By the time the meeting was adjourned, Tessa felt like a child at Christmas. Her gifts this day had been the friendship of these women, except, of course, the sour-faced Trudy. In spite of that snub, she carried a feeling of acceptance with her out the door. Happiness welled up inside her, sweet as warm molasses.

"Well, now, that went pretty well, didn't it?" Margery said, settling in the coach once more.

Tessa smiled. "Yes, it did."

"Alan will be pleased." She wafted her fan. "He's been after me to make friends in town. *Women* friends."

Tessa looked down, pretending not to notice Margery's emphasis on "women." "What he doesn't understand is that *he's* the friend I want the most," Margery added.

Tessa glanced up, surprised at the pensive tone of her friend's voice. "He's always so *busy*," Margery continued. "Always off on patrol or working on reports. He never has much time for me."

Tessa had a sudden picture of beautiful, flamboyant

Margery, fawned over by everyone but the man she needed attention from the most. What better way to wound someone with such a flirtatious nature than by ignoring her? The poor major probably had no idea what he was doing. "I'm sure he doesn't mean to hurt you," Tessa said. "I know he loves you very much. If you could have seen the way he spoke about you—"

"Yes, he loves me," Margery answered with a nod, "but he doesn't need me. And the truth is, I do need him, so very much." She looked away, staring out the window, but not before Tessa saw the shine in her eyes that spoke of unshed tears.

"Oh, listen to me. Going on and on about myself." Margery turned to face her again, a bright smile once more in place. "Let's talk about you. You and that *handsome* Mr. Fox."

Tessa shifted in the seat. "There's nothing to talk about," she said. "He's helping me with the ranch work."

"Yes, but what else?" Margery leaned forward, her voice lowered to a conspiratorial whisper. "I mean, you're a young widow, he's a good-looking, healthy man . . ."

Tessa flushed. "I don't know what you're talking about," she said stiffly, though of course she had a very good idea.

Margery sat back, and her smile faded. "I've gone and offended you, haven't I? I didn't mean to at all. It's just that . . . well, seeing the way you looked at each other yesterday . . . I thought . . ." She shook her head. "Of course, it's absolutely none of my business anyway. Forget I asked."

"What do you mean, the way we looked at each other?" Tessa blurted. Was she giving off silent signals? Could people tell just by looking that she and Micah had kissed?

"You know." Margery waved her hand. "You just looked like . . . like you were *fond* of each other."

Tessa averted her gaze. "Micah and I are friends, of course."

"Friendship is a very good start to love, I'd say."

Tessa's heart jumped in her chest at the word. "That's ridiculous. Impossible."

Margery looked amused. "It's been possible since Adam and Eve, dear. It's what men and women are made for."

"Micah and I could never be anything more than friends."

Margery frowned. "Why not?"

Tessa spread her hands in her lap. "You saw those women back there. They welcomed me. Made me a part of what they're doing. I've never had that before." She looked at Margery, pleading for understanding. "Do you think they'd be so welcoming if I married a half-breed and lived with him openly?"

"Whoa, Nelly." Margery threw up her hands. "Who said anything about marriage?" She leaned over and patted Tessa's hand. "You poor thing. You've really got it bad, don't you?"

Tessa closed her eyes, her cheeks burning. What had she done? "Don't worry," Margery said, still patting her. "Your secret is safe with me."

Will found Reverend Deering in the church, wearing a leather apron and polishing a pair of brass candlesticks. *"Don't they have a sexton to do that sort of thing?"* he asked, settling invisibly into the front pew.

Deering almost dropped a candlestick. He set it carefully back on the altar and looked around. "Is someone there?" he asked.

"I've got another job for you, Deering," Will said, choosing to ignore the question of his identity.

Deering dropped to his knees, hands clasped in prayer. "Yes, Lord. Whatever you want me to do."

"I think it's time you paid another visit to Tessa Bright."

The preacher smiled. That was a good sign. "I was

thinking that very thing myself this morning, Lord.'' His expression sobered. ''Of course, that was probably due to the leading of your Spirit.''

''Maybe we can save that theological discussion for some other time,'' Will hurried on. *''I want you to go visit Tessa Bright again, and this time pay attention to what you see out there. Look around the ranch and think about what you would do with it if it were yours.''* A man with a good eye for horseflesh, like Deering here, would be sure to see the possibilities in the ranch. If Deering could fall in love with the ranch, persuading him to marry Tessa would be easy. *''That ranch could be yours if you listen to me,''* he added, just to make sure the preacher got the point.

''Of course I'll listen to you, Lord.'' He hesitated for a moment, brow furrowed in concentration. ''Should I talk to Micah Fox while I'm there, Lord?''

''Fox?'' What did *he* have to do with anything? *''Why do you want to talk to him?''*

''I just thought he might give some . . . you know, useful information.''

Oh. That was all. Deering probably wanted to ask Fox about the horses or the hayfields or something. *''All right. Talk to him. But don't forget to talk to Tessa, too. A pretty woman like that deserves your attention.''*

''Of course, Lord. Whatever you say.'' He stayed on his knees, head bowed. Will realized he was waiting to be dismissed. *''That's all, Deering. Amen. Go in peace. Get to work.''*

Deering jumped to his feet and headed for the door. Will had a sudden vision of him galloping up to Tessa's doorstep still wearing the stained leather apron. *''Deering!''*

The preacher froze in his tracks. ''Yes, Lord?''

''Don't forget to put on a clean shirt and comb your hair.''

''Yes, Lord.''

Will watched him leave. This might take a little more effort than he'd first suspected. He decided to follow along, just in case the preacher got sidetracked along the way.

An hour later, Reverend Deering, freshly shaved and combed and smelling of the cologne Will had "accidentally" dumped on him, rode through Tessa's front gate.

Tessa emerged from the barn, rake in hand, Micah right behind her. She had straw in her hair and manure on her shoes. Will groaned silently. He'd spent so much time getting the prospective groom ready, he'd forgotten to make sure the bride was equally presentable. Too bad he couldn't pull his God act on her. Knowing Tessa, though, she wouldn't listen at all. She'd developed a disturbing stubborn streak, of late.

"Hello, Reverend Deering," she said as the preacher swung down off his horse. "What can I do for you this afternoon?"

"I . . . I just felt the need to ride out here and . . . and talk to you." He looked around him. "I wanted to see more of your ranch."

Fox scowled at the preacher but said nothing. The bruising around his eye had faded to a sickly yellow.

"Well, I'm sort of busy right now." Tessa looked down at her manure-caked gloves.

"Please, Mrs. Bright. It's important. If I could just have a few moments of your time."

She shrugged and began peeling off the gloves. "All right."

Fox shook his head in disgust and went back into the barn.

"Let's go for a walk." Deering motioned out across the pasture. He tied his horse to the corral fence, then led the way toward the expanse of open land. Tessa fell into step beside him, and Will trailed silently after them. A hot breeze bent the knee-high grass in undulating waves, filling the air with its clean summer scent. Grasshoppers sprang up in their path, whirring off in every direction like spring-loaded missiles. Deering waited until he and Tessa were halfway across the field before he found his voice again. "So, tell me more about the ranch," he said.

Tessa plucked a stem of gramma grass and began to strip the seed head. "I have two sections, bordered on one side by Pony Creek and on the other by the Clear Fork reservation."

Deering's face brightened. "You mean the Indian reservation comes right up to your property line?"

She sighed. "I know what you're thinking, but there's no danger. The Indians cross over to hunt sometimes, but they never bother us."

"Why, that's ideal," Deering murmured. "And do you know some of these Indians personally?"

Indians again! Did the man ever think of anything else? Will considered tripping him or distracting him in some other way. He hadn't brought the preacher all the way out here to talk about Indians!

"I know some," Tessa said. "And others who aren't on the reservations."

"I thought all Indians were required to live here or on the Brazos reservation further north."

She tossed aside the now-shredded grass stem. "Technically, yes. But realistically, as long as they leave the white settlers alone, they're allowed to come and go as they please. Most of the smaller tribes do keep to reservation land."

Will yawned. He hadn't enjoyed politics in life—now that he was dead, all that talk of public policy held even less interest. He fetched a pebble from the ground and launched it at Deering's back, striking him right between the shoulder blades.

"Ouch!" Deering straightened, wincing.

"What is it?" Tessa looked concerned.

"Must have been . . . a bee or something." The preacher felt gingerly at his back.

"Turn around and let me see." Tessa smoothed her hand over the spot Deering indicated between his shoulder blades. "I don't feel anything. Lift your shirt."

Deering blanched. "I really don't think—"

"If the stinger is still in there, we'll need to get it out," Tessa said. "Now come on. Let me take a look."

Ah, this is more like it, Will thought. *Get that preacher suit off of him, and maybe Deering would begin to think like a man and see Tessa as more than just a fount of information about Indians.*

After another moment's hesitation, Deering unbuttoned his collar and shirt. Tessa helped him pull his shirttails from his trousers and lifted up the shirt and undershirt. The preacher's skin was very pale, but firm and well muscled. Here was a man who had lifted more than books and pounded more than pulpits in his day.

Tessa frowned at the small red mark in the middle of Deering's back and brushed her hand over it lightly. "I don't think it's a bee sting," she said. "It looks as if it will be all right."

"Now turn around and face her," Will whispered, his ghostly lips right next to Deering's ear. *"Doesn't she look as if she'd like to be kissed?"* If he had to coach the preacher every step of the way, then, by golly, he would.

Deering looked alarmed. His face blanched, then reddened, but at least he did turn and face Tessa. Suddenly they were standing nose to nose. Will smiled to himself. *All right. Now he could let nature take its course.*

He was so intent on choreographing matters with Tessa and Deering that he didn't hear the horse approaching until it was too late. Micah came galloping toward them on the roan mare like a brave on the warpath.

Chapter Eight

Tessa gasped and sprang away from Deering, who busied himself trying to straighten his clothing. Micah glared at the preacher. "Is something wrong? I heard you cry out, then saw Tessa examining you."

She would no doubt have been kissing *him if you hadn't interfered,* Will thought grumpily. Well, he knew how to deal with Micah. He stepped forward and laid a ghostly hand alongside the mare's flank.

As if touched by a brand, the horse sprang back and tried to run. Micah reined her in sharply, legs gripping the saddle in a show of expert horsemanship. "I'd better take her back to the barn," he called. "If you're sure you're all right?"

"We're fine," Tessa said. After Micah rode off, she studied the ground around them. "There must be a hornet's nest or something near here. That mare acted as if she'd been stung."

"It's a sign," Deering said.

Tessa stared at him. "A sign?"

Will groaned. If anybody heard him, they would think it was the wind. "It's one more sign that this is the place for me to begin my mission." He moved toward Tessa, arms outstretched as if to gather her near. "The Lord sent me here today to talk to you, Mrs. Bright. He directed me to look about your land to see what use I might make of it. Now I know that this is the place he wants me to build my chapel."

"Your chapel?" Tessa asked.

Will glared at Deering. He hadn't said anything about a chapel.

"I was in the sanctuary this morning, polishing the candlesticks and meditating on Matthew 5:16: 'Let your light so shine before men, that they may see your good works, and glorify your Father which is in heaven,' " Deering said. "The Lord came to me and sent me here."

"The *Lord* sent you here?" Tessa looked around, as if she knew Will was listening.

"Yes. I knew then that this was the place I was supposed to set my light, the light of the word of the Lord to the Indians. You can help me spread that word by introducing me to the Indians you know."

Tessa frowned. "I don't know . . ."

Will picked up another pebble and aimed it at Tessa. He meant to graze her arm, but ended up hitting her shoulder instead. She jumped and cried out. "Whatever we do, we'd better get out of here," she said. "These hornets are vicious."

"Don't think of it as a hornet," Deering said, following her across the field. "Think of it as a sign from the Lord."

"A sign in a hornet sting?"

"He works in mysterious ways, Mrs. Bright."

"I'll keep that in mind, Reverend."

"What about my chapel?"

"I'll think about it. Right now, I think you'd better go home while I . . . I'll have a little chat with the Lord myself."

"You do that, Mrs. Bright. I believe all things are possible through prayer."

"Yes, Reverend. I believe that, too." She watched the preacher walk away, then stalked toward the house.

Once inside, she went into the kitchen and poured herself a cup of water. "Out with it, Will," she demanded. "Did you tell that poor man to come here and build a chapel?"

"Not exactly." He pulled a chair back from the table and settled in it. Even though he didn't actually need to sit, he thought doing so might encourage Tessa to join him. *"I did suggest he ride out here and take a look around. I'm trying to get him interested in the ranch."*

"The ranch." She set her cup on the table with a loud thump.

"And you, too, of course." He chuckled. *"I thought for a minute there he was going to kiss you."*

"I do *not* want to kiss Reverend Deering!" She sounded truly horrified, her voice rising an octave on the last syllable.

"You didn't seem to have much trouble kissing Fox the other night."

She dropped into a chair, white-faced. "You were spying on me!"

"Actually, I was spying on Fox, and you happened to come along."

She glared in his direction. "You took him into town, where you knew there'd be trouble."

"I just wanted him to see the attitude of people around here, to recognize that he's bad for you."

"Don't you think I know that already? I'm not a child, Will."

No. Not a child. He rose and came to her, close enough that his cold breath stirred her hair. How long had it been since he'd been able to touch her without her flinching from the chill. *"I know,"* he said softly. *"I just want you to be happy again."*

She nodded. "Then trust me to make the right decisions for myself. And leave Reverend Deering and Micah alone."

She waited for him to make that promise, but he couldn't. He'd come back to watch over her and he had no choice but to do so. She wouldn't understand, so he left her in silence. Sometimes it was better that way, when to speak would only hurt her more.

Micah hefted his saddle off the mare and tossed it onto the saddle rack. He stripped off the saddle blanket and began rubbing the horse's lathered hide with straw, his fingers probing for a hornet sting or saddle bur that might have caused her to buck so suddenly. All the while he worked, his brain was feverish with images of Reverend Jonathan Deering standing in the pasture with his shirt half off, about to pull Tessa into his arms.

"Did you find out what startled her?"

He looked up and saw Tessa silhouetted in the barn door, sunlight tracing her every curve. His mouth went dry, and his muscles tightened with need. Forcing his eyes away from the vision, he shook his head, tossed aside the handful of dirty straw, and swatted the mare's rump to herd her into the stall.

Tessa came to stand beside him as he fastened the stall door. "What did the preacher want?" he asked. As if he didn't already know. What would any man in his right mind want from Tessa? He looked down at her, at the delicate curve of her shoulders and the soft white skin at the base of her throat, skin he longed to kiss.

"He wants to build a chapel on my land. A chapel for the Indians."

Micah grunted. "That's all?"

She glanced at him. "What did you think?"

He bent and scooped the saddle blanket from the floor, shook it out, then draped it over his saddle. "What was I supposed to think with him standing there so close to you, half undressed?"

"I was looking for a hornet sting!"

He glanced at her. Why was she smiling like that? "I do believe you're jealous," she said, coming to stand beside him once more.

"Why should I be jealous?" He moved aside, but she followed. He didn't want to be so close to her, so close to memories of the way she felt in his arms, the way she tasted, the smell of her. He half turned away, so that she wouldn't see the state she'd brought him to, just by standing next to him. "Are you going to let Deering do it?"

"Do what?" She leaned toward him, the simple words taking on a wealth of illicit meaning in his mind.

"Are you going to let him build a chapel?" he snapped.

She straightened. "I think I'll ask the Indians first."

He blinked. Indians? Was she talking about him? "What Indians?"

"You'll see. They'll be coming to visit soon." With an enigmatic smile, she turned and walked away, leaving him curious and confused, physically and mentally frustrated.

When a woman can do that to you, he thought as he stared after her, *then you are in serious trouble.*

Two days later, Micah was surprised to find Tessa in the kitchen, sweating over a blazing stove. "What's going on?" he asked, staring at plate after plate of cookies cooling on the table, chairs, and counter.

"Getting ready for company." She spooned globs of dough into a pan.

He picked up a cookie and bit into it. "Are you expecting an army of children?"

She shook her head. "Do you like the cookies? I got the recipe from Ada Drake."

He nodded and smiled, not at the cookie but at the appealing picture she made standing before him, her cheeks flushed with the heat, a smudge of flour on her nose. He caught her gaze and held it, knowing he was looking at her too long but unable to stop. Was it only because he knew he couldn't have her that he wanted her so? Was he imagining that he read the same wanting in her eyes?

In the end, she turned away and began once more carefully measuring cookie dough into the pan. "I need you to bring all the horses into the corral this afternoon, where we can keep a close eye on them," she said. "And make sure the fence is in good repair and the gates are strong."

"All right." He claimed another cookie and left, wondering about guests who would require dozens of sugar cookies and a reinforced horse corral.

His answer came in the early afternoon, with the arrival of half a dozen Indian braves and assorted horses, dogs, and boys. Micah regarded them warily. They wore no paint, and it was unlikely they'd launch a raid in broad daylight. "These are the friends I told you about," Tessa said, coming out to stand beside him.

The Indian party halted just outside the picket fence surrounding the house. The men dismounted and left their horses with the boys, then came into the yard to stand before Micah and Tessa. He recognized Drinking Wolf, the warrior who had brought the venison. An older man next to him was some kind of chief, judging by the eagle feathers tied in his scalp lock. Tessa introduced him as Tabapahdua—Sun Bear. He was an imposing figure, easily matching Micah in height, with a deep-muscled chest. He wore deerskin leggings and breech-clout, with three rings of silver in each ear and a streak of red paint defining the part of his hair.

Tessa stepped forward, smiling. "It is good to see you," she said, making the sign for greeting.

"It is good to see you also." Sun Bear spoke in Comanche, translating the words to sign. He glanced at Micah. "Esahiwi told us you had a new man."

Either Tessa did not understand the words, or she chose to ignore them. "I am not her man—yet." Micah surprised himself with the comment, made in Comanche. He told himself he said it because he wanted the chief to know Tessa had a protector.

The chief raised one eyebrow and glanced at Tessa. "It will not be many moons," he said. "She has been without a man too long."

Tessa frowned at them. Sun Bear had stopped speaking in sign. "It is good of you to come today," she said, picking up the conversation again, her hands moving gracefully to translate the words into motions.

The chief glanced at Micah, who indicated Tessa alone knew the purpose of the day's meeting. Sun Bear grunted. "I came because I think maybe you are ready to hand over the horse you owe me."

Tessa smiled. "First we eat. Then we talk."

She left them to arrange themselves in a semicircle on the ground in front of the porch. Micah started to follow Tessa inside, then decided maybe he should keep an eye on the chief. What was all that about Tessa owing him a horse? No wonder she'd insisted her stock be brought in close to the house.

The rest of the men joined Sun Bear and Micah on the ground, while the boys continued to watch over the ponies outside the picket fence. The chief glanced at Micah. "You are not from here," he said. "Who are your people?"

Micah hesitated. The simple question had a number of different answers. He'd been born into his father's tribe in the Texas panhandle near the Canadian river, and lived with his white aunt and uncle in East Texas from the age of twelve, until he left them at seventeen to join the Army. He'd spent the next decade trying to find his place among soldiers and scouts at half a dozen different posts. He had never felt he truly belonged to any of those places, yet he thought he knew what Chief Sun Bear wanted to know. "Kiowa," he said. "My father was Winter Fox, a warrior under Little Mountain."

Recognition flashed in Sun Bear's eyes. Kiowa and Comanche had been allies for decades. Little Mountain's reputation as a fighter was well known and respected. Sun Bear leaned forward, studying him. Micah held himself still, not flinching under the piercing gaze. "Your mother was white?" the old man asked after a while.

He nodded. *And half of me is white. Does that make me your enemy?*

The chief sat back and nodded, a thoughtful expression on his face. "I had a white wife once. She was soft and smelled nice. But not pretty like a real woman." He cut his eyes to Micah. "For a half-breed, maybe just right."

Everyone laughed. Even Micah found himself unbending enough to crack a smile. Sun Bear sat with the relaxed posture of a man comfortable with his own authority. For now, at least, he posed no threat and expected none in return.

Will rolled his eyes at Sun Bear's "joke" about Fox and Tessa. The old guy thought he was such a card. But he'd been a good friend, to him and to Tessa after Will had died. Will wouldn't ever forget that.

Tessa came out with platters of cookies and began distributing the sweets among the men. Will examined the platter with interest. Must be a new recipe. The Indians chowed down with approval, but then, he'd never seen anything they didn't like, at least when it came to Tessa's cooking.

Or Tessa herself, for that matter.

Right after he'd died, the old chief had come to Tessa and asked her to be his wife. He had promised her many horses of her own and a new deerskin dress every season. Tessa had been shocked at first, then amused. But Will had seen nothing funny about the proposal. If things on the ranch got bad enough, would Tessa consider taking the old chief up on his offer?

That was when Will had decided to make himself known to Tessa. Up until then, he'd watched over her from a distance, not wanting to frighten her. But after Sun Bear proposed, he felt he had to let her know he still intended to keep looking after her.

He wandered among the Indians, searching for the faces of friends. He'd thought about going to the trouble of materializing and visiting with some of his old pals. He could have said he was Will's hermit brother or something.

It might have worked with a group of whites, but the Indians were a sharp-eyed lot, and superstitious to boot.

They might have recognized him for what he was. They didn't pretend not to believe in ghosts and spirits and such, like white people did. But they tended to stay far away from such things. The knowledge he was here might run them off for good.

So he contented himself with remaining invisible and playing harmless tricks to pass the time. He sat near Drinking Wolf until the half-naked youth developed goose bumps and had to get up to keep from freezing. He stole cookies off Little Dog's plate when he wasn't looking and crumbled them into pieces on the ground.

After all, a ghost denied earthly pleasures had to take his fun where he could find it.

Sun Bear leaned toward Micah once more. "She is a good woman, even for a white woman," he said. "She has very many horses and is a good cook, too."

Micah followed the chief's gaze toward Tessa, who was still handing out cookies. He nodded, holding in his smile. The chief sounded for all the world like a proud father trying to convince a young suitor of the merits of his daughter.

At last all the cookies were eaten. Sun Bear stood, brushing crumbs from his breechclout and leggings. His men rose also, as did Micah, and Tessa came to stand with them. "Is today the day you hand over the horse you owe me?" Sun Bear asked, eyes twinkling with suppressed mirth.

Tessa shook her head. "Not today."

The chief folded his arms across his chest. "Then maybe today is the day you decide to be my woman. I will let you keep your own horses."

The words sent Micah reeling. He opened his mouth to protest, but Tessa's smile disarmed him. "Your offer is very generous, but I must decline. Today I asked you here because I need your advice."

"Ah." Sun Bear nodded. "What kind of advice?"

"There is a man in town, a holy man among my people. He wants to build a special building here on my land. A place for the Indians to come and listen to this holy man speak about the Great Spirit.''

Sun Bear bowed his head, considering her words. ''And what else will this man do besides speak?'' he asked after a moment.

''That is all. He believes he has been sent with a message for your people.''

Sun Bear arched his eyebrows. ''Why would the Great Spirit send a white man to speak to us?''

Tessa shrugged. ''I don't know. What should I tell this man?''

''If he builds this special place, what will he require of the Indians who come there?'' Sun Bear asked.

''Only that you listen.'' She cupped her hand to her ear in the familiar sign.

Sun Bear shook his head. ''White men have said things like this before. Their requests are simple, seem easy to meet. But they always want more, and it is never to our benefit, only theirs.''

''Then you want me to tell him no?''

Sun Bear looked thoughtful. ''I will have to consider this more.'' He turned to Micah and addressed him in Comanche. ''In a few sleeps, when the moon is full, we will have a hunt. You must come and celebrate with us.''

Micah would never have thought to ask such a favor, and the appeal the offer held for him startled him almost as much as the invitation itself. He tried to hide his confused feelings behind a blank expression. ''Where is your camp?''

''It is along the creek.'' The chief sketched a crooked waterway in the air with his hands. ''Turn away from the river to follow the creek when you come to an old cottonwood that has been struck by lightning.''

Micah nodded. ''I will be honored to come.''

Sun Bear turned back to Tessa and addressed her in sign. ''You will come with this man to our camp. Bring this holy man of yours with you, also. I would like to meet him.''

Tessa glanced at Micah, obviously puzzled by the invitation, but she nodded. "I will be honored to come."

The chief looked satisfied. "It is time to go now."

Micah and Tessa stood in the yard and watched them mount up and ride away. "What did he mean when he said I should come with you?" Tessa asked.

"He invited us to come to a hunting celebration in a few days. When the moon is full."

Her eyes widened. "He's never done anything like that before."

"How long have you known him?" Micah turned toward her.

"Three years."

He waited, but she didn't elaborate. Perhaps she enjoyed teasing him this way, making him probe for information. "What did he mean when he said you owed him a horse?"

She smiled, though her eyes looked sad. "My husband first met Sun Bear when he caught him trying to steal some of our horses." She raised her head, and Micah followed her gaze to the stout corral, where a dozen glossy-coated animals milled about. "My husband stopped him and surprised him by speaking to him in sign. He convinced Sun Bear that he was a friend, not an enemy. The two talked a long time, then my husband brought him up to the house to eat." Her voice trailed away, and Micah knew she was lost in thought, remembering another time, a time when she had been in love with someone else, before she had even known he existed. He looked away, fighting back an unreasonable jealousy.

"Sun Bear always said that if my husband had not stopped him that day, he would have had a fine new horse," she continued. "They always joked that one day, Sun Bear would have his horse."

"And the cookies?"

She laughed. "I happened to be baking cookies the day Sun Bear arrived, so I offered him some. He ate every one and asked for more." She crossed her arms over her chest and leaned back against the corral. "After

the first time, I always tried to have sweets to serve
him.''

''And you learned Indian sign?''

She nodded. ''I made the old man teach me.''

He frowned. That old hermit again! ''He taught you
to sign? Why didn't your husband teach you?''

She looked away. ''He . . . he taught us both. The hermit taught us both.''

Don't turn away from me like that, he thought. With
every question he asked, the feeling grew that there were
things she had not told him, important details of the
picture she'd chosen to leave out. Yet he couldn't stop
himself from asking more, hoping somehow she would
take him into her confidence. ''What about Sun Bear's
proposal that you be his wife?''

She laughed. ''Oh, he's not serious!''

''Actually, I think he is.'' He'd seen the admiration
in the old chief's eyes when he looked at Tessa, an af-
fection colored with a desire that matched the feeling
Micah carried in his own heart.

Tessa blushed and smoothed her apron, which wasn't
the least bit wrinkled. ''You're full of questions this afternoon,'' she said. ''Now I have one for you. What did
Sun Bear say to you?''

''When?''

''I saw you talking together while I was inside getting
the cookies.''

He met her gaze, challenging her to read his feelings.
''He wanted to know if we were married.''

Her eyes widened with shock—or was that fear?
''What did you tell him?''

''The truth.'' But not the whole truth, of course.
''Would you rather I'd lied?''

She dropped her gaze and fussed with her apron again.
''I was just curious.''

He clenched his hands into fists to keep from reaching
out and capturing her restless fingers in his own. ''He
thinks we make a good pair.''

''Oh he does, does he?'' She looked away, but not

before he caught the hint of a blush on her cheeks. When she turned toward him again, however, her expression was more guarded. "Was your mother or your father a Comanche?"

So she had been wondering about him. The thought pleased him. "Neither. I'm half Kiowa."

She looked puzzled. "Then where did you learn to speak Comanche?"

"I learned it when I worked for the Army." He could play this game, too, forcing her to pull information out of him one piece at a time. "Speaking of the Army, do they know about your friendship with the Indians?"

She shrugged. "I've never tried to keep it a secret. Besides, Sun Bear and his people aren't classified as a hostile tribe."

"There are a lot of people who wouldn't agree with you." He squinted down the drive, toward the settling dust, all that was left of the Indians' passing. "I've heard talk of Texans petitioning the government to do away with the reservations altogether and move the Indians out of state, the way they did the tribes in Florida and Mississippi."

"Sun Bear's people were here before any of us. This is their land. I don't see why we can't share it."

"I doubt that idea appeals to the Indians any more than it does to Texans," he said.

"I don't see any point in fretting about something that hasn't happened yet." She turned back toward the house.

She was either pitifully naive or determined to ignore the obvious. He followed her, intending to force her to admit the risk she was taking by befriending Sun Bear and his people. "Did you notice one of the boys tending the ponies was a captive?" he asked. "A Mexican, from the looks of him."

She stopped at the edge of the front porch and glared at him. "What are you trying to say?"

"These people are warriors. They're used to going where they please, doing whatever they like. If the government.thinks it can control them by putting them on a reservation, it's dreaming.''

"Just like no one can tell you what to do, is that it?''

He bristled. "What do you mean by that?''

She met his gaze with a hard look of her own. "I heard about the fight in the saloon. How Gabe Emerson asked you to leave and you wouldn't.''

That again! He couldn't believe she was bringing it up now. "Emerson didn't ask. He ordered. And backed up his words with a loaded sidearm.''

Her expression clouded. "I don't want you stirring up trouble in town.''

He resented having to defend himself this way. "I just went in for a beer. The bartender didn't have any trouble serving me, so it was none of Emerson's business.''

"Just be more careful next time.'' She put her foot on the bottom step. "I'm going in now. I'm tired.''

He watched her walk across the porch. Was Tessa concerned for his safety, or just for her own reputation? He might have asked her, if he hadn't been afraid her answer would bother him more than not knowing.

Chapter Nine

Micah was currying the Morgan gelding the next morning when Tessa came out and asked him to hitch up the wagon. "I used all my sugar and flour baking for Sun Bear," she said. "I need to go into town to buy more."

"I'll drive you," he offered. The idea of an outing with Tessa appealed to him.

She avoided his gaze, her attention focused on the horse. "That's sweet of you to offer, but, really, I can manage just fine on my own."

Her resistance made him stubborn. "I want to come with you." He put away the curry comb and took the harness from the wall. "I need to pick up a few things myself."

"All right, then," she replied, but she didn't sound particularly pleased. She retreated to the house. Her uncharacteristic coolness irritated him. Was she still upset about the argument they'd had last night?

It wasn't even an argument, he told himself as he buckled the harness onto the wagon horses. He'd only been trying to make her see what a chance she was taking in befriending the Indians.

The same chance she was taking by remaining friends

with him. The truth gnawed at him. No wonder she preferred to go to town alone. He flexed a horse collar over one knee, then slipped it over the head of the wheel horse. Tessa was just too polite to come right out and refuse him. If he was any kind of gentleman, he would let her off the hook and offer to stay home.

But no one had ever accused him of being a gentleman. He fit the collar on the horse and fastened the rest of the harness. He *wanted* the chance to be with Tessa like any other man. He wanted to drive into town with her by his side, to bask in the warmth of her smiles, to see envy in the eyes of other men they passed.

He left the horses in the stalls and went to wash his face and comb his hair. At the last minute, he decided to put on a clean shirt, a dark-brown homespun that had belonged to the late Mr. Bright. As if this extra care with his appearance could change what Tessa and the townspeople thought of him.

By the time he'd hitched the horses to the wagon, Tessa was waiting for him on the front porch. She wore a dark-gray dress he recognized as one she'd worked on many an evening as they sat together. Somehow, even with one arm in a cast, she'd managed to grip the fabric in her fingers and work the needle through the layers. He'd admired her determination, though he'd never thought until now to tell her so.

"You look very pretty," he said as he helped her into the wagon, the words feeling awkward on his tongue. He'd never been one for handing out flattery.

She flushed a becoming pink and smoothed her skirts. "Thank you. It's really an old dress, but I made it over from a pattern I found in *Peterson's Magazine*."

"Well, you did a good job."

She rewarded him for these words with a smile that made him feel six inches taller. Why had he been so stingy with his praise before?

They set off at a fast clip, Micah deftly guiding the horses around the roughest places in the road. Tessa raised a ruffled parasol against the sun's glare. He couldn't remember seeing a prettier picture. The soft floral scent of her perfume enveloped him, and he was uncomfortably aware of the narrow distance between them. He had only to slide over a few inches, and they would be sitting thigh to thigh . . .

He resolutely turned his mind away from such thoughts. Maybe while Tessa was shopping he needed to pay another visit to the saloon and find Tina or another of her ilk to provide a little physical release.

But that idea held no appeal to him. It was as if kissing Tessa had spoiled him for any other woman. He hazarded a glance at her and found her gaze fixed on him, a thoughtful expression in her eyes. "Is something wrong?"

"I was just thinking how little I really know about you," she said softly.

He leaned forward, elbows on his knees, reins relaxed in his hands, his very casualness an attempt to hide the turmoil of his thoughts. So she had been thinking about him. The idea made his spirits soar, though he dared not reveal as much. "What do you want to know?"

She stared out over the summer-dry prairie, as if sorting through a number of questions in her mind. "Your name. How did you get your name? It seems so unusual for an Indian."

"My mother said I was named for the Old Testament prophet." The wagon seat creaked as he propped one foot on the footboard. Over the years, his memory of his mother's face had softened and blurred, but he could still recall her bright red hair; hair that had probably saved her life, since the Kiowa seemed to regard redheads as particularly favored. She had green eyes, too, like his own. "She was a preacher's daughter. Just before she was captured, she had memorized all the books of the Bible. After a while, it was about all the English she remembered."

A startled look flashed into Tessa's eyes, fading quickly to sadness. She hadn't expected that, had she? To hear that his mother was a captive. She'd no doubt craved some more romantic story, not this harsh reality. "Later on, a trapper told my father the word meant a sharp, shiny stone," he continued. "He liked that."

"What happened to your mother?"

He slid his thumbs along the reins. "She died when I was thirteen."

"And your father?"

"He was killed. By soldiers."

Tessa put her hand to her mouth, but not before a gasp escaped. Micah looked at her, an old pain pricking him, like a buried thorn. She opened her mouth, then closed it without speaking. He knew what she wanted to know, and suddenly he *wanted* her to know. "I was twelve or so when it happened." It had been the summer after his first buffalo hunt, or rather the first hunt in which he had been allowed to do more than hold the horses. "We were camped along a river. Troops rode in and began killing everyone."

He used to dream about that day, although he hadn't in a long time. Panic had swept through the tents, as children's screams and women's wails mingled with the shouting of the soldiers and the deadly thunder of their guns. His father had been one of the first shot. At the same time, soldiers began setting fire to the tents. "My mother grabbed me and my baby sister and raced for cover along the river." They had lain amongst the reeds, half submerged in shallow water, the stench of burning buffalo hides filling their nostrils, the wails of the dying and grieving buffeting their ears.

"We stayed hidden for a long time, until some soldiers found us and recognized my mother as white. They took us to a fort and eventually located my mother's sister. She and her husband took us in."

He'd been afraid of Aunt Mag and Uncle Eb at first. They'd both been big, stern people. He hadn't realized until he was much older the courage and kindness they'd demonstrated in taking in Mag's long-lost sister and half savage children.

"And your mother died a year later?"

Tessa's gentle prompting pulled him back to his story. "She and my sister died of cholera that next summer. My aunt and uncle raised me." He'd been terrified they would send him away, or abandon him the way the Kiowas sometimes did old people who became a burden to the group. But Aunt Mag had taken his hand after the funeral service and told him he had a responsibility to grow up into a man his mother could be proud of, and she intended to help him do just that.

He doubted his mother would see much to be proud of in the rootless wanderer he'd become. He could only hope that she would understand what had brought him to this point.

He stopped speaking, and Tessa bowed her head. He wished he could reach out and take her hand; he wished he could risk taking that much comfort, but fear paralyzed him—fear that she might rebuff him, or that once they touched they might never release their hold on one another.

They reached the edge of town, and as the wagon rolled past houses and storefronts, he noticed people staring at them. He wished he could pretend people were staring because they were such a handsome couple, but he knew better than that. They were wondering how a white woman like Tessa could associate herself with a man like him.

He parked the wagon in a lot across from Wilkins's Mercantile. "You take care of your shopping," he said. "I'm just going to look around."

"Where are you going?" she asked, looking worried.

"Don't worry. I'll meet you back here at noon." He didn't know where he was going. It was obvious that there was no place in this town where he was welcome.

He left the wagon and started walking down the street, looking idly into windows of stores he passed. Two women approached, and he raised his head to greet them politely. But when they caught sight of him, they gasped and hurried across the street.

He reached the saloon. A glimpse through the batwing

doors showed little activity this time of day. The bartender sat behind the bar, reading the paper. Micah had heard the man was the biggest donor to the Library Society's cause. Was it because he loved to read or because he was trying to buy his way into respectable society? Perhaps that was Micah's problem: He hadn't neither been born into wealth or discovered it later.

He started to go inside, then resolutely turned around. Why purposely stir up trouble?

At the opposite end of town from the saloon sat the church. As Micah neared the steepled building, a familiar voice hailed him. "Mr. Fox! I wonder if you might help me for a moment?"

Micah didn't much like Reverend Deering, but he had to admit the man was the only one who'd been halfway civil to him, outside of Tessa and perhaps the bartender. He found the preacher in the shade of an oak beside the church, attempting to snub the bay gelding to the rough-barked trunk. "If you could just hold him a moment while I examine his hind foot." Deering handed over the reins.

"This is a fine-looking horse," Micah said as he held the animal steady and stroked the aristocratic nose.

"It was a gift from the people of my previous congregation," Deering explained as he bent over the horse's left hind foot. "A token of their esteem."

Micah thought of his Mexican silver saddle. The officers at Fort Inge had presented it to him after he'd saved a group of them from ambush along the Nueces River.

"They knew I'd need a good horse if I was to carry out my calling."

"Your calling to preach to the Indians?"

"Of course." Deering straightened, a thumb-size ball of clay wedged on the end of his knife. "No wonder the poor beast was lame."

What would it be like to know exactly what you were supposed to be doing with your life, Micah wondered. On the day he'd been presented with the saddle, he thought he'd found his rightful place in the world, with work he enjoyed, men who respected him, and an enjoyable affair with a beautiful woman.

Less than a month later, he'd been sneaking away in the middle of the night, his happiness blown away like so much chaff in the wind. "How do you know preaching to the Indians is really your calling?" he asked.

Deering wiped the knife on his trouser leg and replaced it in the sheath at his side. "I suppose it comes from hours of prayer and meditation on the Lord's will." He glanced up at Micah. "But the truth is, when you've found your calling, there really isn't anything else you *can* do. Every road keeps leading you back there." He relieved Micah of the horse's reins. "Thanks for your help. Why don't you come in, and I'll make a fresh pot of coffee? It's time we sat and had a real visit."

Micah followed the preacher toward the little parsonage behind the church, Deering's words crowding his thoughts. The roads he'd been following had led him to Tessa, but how could he know that wasn't just another layover on a journey that didn't seem to be taking him anywhere?

After Micah left her, Tessa crossed the street and started toward the mercantile. Micah's story had filled her with a wrenching sadness she was having trouble shaking off. She felt for the orphaned boy and the outcast man. She knew what it was like to want acceptance among a people who turned their backs on you, and the realization frightened her. She didn't want to care that much about him. Whereas she had thought his handsome face and body might be her downfall, she was beginning to see that the real danger lay in the way he touched her spirit. These growing moments of empathy between them tempted her more than the physical passion they shared. But she ought to know by now that the pleasure of giving in to her longing wouldn't be worth the pain that came later.

"Good morning, Mrs. Bright." Ada Drake hailed her from the steps of the store.

Trying to dispel a lingering feeling of regret, Tessa pasted a smile on her face and returned Mrs. Drake's greeting. Still smiling, she entered the store.

"Hello, Mrs. Bright." Bob Wilkins, the proprietor, looked up from cutting a plug of tobacco for Milo Adamson. "Be with you in a minute."

"What a lovely dress." Ammie Smith passed on her way out the door and gave Tessa a friendly smile.

"We have some new sateen muslin you might be interested in," Mrs. Wilkins told her as Tessa walked through the dry goods department.

This onslaught of friendliness made Tessa feel two inches taller. How different this was from the days when she'd entered the store and spoken to no one, and no one had spoken to her. She supposed she had Reverend Deering and the Library Society to thank for the change, though perhaps her own attitude had aided the transformation as well. It was much easier to smile and make small talk now that she no longer saw the townspeople as her enemies.

"Mrs. Bright, I wonder if I might ask a favor of you?" Mamie Tucker hurried up to her as Mr. Wilkins was wrapping the last of Tessa's order.

"Certainly, Mrs. Tucker." Tessa smiled at the young woman in the white ruffled sunbonnet. "What is it?"

"I was wondering if you would agree to host the next meeting of the Library Society. It's Tuesday after next. I volunteered to do so, but my oldest, George, has come down with a summer cold, and I know from experience it's bound to work its way through all four children before it's done."

Entertain the town ladies in her home? Tessa's smile wavered, and she swallowed hard. "All right." She took a deep breath and nodded. "I . . . I'd love to."

"Wonderful." Mrs. Tucker squeezed her hand. "See you Sunday, I'm sure."

Tessa turned back to the storekeeper. "You'd better

add another pound each of tea and sugar to my order.''
She stood taller. ''I'm hosting the Library Society in my
home week after next.''

''Will do, Mrs. Bright.''

She'd scarcely had time to recover from the shock of
Mrs. Tucker's request when a familiar voice assailed her
from across the room. ''Tessa, darling. How delightful
to see you!'' Like a falcon descending on an unsus-
pecting dove, Margery Finch swept through the door and
made a beeline for her friend. ''I'm so glad you're here!
You can help me find the perfect ribbon for my hat.''

''Margery. How nice to see you.'' Tessa smiled and
allowed Margery to lead her along to the hat section,
where Mrs. Wilkins stocked a variety of ribbons, feathers, stuffed birds, and other millinery ornaments.

''Did you come to town alone, or did you bring that
handsome redskin with you?'' Margery selected a spool
of ribbon and held it up to the light.

Tessa flushed. ''If you mean Mr. Fox, he's in town
somewhere.''

''Well, of course I mean Micah Fox. Or are you hiding more than one good-looking Indian on your place?''

Conscious of the stares of those around them, Tessa
steered Margery to the end of the aisle where she hoped
they'd have more privacy. ''Did you come all the way
into town just to buy a hat ribbon?'' she asked.

Margery shaped her pretty mouth into a pout. ''Alan
is away on patrol, and I'm bored half out of my mind.
So I thought I'd have one of the boys drive me into
town to see what fun I could stir up.''

Tessa looked toward the door. The ''boy'' in question
was a middle-aged sergeant who gazed after the major's
wife with a smitten look on his face. Tessa frowned. She
started to say something about how happily married
women shouldn't be so interested in fun with the
''boys,'' but thought better of it. ''I'll have you and Alan
to dinner at my house soon. I know you'll enjoy that.''

''Oh, yes, I will.'' Margery tried a red ribbon, then

selected a blue. "Maybe we should find Micah and persuade him to take us to dinner now."

"I'm afraid I'll have to pass on that offer today, Mrs. Finch."

Tessa was never going to get used to Micah's ability to sneak up on her. He was almost as bad as Will! She whirled and saw him standing at the end of the aisle, Reverend Deering at his side. "The reverend wanted a word with you, Mrs. Bright," Micah said formally.

Deering beamed and advanced down the aisle to them. "Mr. Fox has relayed your kind invitation to visit one of the Indian encampments," he said.

"Uh, yes. That's right. Chief Sun Bear has invited us to visit his camp. He wants to meet you."

"And I am excited about the opportunity to meet him. Such an important personage could no doubt be a valuable ally in my mission work."

Tessa craned her neck to look over the stacks of boxes and cans on either side of them. The aisles seemed uncommonly full. No doubt, within half an hour, it would be all over town that Tessa Bright and her half-breed ranch hand intended to pay a social call on a bunch of Indians. At least with Reverend Deering along they could pass it off as missionary work. "I'm happy to help you with your work anytime, Reverend," she said loudly.

He grinned and pumped her hand. "Thank you, Mrs. Bright, and God bless you."

Tessa sincerely hoped Deering was in touch with someone other than Will when he said his prayers. While Micah collected her purchases, she swept out of the store, followed by Deering and Margery. "I'll send that invitation soon," she told Margery as she climbed into her wagon. "I hope you have a nice afternoon in town."

"I'm sure I will. I'm going to get the good reverend here to show me around." Margery linked arms with a red-faced Reverend Deering. "You all be careful driving home, now."

Micah took up the reins, and they set out. Tessa

waved to a few people they passed, then sank back against the seat. "I guess it's just as well Reverend Deering's going with us," Micah said. "Maybe it will keep people from talking."

"Yes," she murmured, a little wistful for the days when she hadn't cared about the opinions of others. Did respectability mean trading in all her freedom? She glanced at the man at her side, at his broad shoulders and the sculpted planes of his face. Or could she find a middle ground somewhere—a middle ground that didn't leave Micah out?

Tessa, Micah, and Reverend Deering set out for the Indian encampment the next morning. "The Lord has blessed us with a perfect day for traveling," Deering declared as they rode along.

Tessa looked past him at the tall grass rippling in a warm breeze, and the sunflowers and white prickly poppies dancing above the grasses and filling the air with a delicate scent. She breathed in deeply. "I wish I could bottle up a day like this and save it."

"What would you do with it if you could?" Micah rode up beside her on Pigeon, who showed no sign of a return to her old runaway habits.

She smiled. "I'd wait for some dark winter morning and take it out and let it loose. I'd remember how all the things that die in winter come back to life in spring." She looked into his green eyes and felt as if something inside her was coming back to life as well. The thought frightened her, but she was determined not to run from it.

"How much farther do you think we have to go?" Deering asked, breaking the spell between them.

"We passed the reservation boundary a little while ago," Micah said. "Chief Sun Bear said to follow the river to a creek with a lightning-struck cottonwood on its banks."

They fell silent again. The gentle rocking of her horse and the heat of the sun sent Tessa into a doze.

"There's the cottonwood!" Deering could hardly

contain the excitement in his voice. Tessa looked up and saw an old tree trunk split in half and lying on the creek bank. The men turned their horses to follow the boulder-strewn watercourse around a bend, and she urged her horse into a trot to catch up with them.

The village appeared suddenly around the curve, a dozen or so buffalo-hide tepees scattered along the waterside, with cook fires and drying frames in front of them. A dozen or more children splashed and raced through the water, while clusters of women worked hides or jerked meat nearby.

A score or more dogs announced their arrival with a furious barking, and a trio of naked children squealed and hurried to their mothers. The rest of the population appeared not to notice the visitors, though Tessa felt sure their gazes followed them across the encampment.

They headed for the tepee in the center of the group. Easily the largest shelter, its bearskin door was thrown aside to let in air and light. A woman worked outside the door, scraping the hair from a hide. At their approach, she rose and went inside.

As they waited, Tessa began to wonder if they should go in also. Just then Sun Bear came out to greet them. "Welcome," he said, a Comanche word she recognized.

A young man came to take their horses, and the chief ushered them into the tent. Micah led the way to a pile of skins opposite the door. They sat cross-legged, with Tessa between Micah and Deering, Sun Bear across from them.

The woman pulled the bearskin door shut behind them. After the brightness and openness of the out-of-doors, the interior of the tepee was dark and stifling. Tessa blinked, trying to focus in the sudden dimness. A rush of odors assailed her—sweat and grease and burning cedar. Sun Bear poked at the small fire in the center of the room and coaxed a thin flame from the embers.

"This is fascinating," Deering whispered. Tessa nodded, afraid to speak.

The woman who had been working in front of the

tepee—Tessa supposed she was Sun Bear's wife—
brought the four of them hide bowls filled with some
sort of meat stew. Micah nodded his thanks and began
to eat with his fingers. Tessa and Deering stared at theirs.
She wondered what kind of meat this was. She had heard
stories . . .

Micah nudged her with his elbow. "Eat it," he said
under his breath. "Do you want to offend your friend?"

Holding her breath, she scooped a chunk of meat onto
her fingers and raised it to her lips. Slightly greasy, a
little chewy, but not very different from beef. She looked
toward Sun Bear and nodded, hoping he would take her
actions for approval.

While she ate, she looked around the tepee. It was
bigger inside than she would have imagined, with raised
areas like beds for sleeping, and stacks of blankets,
pouches, and bowls arranged around the room. Soon
more Indians began arriving and taking their places. Out
of the corner of her eye she saw a number of men, some
of whom she recognized from their visits to the ranch.
They wore solemn expressions, though whether suspi-
cious or merely dignified she couldn't judge.

When they had finished eating, the woman came and
removed their bowls and brought a pipe. Sun Bear made
a ceremony of lighting the little clay bowl, holding it
out to the four directions, and saying words that she took
to be a kind of prayer.

She held her breath as the pipe came toward her, but
Micah did not offer it to her, passing it on to Reverend
Deering instead. The preacher took a small puff on the
pipe and began coughing, but he smiled and nodded and
passed it to the next man.

As the men talked, Tessa studied the other occupants
of the room. She was one of three women in the tepee.
She'd already decided that the older woman who had
waited on them was Sun Bear's wife. A younger, prettier
woman tended a baby in a cradleboard. Was she the
chief's daughter?

The older woman met Tessa's gaze with a challenging

stare, but the younger woman smiled before turning her attention back to the baby. Tessa could see little more of the child than a thick shock of black hair on top of its head. The rest of it was laced into the cradleboard. There'd been a time, when her marriage to Will was still young, when Tessa would have felt a sharp pang of envy for the woman with the baby. Over time, she had come to accept that she might never have children of her own. Acceptance took the edge off her pain, though nothing could wipe it away completely.

She turned her attention to the men once more, watching their faces as they spoke.

"What are they saying?" Reverend Deering leaned over and whispered in her ear.

She shook her head. "I don't know."

Micah's face was as unrevealing in its expression as those around him. Tessa watched him as if seeing him for the first time. With his long black hair, his skin gleaming brown in the firelight, he could easily have been one of the chief's warriors, for all he was dressed in white men's clothes.

He spoke in the low, guttural tones of the Comanche language and leaned forward to study a drawing the chief made in the dirt. Tessa felt a heaviness in her stomach. She had thought she was coming to know Micah better, and yet she knew so little. He seemed to have forgotten about her, though she was sitting close enough to touch him.

She felt a light hand on her shoulder and turned to see the younger woman standing behind her, smiling. She beckoned Tessa to follow her. With a last glance at Micah and a farewell wave to Reverend Deering, Tessa followed the Indian girl out into the bright sunlight.

The girl had the baby strapped on her back now, a headband holding the cradleboard steady. She faced Tessa outside the tent, and the two women studied each other. They were about the same height, similar in build, but the similarities stopped there. The Comanche woman's hair was dark and shiny with grease, parted in the middle and chopped off to chin length. She reached out and gently patted Tessa's own piled hairdo and giggled.

Tessa smiled nervously and glanced back over her shoulder at the tepee. Her new friend made a face and made a sign with her hands like a gobbling turkey, and another sign for time passing. Tessa nodded. "You're right. They'll talk like that for hours."

The girl pointed to herself. "Queneceah," she said, making the signs for "eagle" and "feather." So her name was Eagle Feather. Then she pointed at Tessa.

"Tessa. My name is Tessa." The name seemed simple, even drab, compared to her new friend's colorful appellation.

Eagle Feather nodded and took her hand. "Tes-Sah," she repeated, leading the way across the camp.

They passed a group of women piling firewood inside a circle of stones, and Eagle Feather explained in sign that they were building a bonfire for the celebration tonight. She made the sign for a buffalo running, then indicated an arrow being fired. Then she showed the buffalo dancing. Tessa could see the action. She wanted to applaud the young woman's storytelling abilities, but she merely nodded in understanding.

They continued across the compound to another tepee, where two older women sat cutting up meat to dry. "Tes-Sah," Eagle Feather introduced her. She pointed to the oldest of the women, whose braids showed streaks of iron. "Tabanavood." Painted Sun. The younger woman, who was plump and round as a dove, was Parriasaermin, meaning Ten Elks.

Tessa nodded in greeting. Eagle Feather began to talk with much animation, occasionally pointing to Tessa and giggling. Tessa heard her own name again and Sun Bear's. Eagle Feather drew in the air a tall, handsome man. Tessa's smile broadened. She was talking about Micah!

Then Eagle Feather pointed to Tessa's hair and touched her skirt. She made a motion like dancing, and the sign for fire and buffalo again. Tessa frowned, confused.

Ten Elks was frowning, too, but Painted Sun grinned a toothless grin and nodded. She stood and took Tessa's hand.

The women led her into the tepee, a smaller tent with its own glowing fire. They smiled and chattered, and Tessa smiled too, unsure what to expect, but wanting to fit in.

Her smile vanished, and she let out a cry when Ten Elks grabbed her dress and tried to raise it up over her head. She pulled away and backed into the corner, staring at her hosts, fighting back fear.

Eagle Feather shook her head and took Tessa's hand again, drawing her out of the corner. She touched Tessa's skirt, then pointed to her own clothes. She said something to Ten Elks, and the old woman lifted a deerskin dress from a bundle of skins on the floor.

Eagle Feather handed the dress to Tessa and indicated she was supposed to put it on. Then she made the signs for a bonfire, buffalo, and a tall, handsome man.

Tessa laughed, understanding dawning. They meant to dress her up for tonight's celebration, as a surprise for Micah. And what a surprise that would be! She obligingly began to unfasten the many buttons down the front of her bodice. Three pairs of dark eyes watched her every move as she removed first the bodice and skirt, then four petticoats and a lace-edged camisole. Possessed by a spirit of daring, she divested herself of her confining corset, too, so that at last she stood before them clad only in stockings, drawers, and chemise.

Eagle Feather reached out and fingered the fine lace and cambric of the camisole, then tried it around her own torso and grinned. Tessa slipped the deerskin dress on over her chemise and drawers. The hide was buttersoft and decorated with hundreds of beads and tiny shells. The fringed hem had little pieces of tin tied on the ends, so that when Tessa walked across the tepee, a sound like bells followed her.

She traded her riding boots for long, fringed moccasins. Then Ten Elks removed the pins from her hair and let it fall loosely around her shoulders. She pushed Tessa down onto a pile of deerskins and set about braiding the brown strands.

Painted Sun brought a pot of red paint and painted a stripe down the part of Tessa's hair, and Eagle Feather wrapped the ends of her braids with strips of beaver fur.

The three women stood back to admire their work. Tessa did not need a mirror to know they had changed her into someone who would truly fit in at tonight's celebration.

Chapter
Ten

Some time passed before Micah realized Tessa was not in the tent. He shot a questioning look at Deering, who, despite not understanding the Comanche language, seemed to be enjoying himself. "Where's Tessa?" he asked.

"She went somewhere with one of the Indian women," Deering answered.

Sun Bear touched his hand and nodded reassuringly. "My wife has taken Tessa to introduce her to the people. She will be well cared for."

He sat back, a little uneasy but knowing he could do nothing about it. He had no reason to think these people meant Tessa any harm, after all.

"Tell them about the chapel I want to build," Deering whispered.

Micah frowned. So far the chief had shown them every courtesy. It seemed wrong somehow to inflict Deering's vision upon them now, to talk of what to them must be one more way of trying to force a white man's ways on them.

"Does the crow man wish to speak?" Sun Bear leaned forward and touched Micah's knee.

Micah smiled at this reference to the preacher's black suit. He nodded. "His name is Deering, and he's one of the white men's holy men."

At the mention of his name, Deering perked up. He nudged Micah. "Tell him about the chapel. Ask him if he'll bring his people to hear me speak there."

"He wants to build a special house on Tessa's ranch and hold a big meeting there," Micah explained. "He wants to know if you will bring your people there to listen to him talk about the Great Spirit."

Sun Bear considered this for a moment. "Will there be good things to eat?"

Micah held back a smile. "Yes."

"And gifts? Gifts for my people?"

Why not? "Plenty of gifts for your people."

Sun Bear nodded. "Then tell him we will come."

Micah turned to Deering. "He says he and his people will come."

"Praise the Lord." Deering looked heavenward.

Micah wondered how much praising the preacher would do when he found out he'd just agreed to feed the whole tribe.

The Indians began to talk among themselves again. "They're talking about hunting, aren't they?" Deering scooted closer to Micah and spoke in a low voice.

Micah listened for a moment, then nodded. In fact, Drinking Wolf was telling a story about killing an old bull buffalo.

"I thought so." Deering smiled with satisfaction. "I used to sit around and listen to my uncles talk. They weren't much different."

The young warrior demonstrated how he had ridden up to the bull and driven a spear between its ribs, aiming for the heart. The bull turned in anger, but the warrior held on, facing down the angry red eyes, feeling the snorting, hot breath.

Micah grunted his approval with the others. How long had it been since he had sat like this? Yet now it seemed only yesterday, when he had hovered on the fringes of the groups of warriors, soaking up their tales, looking toward the day when he would be the one speaking, the one to receive the congratulations for his hunting prowess.

He remembered his first hunt, the summer he was twelve. He was allowed to ride with the men, to carry his own spear and bow. He knew it was a test, to see if the half-white boy had what it took to be a man, to provide for his family and protect his people. To be a warrior.

He had not slept the night before the hunt, but stayed awake into the early hours, praying for help from the spirits. The next morning, as the hunting party gathered within sight of the great herd, his pony danced beneath his knees, the way Micah's heart danced within him.

His father had looked at him, a grave, proud look, and nodded in encouragement, before the group began to fan out, to encircle the indifferent herd. The only sounds were the striking of a horse's hoof on rock, or, as they drew nearer, the placid chewing of the herd. They pulled their circle ever tighter, until Micah could make out the calves grazing in the center of the group, and smell the dusty scent of the animals.

One old cow raised her head and stared right at him, and he was frozen, fixed in that steady gaze. Then she threw back her head and snorted, and the herd began to mill about in confusion.

With a triumphant cry, the men surged forward, lances raised, bows drawn. Micah's hands trembled as he fitted an arrow in his own bow and aimed for the nearest animal.

His arrow merely glanced off the tough hide. He took a deep breath and fitted another arrow, guiding his pony with his knees until he felt he was almost close enough to reach out and touch the snorting, stamping beasts.

He willed himself to stay calm and remembered his uncle's instructions to aim between the ribs, toward the heart. He released the arrow and stared as it hit the hide and pierced it. Then the cow was on her knees, falling.

Then she was dead.

With a whoop, Micah rushed forward to claim his kill. A second cry answered his own, and he looked up to see his father, bow held over his head in triumph. Boy and man grinned at each other before whirling their horses and returning to the fray.

It was barely a month later that he stood in the ruins of his village, staring at the bodies of his father and uncle, and smelled the burning hide of the very buffalo they had slain that day.

A hand on his shoulder pulled him back to the present. He looked up to see Sun Bear staring at him thoughtfully. "You were far away from us."

Micah nodded.

"Where were you? Was it a vision?"

"Only a vision of the past." He glanced at his host. "I was thinking about what it is to be an Indian."

"Tonight you will be an Indian again." He stood and nodded toward the door. "Come. We must prepare."

Tessa could hear the singing long before she and Eagle Feather reached the bonfire. Men's voices rose and fell to a minor melody accompanied by a steadily beating drum and the crackle of the roaring fire. Though she did not understand their words, she felt drawn to them, pulled into that circle of people and light until the music wrapped around her, seeming even to flow through her.

A group of women on one side of the fire moved over to make room for her. She recognized Ten Elks and Painted Sun. The latter surveyed her and nodded solemn approval. Tessa searched the crowd for Micah but did not see him.

She spotted Reverend Deering, however, and shrank back from the sight of him. What would he think, seeing her dressed this way, with her hair down and her scalp painted? He was seated on the other side of the fire, red-faced from the heat, in the midst of a cheerful group of older men, who plied him with strips of buffalo meat and gourds full of no telling what beverage. In any case, he seemed to be enjoying himself immensely, laughing when the men laughed, eating and drinking, and taking in the strange sights like a wide-eyed child. His face showed no recognition when his gaze passed over Tessa, and she allowed herself to relax a little.

Eagle Feather lightly touched her hand and nodded toward the northeast side of the circle. Sun Bear sat among his men, wearing a headdress made of a buffalo head. Next to him stood a tall man, dressed only in a beaded breechclout and low moccasins. Streaks of red paint striped his cheeks and nose, and more red paint highlighted his muscular chest. A black feather hung from his scalp lock, and strips of rawhide bound his braided hair.

Tessa's breath caught in her throat as she stared at the man, unable to look away. His eyes met hers, eyes as green as spring grass. They shone with a feverish excitement. She wondered if he had drunk from the gourds passed among the men, or if it was only being here, in those clothes and with these people, that made him look so vibrant and aware.

From the admiring looks and whispered comments of the women around her, she knew she was not the only one who had noticed the handsome warrior. Her heart seemed to beat in rhythm with the ever faster pounding drums as she watched him move with the other men to a place on the west side of the fire. She knew she would never look at him again without remembering him this way, tall and proud, his perfectly formed body gleaming in the firelight.

The singing stopped, but the drum continued its steady throb. From a distance came cries and the sound of running feet. Startled, Tessa turned to watch the approach of half a dozen young men, three wearing buffalo heads and skins, the other three carrying spears and bows. The hunters chased the buffalo around the fire, whooping and hollering, dancing and leaping. First one then the others rushed forward to strike at the beasts with spears. They pretended to draw arrows and fire them into the hides.

One by one, the buffalo sank to the ground, and the young men claimed their prizes. As the last one fell, the crowd let out shouts of celebration. First the men and then the women were drawn into a dance around the fire. Tessa found herself pulled along with the crowd. Awkwardly at first, then with more confidence, she joined in the slow, shuffling steps of the dance, moving in rhythm with the chanting.

This was so different from any dancing she had done before. The sedate waltzes and more lively quadrilles she'd always known did not require the participation of every part of her the way this deceptively simple Indian dancing did. It was as if she had relinquished control of her body to this other woman, this Indian squaw. Tessa herself could only look on in wonder, surrendering herself to the sensations that engulfed her. She felt the heat of the fire, tasted the warm juices of the meat that was handed to her. The music pulsed through her, and her nose was filled with the perfume of roasting meat, woodsmoke, and sweating bodies.

A man came up beside her and offered her a drink from his cup. She raised her head and smiled, thinking it was Micah, but the eyes that met hers were as black as coal and as shiny as river stones.

She stumbled, losing her place in the dance, and looked around for Micah. At last she spotted him seated on a rock, holding a bowl of food, a lovely young woman kneeling on the ground in front of him. He said something that made her laugh, and she leaned forward, her hand on his leg. Tessa's stomach twisted, and she quickly looked away.

The Indian beside her touched her arm and made the sign for a tepee. She realized with shock that he was asking her to come with him to his home.

She flushed and shook her head, backing away, running into other dancers. The Indian did not pursue her.

He shrugged and moved off down the line, perhaps to find a more willing woman.

Tessa looked back at Micah, but the rock where he had been sitting was empty. Frantic now, she moved out of the circle, away from the crowd. She saw Reverend Deering, talking in clumsy sign with two old Indian men, and started to go to him, then thought better of it. She stood on the edge of the firelight, watching as couples departed the circle. Eagle Feather moved toward the tepees, followed closely by Sun Bear.

Had Micah left, too, with the pretty young woman? Was he even now in her tepee, making love to her in a language Tessa could not understand?

She swallowed hot tears and shook her head. Why shouldn't he go with the woman if he wanted? He was a handsome, healthy man.

She hugged her arms across her chest and walked away from the camp, toward the river. The music of water rushing over rocks did little to soothe her troubled thoughts. She doubted if there was a woman here tonight who would refuse to share her blankets with Micah. *Does that include me?* she wondered. *If that Indian brave who asked me to go with him had been Micah, would I have gone?*

She closed her eyes, and the memory of Micah's gleaming body sent a rush of feeling through her. How could she have said no to him?

But Micah hadn't asked her to go with him. After all, she was a white woman, different from him and from these people with whom he seemed so at home. That was what she wanted, wasn't it—to keep a distance between them, to show the white world, the town women, that she belonged in their circle? She had wanted that, even if it meant turning her back on a chance for love.

The word frightened her, but what other word was there for the connection she was beginning to feel with Micah? She hadn't asked for this, hadn't sought it out, yet she felt pulled toward him like a leaf carried along on a flooded stream.

She did not know how long she walked by the water, fighting the confusion that welled up within her. Weariness finally drove her back to Sun Bear's tepee. She hesitated to raise the bearskin door, listening for sounds of movement from inside. When all she heard was gentle snoring, she raised the flap and entered.

A small blaze flickered in the fire ring. Micah sat beside it, stirring the embers with a blackened stick. "There you are," he said, relief in his voice and on his face. "I was debating going to look for you."

He still wore his Indian clothes—the breechclout and moccasins, though he had added a calico shirt in deference to the night chill. The skin of his thighs looked like burnished bronze in the dim light.

Tessa sat a little ways from him. She stared at the fire, afraid to look into his eyes. "I went for a walk. Down by the river."

He poked at the fire. A feeble trail of sparks rose toward the smoke hole. "I thought maybe you'd gone to spend the night somewhere else."

Her face grew warm. "No," she whispered. "I wouldn't do that."

"You were asked, weren't you?" His voice grew rough. "You don't know how beautiful you look. All the men were staring, asking about you."

She hunched her shoulders toward the fire, afraid to take his flattery seriously. "I thought you had gone off with some pretty Indian woman."

He didn't say anything for so long that she thought she had hit upon the truth. She swallowed tears and blinked to clear her vision.

"No, I couldn't do that," he said after a long while, "knowing I wasn't going to stay."

She looked at him at last. Shadows danced across his face, hiding his expression. "I thought maybe you *would* stay. You seem so . . . so at home here."

He shook his head. "Tonight was . . . different. It make me think. But I can't go back."

She heard the regret in his voice and the things he left

unsaid. He didn't belong here. He didn't belong in Pony Springs. Where was the world where Micah Fox belonged?

There were so many things she wanted to say, but she could find words for none of them. Across the fire from them, she saw Reverend Deering, snoring beneath a buffalo robe. Further back from the fire, Sun Bear and Eagle Feather lay entwined even in sleep. Another dark shape slept apart from them—wife number one, Tessa guessed. If she and Micah had been alone . . . she shook her head. No use thinking that way.

"I'm tired," she said. "I think I'll get some sleep." She went to a pile of skins near the door and lay down. She closed her eyes, but sleep did not come. She was still awake a little while later when Micah came and stretched out near her.

The whole camp turned out the next morning to say good-bye to the visitors. Reverend Deering, looking only slightly disheveled from the previous night's revelry, made a speech full of flowery language, inviting the Indians to visit his chapel when it was completed. Tessa suspected Micah didn't bother to translate most of it, though she was sure the gist of the message was delivered. Sun Bear presented the preacher with a beaded pouch, which pleased Deering immensely.

Eagle Feather insisted Tessa keep the deerskin dress as a gift. She grinned with delight when Tessa handed over the lacy camisole and two of the petticoats as her own token of friendship. Micah gave the chief a bone-handled knife and received a buffalo-horn drinking cup as his gift.

What with the speech-making and gift-giving, the leave-taking took a good part of the morning. The sun was high overhead by the time Deering, Micah, and Tessa reached the split cottonwood and turned for home.

They spoke little. Deering looked tired, and Tessa was too full of emotion to speak. Micah was silent too—the silence of one whose mind is far away, lost in thought.

He had changed back into his everyday clothes, but she still detected traces of paint on his face. She couldn't look at him without an aching heaviness in her breast, the ragged pain of regret for opportunity lost.

Opportunity for one night of passion or for something more? She forced her thoughts away from the question. No good would come of answering it.

They were not yet off the reservation when Micah stopped and pointed in the distance. Tessa squinted and focused on a cloud of dust moving toward them.

"Looks like we've got company." As Micah spoke, he drew the rifle from its scabbard on the saddle and laid it in front of him.

The cloud grew larger, until she could make out the blue tunics and yellow-striped pants of a mounted patrol. Their horses were damp with sweat, and dust caked man and beast. "Halt!" A man at the front of the formation stood in the saddle and gave the order.

Tessa recognized Major Finch, his face streaked with dirt and sweat. "Major, is something wrong?" she cried, something in his expression alarming her.

Finch blinked for a moment, as if trying to place her, then his eyes widened. "Mrs. Bright. I didn't expect to see you out here."

"We've been visiting Chief Sun Bear's band." Reverend Deering seemed pleased to make this announcement.

Finch's eyes narrowed. He looked at each of them in turn, coming to rest finally on Micah. "What business do you have with the chief?" he asked.

A muscle on the side of Micah's mouth twitched, the only sign that the major's scrutiny angered him. "We were paying a social call," he said evenly. His gaze flickered over the mounted men ranked behind the major. "Why do you want to know?"

"I'll ask the questions." Finch rode closer. "Now tell me what you were doing on the reservation."

Before Micah could answer, Deering interrupted. "I intend to start an Indian mission," he declared. "I invited the chief and his people to join me.''

"And what were you and Mrs. Bright doing?'' the major asked Micah.

Micah's expression looked murderous, but the major never flinched. Tessa held her breath, fearful the tense silence around them would erupt in violence. Once again, the preacher spoke first. "Mr. Fox acted as my interpreter,'' he said.

"And Mrs. Bright?'' The major looked as if he were fast losing patience.

"I went because Sun Bear is a friend of mine,'' she said. She looked back over the column of soldiers. They all bore the same intense expressions of men with a mission. They bristled with weapons; even the horses were hung with extra ammunition. A cold chill speared through her. "What is going on, Major?'' she asked again, trying to hide her agitation.

"Margery is missing.''

She swayed in the saddle, as stunned as if the words had been rocks thrown at her. "When?'' she said with a gasp. "How?''

He rode closer, as if to keep his men from overhearing. "She didn't return from shopping yesterday.'' He hesitated, then added, "Sergeant Adkinson was with her.''

Foolish, foolish woman! Surely Margery had not run away with this sergeant?

"Why aren't you checking the stage stations, instead of looking for her here on the reservation?'' Micah spoke for the first time since the soldiers' arrival.

Finch scowled. "Sergeant Adkinson is a married man with five daughters. He has been with me since my first post. I have no reason not to trust him.''

"But you don't trust your wife.'' Micah's voice held a note of bitterness.

Finch's eyes sparked with anger. "I am aware that my wife is a young, beautiful woman, married to an older man with little to offer her in the way of material pleasures or entertainment. Such a woman might be led astray by an unscrupulous wanderer, a man who might take advantage of past friendship . . .''

Tessa listened to him with growing alarm. ''Major, what are you talking about?''

He flushed and cleared his throat. ''Lieutenant Hamilton mentioned . . . rumors . . . that my wife and Mr. Fox had a . . . relationship. While they were both at Fort Inge.''

Tessa stared at Micah. ''Is this true?''

She saw in his eyes that it was. The pain she felt surprised her, like a killing wound from a friend. Margery's insistence on seeing Micah again made sense now. Had she intended for them to be lovers once more? Had she succeeded?

''It doesn't have anything to do with what has happened to Mrs. Finch today,'' Micah said. He turned away from her, toward the major. ''She hasn't been with us. She isn't with Sun Bear and his people either.''

''Then where is she?'' Finch's voice shook.

''I suggest we pray,'' Reverend Deering said, bowing his head. No one moved, Micah and the major glaring at each other.

''Gentlemen! Bow your heads while I ask the Lord's assistance in this matter.'' Tessa didn't know when she'd heard such a note of authority in the preacher's voice. Automatically everyone around them, including Micah and Major Finch, bowed in prayer.

Tessa bent her head, but she didn't close her eyes. She couldn't stop watching Micah, wondering what other secrets she had yet to learn about him.

Will was amusing himself by sneaking up on jackrabbits and sending them bounding away when he came upon the Army ambulance parked in the middle of a field. A sad-looking man in a uniform appeared to be arguing with a beautiful woman in a blue dress. *Those two certainly don't look like they belong together,* he thought as he drifted closer.

''Mrs. Finch, I really do think it's time we headed

back for the fort,'' the man was saying. The fringe of
hair around his ears stood out in all directions, as if he'd
run his hands through it over and over again. "The major will be having conniptions."

"If the major is so worried, then he can come get me
himself." The woman sat on the ambulance steps, arms
folded across her ample bosom. She was altogether
lovely, with red-gold curls and creamy skin. Even her
button nose, though reddened by the sun, was just about
the cutest nose Will had ever seen.

The soldier—Will noticed the sergeant's stripes on his
tunic now—pulled out a limp handkerchief and mopped
his shining brow. "Pardon me, ma'am, but how will the
major know where to find us?"

The woman straightened, stretching her legs out in
front of her. "I left him a note." Shielding her eyes with
one hand, she gazed up at the sun overhead. "I don't
know why he hasn't shown up by now. I don't appreciate being left to spend the night out here on the prairie."

The sergeant turned away, though Will thought he
heard him mumble something about "it ain't exactly
been a picnic for me, either." The woman jumped to
her feet and began pacing back and forth in front of the
ambulance. "What could be keeping him?"

"Maybe he hasn't seen the note." The sergeant
climbed into the driver's seat of the ambulance and sat,
chin in hand. "Where did you leave it?"

"On his pillow, of course."

The sergeant shook his head. "Excuse me, ma'am.
But if the major is worried about you missing, he isn't
likely to have gone to bed, is he?"

She halted her pacing and looked up at him. "I . . . I
never thought of that."

The sergeant sighed and looked off across the prairie.

The woman kicked a rock, sending it right through
Will and bouncing over the ground. "All right, then,
we'll go back."

The sergeant wasted no time gathering up the reins.

''The major'll have my hide,'' he muttered as he waited for the woman to take her place inside. ''That is, if my wife doesn't skin me first. I'll be busted so low I'll be cleaning horse stalls for the rest of my life.''

The woman mounted the steps of the ambulance and slammed the door behind her. She dropped onto the tufted seat, almost landing in the now-materialized Will's lap.

''Ahhh!'' She squealed and drew back. ''Who are you?'' she demanded.

Will tugged his forelock and bowed. ''Just call me Will.'' He smiled broadly. ''Everyone does.''

''Amen.''

Major Finch raised his head as soon as Reverend Deering closed the prayer. ''What are you going to do now?'' Tessa asked.

Finch's shoulders sagged. ''I don't know. We've divided the area into sections and have been canvassing them half the night, but we haven't made much progress.''

''In East Texas, when someone was lost, they'd track them with bloodhounds,'' Deering said.

''We don't have any bloodhounds here.'' Finch paused, his eyes growing more animated. He turned to Micah once more. ''But we do have you.''

Micah looked wary. ''What about me?''

''You were a tracker for the Army at Fort Inge, weren't you?''

''What about the men you have working for you here? One of them could help you.''

Finch nudged his horse forward, until his face was only inches from Micah's. ''But you *know* Margery. You'd have a better chance of finding her.''

Someone who knew him less well would not have recognized the emotions Micah wrestled with now. But Tessa saw the telltale tension around his mouth, the tightness in his jaw, the way his knuckles whitened around the reins. The man who had previously insulted him now asked for help. Would pride have kept him from relenting if the woman missing was not one he had loved—one he might love still?

"All right. I'll do it. I'll ride with you back to the fort, and we'll start from there."

"I'll go with you," Reverend Deering said.

"So will I," Tessa echoed.

Micah shook his head. "There's nothing you can do to help. Best go back to the ranch and wait."

Tessa raised her chin, daring him to refuse her. "Margery is my friend. If she's hurt or in trouble she'll want a woman near her."

"It's my duty to go where I'm needed to offer spiritual comfort and guidance," Deering said.

"You can both wait at the fort," Major Finch said. He took up the reins and turned his horse. "We've wasted enough time talking. Let's go."

They rode at the head of the column of soldiers, no one speaking. Micah sat with his eyes straight ahead, scanning the landscape, perhaps for some sign of Margery or the Army ambulance. Reverend Deering kept his head bowed, his lips occasionally moving in silent prayer.

Tessa tried to pray too, for Margery's safety and for her own forgiveness. Her thoughts were like a twisted skein of yarn. Pull one strand and no telling where it would lead. One moment she was fearful for Margery's safety, the next she was angry at her friend for trying to seduce Micah right before her eyes. Then she felt remorse, knowing she had no claim to Micah. He had promised her nothing beyond a pledge that he would stay with her until her arm healed. She had given him nothing in return but his pay at the end of each week and a place to sleep.

The picket greeted them at the gate of the fort with word that no news had arrived regarding Mrs. Major Finch or Sergeant Adkinson. Men stopped to stare as the three civilians rode in alongside the major, but none said a word as he led them toward his quarters. "The last time I saw her was two days ago," he told them as they halted before the neat white house. "She said she was going into town to buy some ribbon to trim a hat."

"I saw her there," Tessa said. "She seemed fine." She gave the major a sympathetic look. "She said she was bored."

Micah swung down off his horse and wound the reins around the porch railing of the major's home. "I'd like to go inside and look around," he said.

"Of course." Finch led the way. Tessa thought perhaps she and Deering should wait outside, but the major held open the door and motioned for them to follow Micah inside.

Tessa stood by the front window while Finch led Micah back to the bedroom. What must it feel like to show that room to a man who had one time bedded your wife? But Margery had not been the major's wife then, had perhaps not even known him. Tessa knotted her hands into fists and pressed them into her stomach, as if she could squeeze out the ugly jealousy that plagued her.

The two men emerged from the bedroom a moment later. Micah held a sheet of notepaper in his hand. He showed it to Tessa. *Darling, I'm so anxious for us to have some time alone. I've gone out with Sergeant Adkinson. Come for me and we will send him back alone. Love, M.*

"How could she be so foolish?" Finch took the note and crumpled it in his fist. "Does she want to ruin me?"

"She only wanted you to herself for a little while." Tessa tried to ease his suffering.

"I don't have the luxury of time to myself! I have men depending on me. A whole community beyond these walls looking to me for protection. I can't just go chasing off across the prairie for some . . . some *dalliance*!"

Micah adjusted his hat on his head. "Come on, we'd better go. Take me to the stables and let's talk to the officer there. Maybe he remembers seeing something."

Chapter Eleven

"What's going on back there?" The driver rapped on the partition separating his seat from the enclosed ambulance.

"It looked like you folks might need some help, so I thought I'd offer my services," Will said graciously.

"Who are you?" the sergeant demanded. "Where did you come from?"

"I'm Will. I'm a . . . a hermit." He nodded toward the prairie outside the coach door. "I live out here."

"Do you know how to get to Fort Belknap from here?" the sergeant asked.

"Of course."

The woman's eyes went wide. She stared at the sergeant. "You mean we're lost?"

"Not anymore." He nodded to Will. "This fellow says he knows the way home."

"Drive straight until you come to the creek, then head left four miles. You'll hit the road to the fort. Turn right and you'll be there in no time." Will settled back against the seat. "I'll go with you a ways, to make sure you don't get lost again."

"Yes, sir." The sergeant turned back around and

popped the reins smartly across the mules' backs. The ambulance lurched forward, and the woman almost tumbled into Will's lap. He steadied her, admiring the soft feel of her curves in his hands. With a rueful sigh, he let her go, knowing she wouldn't have felt his touch anyway, beyond the inevitable sensation of bitter coldness.

The woman sat across from him, her arms folded across her stomach, eyes on the landscape outside. "Now you know my name, perhaps you'll tell me yours," Will said.

"It's Margery. Margery Finch." She barely glanced at him. Her eyes were sapphire blue, but marred by dark rings beneath them, as if she'd spent a sleepless night.

"Well, Miss Margery, you appear quite downhearted. I wonder if I might be of help."

She shook her head. "I doubt it. What do hermits know about being married?"

"I wasn't always a hermit. I was married for seven years to a fine woman."

Her mouth drooped. "I'll bet she never ran off from you."

He shook his head. "No, she wouldn't have done that. She was just a girl when we wed. Her family disowned her for taking up with me. I was all she had."

Margery's face softened. "I'll bet you never spent all your time working, ignoring your wife."

Will rubbed his chin. Becoming a ghost hadn't exactly given him any insight into women. "Well . . . I did work a lot. A man's got to eat, after all. It's a hard life out here." He straightened. "But she worked with me. Right alongside."

Margery looked sadder still. "I can't very well help my husband in his work."

"What does your husband do?"

"He's commander of Fort Belknap."

"Ah, well, sure you can help him."

"How? He'd never let me go on patrol with him, and as for fighting—"

"Not that. You can help him by doing nice things for his men, so they'll want to stay loyal to him. You can help out in the camp hospital, and entertain the other wives, take up good causes."

She sank back on the cushions, pouting. "None of those things sound like any fun."

Will chuckled. "That's why they call it work, ain't it?"

She said nothing for a long while. The coach reached the creek, and the sergeant bent down once more. "Turn here?"

Will nodded. "Turn here."

They had traveled another few hundred feet when Margery spoke again, her voice so soft he barely heard it above the creaking of the coach. "But how can I get him to love me?"

Will scratched his head. "You don't think he loves you now?"

She shifted in her seat. "He comes from a very fine family back east. I'm just a soldier's daughter. My father worked his way up in the ranks. I never went to some fine eastern finishing school." She sniffed. "I'm loud and I'm brash. I like bright colors and lively music. I always stand out in a crowd. I never minded not fitting in before, but now . . ."

"Maybe he loves you *because* of all those things."

She looked at him, blue eyes brimming with tears. "But how do I know he does?"

Women made Will nervous when they cried. He could feel himself fading fast. If he didn't watch it, he was going to disappear right in front of her eyes and scare the bejeebers out of her. "Why don't you just ask him, then?" he blurted.

She frowned. "I couldn't do that."

"Don't see why not. You seem to have a firm enough command of the language."

She studied him through lowered lashes, a look that would have made a more earthly man all hot and bothered. As it was, even Will was starting to feel a little sweaty. "Did you and your wife ever talk like that?" she asked. "About what you liked and disliked about each other?"

He pondered the question a minute. "No, I can't say that we ever did." It hadn't seemed particularly necessary.

"Then you never really knew her." Margery sounded sad. "If you never asked her, how could you know what was going on inside her head?"

"I just did!" Though beautiful, Mrs. Finch was beginning to wear on his nerves. "I knew everything about her. Everything that was important to know, anyway."

"Who goes there?" The sentry at the Fort called for the password, but Will could already hear the cry going out for Major Finch.

"I'd best be saying good-bye," he said.

"No, you must stay and let us properly thank—" Before she completed the sentence, the door was thrown open, and Alan Finch was pulling her into his arms.

Will vanished and drifted away. In a minute, they'd all wonder what had become of the old man, but he doubted if they'd try too hard to find him.

He looked back over his shoulder once, at Margery and her major embracing. Would she take his advice to talk to her husband?

Would things have been different for him and Tessa if they'd talked? It hadn't seemed necessary at the time. He always knew how to take care of her, and she let him. Why should things be any different now that he'd passed on? He was still older than she was, and wiser. He could still look after her. Of course he could.

Deering decided to stay at the fort, while Micah and Tessa elected to return home. Tessa rode sedately from the palisaded walls, but she felt inside as if she was racing toward the sanctuary of her home. She longed for the days when she had hidden there alone. The pain and confusion she felt right now seemed a poor trade compared to the peace she'd known then.

Micah rode ahead of her, silent as a statue. She stared at his back, wondering what thoughts and emotions his impassive expression concealed. Even Will, for all his dour stubbornness, had never made her feel so at sea, not knowing what she should think or do.

At the ranch, she left Micah to unsaddle the horses, while she escaped to the house. She went through the motions of preparing supper, fighting a weariness that made her want to crawl beneath the covers and sleep. When she awoke, things might be normal again.

The door opened, and she heard Micah's boots scrape on the rug. Keeping her back to him, she measured corn-meal into a bowl and selected an egg from the basket on the counter. "Tessa, about Margery—" he began.

The egg broke against the edge of the bowl, shattering instead of cracking, bits of shell drifting into the corn-meal, gooey white coating her fingers. She grabbed a rag and began cleaning up the mess. "I'm really busy right now," she said. "I don't have time to talk." Plucking the last of the shell from the bowl, she dumped in half a cup of water and began beating the mixture furiously. "I have a million things to do to get ready for the Library Society meeting here tomorrow."

He moved closer, casting his shadow over the table where she worked. She gripped the fork tighter, beating the batter into toughness.

"I just want you to know it's over between us. It was over a long time before I came here."

She slid the bowl onto the table, not trusting herself to hold it anymore. "Why do you want me to know that?"

"Because it seems to matter to you."

She grabbed a skillet from the stove and dumped the batter into it with jerky movements. "Well, you're wrong. It doesn't matter to me at all. What you do is your own business. Why should I care at all?" She knew she was talking too much. She should be quiet, but she couldn't stem this flood of feeling that manifested itself in an outpouring of words.

He came up behind her, close enough to touch her, but not touching. His breath stirred the hairs at the back of her neck, sending tremors down her spine. "It matters to you," he said. "Just like it matters to me that you didn't sleep with that brave who asked you."

"No, it doesn't," she lied, holding on to the edge of the table. "It doesn't matter."

He said nothing for a long moment. She could feel the heat of his gaze on her, willing her to turn and face him, but she was rooted to the floor, unable to move. Finally he turned and walked out the door, closing it gently behind him.

She sank into a chair and buried her face in her hands, not moving for a long time, until the cornbread started to burn, and she got up and threw it out.

The members of the Pony Springs Library Society began arriving at ten the next morning. Mamie Tucker, whose children were well enough to be left with their father for a few hours, arrived first in a trim black buggy, followed shortly by Ammie Smith and Ada Drake in the Drakes' piano box buggy. Trudy Babcock, enveloped in a scented cloud of Jasmine Nights, steered her old-fashioned cart into the shade of an oak and issued stern instructions to Micah on the watering of her horses. Margery Finch arrived last, in an Army ambulance with two soldiers as escorts. She looked as lovely as ever, in a yellow silk frock and matching bonnet, though Tessa wondered at the dark shadows beneath her eyes that a brave dusting of powder did little to conceal.

The meeting convened in the parlor, where Tessa served tea and cakes. The women were gracious, complimenting her home and her hospitality. "That is such a beautiful gate at the entrance to your place," Ammie Smith said. "Wherever did you get it?"

"Thank you. My husband made it shortly after we built the house."

"Well, he was quite an artist, I'll say that," Miss Smith said.

"Making a gate out of iron isn't such an art, if you ask me." Trudy sniffed. "My Jackie could do the same if he wanted to. If I lived this close to the reservation, I'd have an iron fence around my whole place." She made a face at Tessa. "I don't see how some people can stand it."

"I suppose all Indians aren't so horrible," Mrs. Tucker said. "Mr. Fox was most gracious when he stabled my horses." She spoke as if the observation surprised her.

"For an Indian, he's one of the *handsomest* men I've seen." Ammie Smith gave her a sly look. "Perhaps that's the real reason Tessa keeps him around."

Tessa flushed and looked down at her lap. She'd hoped to be spared such talk today, but obviously that was not to be. "Is it true you visited an Indian tribe?" Trudy asked.

Tessa raised her head to find all eyes on her. The women's expressions ranged from shock to avid interest. "Yes," she reluctantly admitted. "I went there on Reverend Deering's behalf." She cringed even as she told this half-truth. Never before had she been ashamed of her friendship with Sun Bear and his people.

"What does Reverend Deering want with the Indians?" Ammie Smith asked.

"He intends to build a chapel for the Indians and wanted to invite them to worship," Tessa answered.

"A chapel for the Indians?" Trudy sounded incredulous. "What an odd idea."

"He feels a call to minister to the Indians," Tessa explained, eager to draw attention away from herself and Micah.

"What a fine Christian gesture," Mrs. Drake said.

Trudy stirred sugar into her tea. "I don't know, Ada. I rather think the heathens are a hopeless lot."

"How did you come to know these Indians well enough to introduce them to Reverend Deering?"

Mrs. Tucker's question caught Tessa off guard. "Oh. Well, my husband traded with them."

"Your husband." Trudy smiled into her teacup. "Why, for a moment I'd almost forgotten—"

"Ladies, I believe it's time to talk of the library." Mrs. Drake came to Tessa's rescue. As president, she stood and called the meeting to order. The treasurer's report showed donations were coming in steadily, with a generous contribution from Major Finch's family, and another from the saloon owner, Mr. Hardy.

"I suppose our husbands have contributed so much to his wealth, he feels he owes us." Mrs. Tucker's remark was greeted by nervous laughter.

Tessa excused herself to brew more tea. "I'll help," Margery said, following her into the kitchen.

If Tessa harbored any lingering feelings of ill will toward Margery after a night of wrestling with her conscience, these vanished upon seeing her friend's woeful expression. Margery sank into a chair at the kitchen table, eyes downcast, shoulders slumped.

Tessa put the kettle on to boil. "Are you all right?" she asked. "You look as though you've been crying."

"It's just the blasted dust in the air." Margery dashed a tear from her eye even as she spoke. "Oh, Tessa, Alan won't speak to me!"

"He's just upset. He'll come around." Tessa sat opposite Margery and regarded her across the table.

She pulled a handkerchief from her handbag and dabbed her eyes. "He's practically put me under armed guard. He says I endangered the lives of everyone at the fort with my foolishness."

"You frightened him yesterday, running off like that."

"I've said I'm sorry. He refuses to believe me."

"Keep saying it. He'll forgive you soon." But Tessa wondered. Had Alan Finch hardened his heart, perhaps in an effort not to be hurt again?

Margery twisted the handkerchief in her hands and gave Tessa a sheepish look. "He says he told you about my affair with Micah Fox."

Tessa looked away, afraid to speak.

"It was a long time ago, I promise."

"When you came here that first day, you didn't care about seeing me, did you?" Tessa said. "You wanted to see him."

"I didn't know you then. And I thought it could be the same between us as it was before." She looked down at her hands, folded on the table. "But it couldn't. Not when he . . . well, not now that I'm married to Alan."

Something in her voice broke through the brittle shell Tessa had tried to erect around her feelings. An unexpected tenderness toward the woman in front of her seeped through. "You really do love him, don't you?"

Margery nodded. "I love Alan. I may not always show it, but I do. And I want him to love me."

Tessa leaned forward and took her friend's hands. "He does love you. I'm sure of it."

The pain around Margery's eyes did not ease. "But I want him to show it. Is that too much to ask?"

"I wish I knew what to tell you, but I don't."

"The old hermit told me I should talk to Alan, explain how I feel."

Tessa sat up straighter. "What old hermit?"

"I met him yesterday, just wandering out on the prairie. He helped us find our way back to the fort, then just disappeared." She shrugged. "I guess he was uncomfortable around the crowd."

"What did this . . . this hermit look like?"

"Oh, he was kind of a stocky fellow, barrel-chested, with long silver hair and pale skin. Didn't look like he'd spent much time in the sun."

Tessa sighed. Leave it to Will to become mixed up in this as well. "And he told you you should talk to Alan?"

She nodded. "He said Alan couldn't know how I was feeling unless I told him. But now he won't even listen to me." Her face crumpled, and she held her handkerchief to her eyes once more.

Tessa squeezed her hands, hoping to offer some comfort that words could not give.

"At least I have *you* to talk to. That helps." Margery

straightened and offered her a brave smile. "And knowing you don't hate me."

Tessa shook her head. "I could never hate you. I don't think anyone could."

"I'd better go wash my face before I go back to the other ladies. I must look a mess."

"You can go up to my room if you want. I'll just finish with the tea and be right out."

"Thanks." She slipped out of the room, and Tessa began arranging clean cups on a tray.

"Do you need any help with that, dear?" Tessa looked up as Ada Drake came through the doorway. The older woman looked around at the orderly kitchen and nodded approvingly. "You've done very well today," she said.

"Thank you." Tessa wondered what in particular she'd done to deserve this blessing. Was it the Darjeeling tea or the frosted tea cakes?

Mrs. Drake moved closer. "I've taken a liking to you," she said, "so I hope you won't mind a bit of unsolicited advice."

Tessa shook her head. What could she say, especially when Mrs. Drake spoke so kindly?

"Mind you, I'm telling you what I'd tell my own daughter." Mrs. Drake patted her hand. "You must get rid of that half-breed. He'll cause nothing but trouble for you."

The words stunned Tessa. "I . . . I can't just send Mr. Fox away," she stammered.

"Of course you can." Mrs. Drake nodded firmly. "If you need help, find an older man, or better yet, a married couple. Mexicans make decent servants if you can't find Negroes. As long as you have that half-breed living here, people will never stop talking about you."

With a sinking feeling in her stomach, Tessa stared at the older woman. Mrs. Drake was right. As long as she and Micah were living here together, no matter how innocent their actual relationship, those with an inclination to speak ill of her would never stop doing so. She could rail against the unfairness of it all she liked, but she couldn't change the way society operated. "Thank you for your concern," she managed to answer.

Mrs. Drake nodded again. "I'd hate to see a young woman like you ruined at such a young age. You've made your share of mistakes, but now you seem inclined to make up for them. I'd like to help you get started on the right path." She offered a kind smile. "Now let's have some tea, shall we?"

Tessa picked up the tray and followed Mrs. Drake out of the room. The older woman's words hammered in her head. *Get rid of Micah.* How could she? But, maybe she'd done her best to run him off already. She'd lied when she told him she didn't care. But lies were like bullets fired from a gun—you could never take them back once they'd been let loose.

Micah watered the horses belonging to the women from town and parked their buggies in the shade. He ignored those who ignored him and gave no more than a polite nod to those few who batted their eyes and attempted to flirt. He knew they saw him as no more than an oddity or an entertainment. He was not a part of their world and never would be.

After seeing to the last of the animals, he walked to the house to eat. He thought he would slip into the kitchen and out again before anyone knew he was there. Just as he mounted the first step to the back door, he heard voices. He started to turn away, but the mention of his own name stopped him. Moving lightly as a cat, he crept forward and listened.

"As long as you have that half-breed living here, people will never stop talking about you." He didn't recognize the woman's voice, though he wasn't likely to forget the self-righteous timbre of it.

Tessa mumbled something unintelligible, and the woman's reply was just as indistinct—something about Tessa's past? Micah leaned against the wall by the door and listened to footsteps leaving the room: an older woman's heavy tread and the lighter tapping of Tessa's heels on the polished floorboards.

An old anger flared in his chest as he stood there. How many times had he been in this position, forever on the outside, looking in, moving on the perimeter of people's lives? Yet he'd never stopped trying to force his way among them, foolishly thinking he could somehow earn their acceptance. He might as well try to change a law of nature as to alter the rules of society.

He straightened, staring at the back door but not really seeing it. The old woman was right about one thing. He and Tessa didn't belong together. Not in any way that was lasting and real. It was time they accepted that and got on with their lives.

He'd promised not to leave her—not yet. But they couldn't go on like this, both wanting each other, mistaking the desire for physical passion for something more enduring.

Things had been so much easier with Margery. There'd never been any pretense between them, and little damage when their time together came to an end. That was the way it should be between two people from different worlds—two people like him and Tessa.

He turned away from the house, a new resolve quickening his step. He knew how to handle things now. He'd arrange it so he and Tessa both got what they wanted: a temporary relationship, to meet a physical need. And when the time came for him to go, they'd both be satisfied. Or at least a certain restlessness would be calmed within them. As for the deeper longing that nagged at the marrow, they'd have to look elsewhere for that, among their own kind, however that might be defined.

Chapter Twelve

Tessa had made up her mind to speak to Micah about Margery. She'd been wrong to avoid the subject; the best thing to do was to clear the air. She had no right to hold his past against him any more than she could lay claim to any part of his future. Still, she spent some time in her room, fussing over her appearance and working up the courage to confront him again. Hair neatly combed and a fresh apron around her waist, she went downstairs to the kitchen to find Micah already waiting for her, a bouquet of wildflowers in his hand.

"I thought you might like these," he said, offering the flowers.

She stared at the bunch of yellow sunflowers and purple gayfeather, and every word of the carefully prepared speech she'd intended to make vanished from her mind. The bright blossoms splayed against his brown fingers, their delicate stems cradled in his palm. He had held her with the same gentleness and strength once. The craving to feel his touch filled her now. A weak "thank you" was all she could manage, before turning to rummage in an overhead cabinet for a vase.

"Let me get that for you." He came up behind her

and reached up to pluck the vase off the high shelf. She froze as his body brushed against her, awareness sharpening every nerve ending.

He moved away slowly, leaving a lingering warmth. She drew a deep, steadying breath, and the scent of him filled her head, an intoxicating mix of soap and leather and clean male skin.

"There. Is that all right?"

She turned and was aware of the filled vase on the sideboard but more aware of him, standing beside his gift. He fixed his gaze on her, eyes languid and intense. She hugged her arms over her chest in a feeble defense against that searching gaze. Her skin burned, as if he could somehow see through her clothing, all the way to her bare skin, or further still to her heart.

"I'm hungry," he said, and the innocent words sent a bolt of heat through her.

"S-supper's ready." She jolted out of her stupor and hastily took her place at the table. For a moment all was quiet, as they set about filling their plates. Tessa began to relax. How odd that she should feel so uneasy. It was only Micah here with her, no different than he'd ever been.

"How did the meeting go?" he asked as he helped himself to fresh field peas.

"The meeting? Oh, it went fine." She focused on cutting into her fried ham, surprised to find her hands shaking. What had come over her? Was it just a release of nerves, now that she'd made it through the trial of hosting all those town women here? "We've collected quite a bit of money so far. Mr. Hardy even made a donation."

"There was a tall young woman in a green dress. Who was she?"

Tessa thought a minute. "That was Ammie Smith." She glanced across the table at him. "Why do you want to know?"

His lips barely curved into the hint of a smile. "She was flirting with me when I brought her horse around."

Tessa clutched the knife and fork until her fingers hurt and went back to cutting her meat. The words that came out of her mouth sounded strained. ''Yes. She mentioned she thought you were handsome.''

He shook his head. ''I've never cared much for such black hair on a woman, really. I prefer brown hair.''

She had thought he would say redheads. The surprise must have shown on her face. She jerked her head up and found herself trapped by his gaze, pinned to her chair like a stunned bird. ''I like hair your color,'' he said. ''Rich brown, like turned earth, or coffee with cream. And brown eyes flecked with gold.''

His voice was low, hypnotic. She had never heard him speak like this. She wished he would stop. The change was too frightening . . . too fascinating.

''I think your meat is cut enough.''

She looked at her plate and saw that she'd reduced her ham to hash. Dropping her knife, she scooped up a forkful, scarcely tasting as she chewed.

''It's a warm afternoon, isn't it?'' He unbuttoned the cuffs of his shirt and rolled up the sleeves to reveal muscular forearms. She had never noticed what slender fingers he had. Strong, yet agile. She forced her eyes away from him, but she could not force away the longing for his touch.

''Aren't you hungry?'' he asked. ''You aren't eating much.''

With trembling hands, she buttered a biscuit and took a bite.

''Wait a minute.'' He leaned toward her and put out a hand. ''You have a crumb. Right . . . there.'' He touched the corner of her mouth with one finger. She jerked at his touch, as if she'd been burned, and a gasp escaped her.

And then his finger was in her mouth, feeding her the crumb, the rough skin grazing her lips. The gasp gave way to a sigh, and she closed her lips around him, caressing him with her tongue, tasting his salty skin.

She watched his eyes darken with desire and felt a

surge of pleasure race through her. He breathed in rough pants, or was that herself she heard?

He jerked his hand away from her, the movement pulling her toward him. She closed her eyes, silently begging him to touch her, to kiss her. Every inch of her burned for his touch; her breasts felt heavy and aching, her body feverish with desire.

The scrape of the chair against the table made her open her eyes. He stood, still breathing hard, and stared down at her. "I'd better go see to the horses," he said and walked stiffly out of the room.

She reached out for him, but he did not turn and see. As the door closed behind him, she sagged against the table, bereft and confused, halfway between screaming and crying, knowing neither would ease the ache within her.

Micah plunged his hands into the water trough and splashed his face. But he doubted if mere water could cool the fire within him. He leaned against the side of the barn, heedless of the water dripping down to soak his shirt. He hadn't meant for things to get so out of hand back there. He'd only meant to tease her with words and looks, to whet her appetite with a taste of what would come later.

She'd responded so readily to his every move. Her wide-eyed nervousness had tempted him to further his seduction. The pleasure of watching her desire awaken had eased his own frustration at waiting for her.

And then, the minute her lips had closed around his finger, he'd been lost. He'd have taken her on the table, heedless of dishes or daylight. But the knowledge of all the warnings she must have heard about living with a savage had stayed him.

So he'd retreated to think and plan some more. He intended to treat her like the lady she was, to love her as tenderly as any storybook hero.

He turned and looked toward the house. Tonight,

when the veil of night would render them both less vulnerable, he would go to her.

Will was inclined to push Fox *into* the water trough. Not that he really thought that would do much to cool the young man's ardor. It had been some twenty years since he'd been Fox's age, but he hadn't forgotten the hold lust could have on a young man.

But Fox needed to ease that particular ache with someone other than Will's wife.

All right, so she wasn't exactly his wife anymore. But she didn't need to be fooling around with some half-breed vagrant. Not when he was setting her up to marry a minister. Deering wasn't the brightest man he'd ever met, but even he would object to his fiancée sleeping with another man.

Fox left the barn and headed for the woodpile. He'd just picked up the ax when Will sauntered around the corner of the house. "I always found chopping wood to be a good way to work off a little nervous energy," Will said approvingly.

Fox gave him a curious look. "I'll be happy to lend you the ax anytime," he said.

"Oh, no. I'm past all that." Will settled himself on a stack of wood. "And I daresay a little good old-fashioned *constructive* work would do you good."

Fox balanced a log on the chopping block. "Is there something in particular you wanted to talk about? If not, I've got work to do." He raised the ax over his head and brought it down, neatly cleaving the log in two.

"I've seen the way you've been looking at Tessa," Will said. "It don't take a mindreader to know what you've been thinking. I'm here to tell you to put a stop to it right this minute."

Fox froze, ax in midair. "I don't know what you're talking about."

"Don't you?" Will broke off a long splinter of wood and began cleaning his nails. "So you're telling me you don't have any interest in bedding her? All your feelings are innocent as a baby's?''

The murderous look on Fox's face made Will glad he was already dead, and thus immune to the implied threat. "What goes on between me and Tessa is none of your business," Fox said.

Will crossed his arms over his chest. "I believe it is. I promised Tessa I'd look after her, and I'm a man who keeps his promises. I can't let her go ruining her life with you."

Fox lowered the ax and looked toward the house. The rattle of pots and pans told them Tessa was doing the dishes. "Answer me one question—did Tessa ask you to talk to me?"

Will shook his head. "She doesn't know anything about this. And she doesn't need to know."

"Then I think you'd better mind your own business." He picked up one of the split halves and brought the ax down again forcefully, sending wood chips flying.

Will stood and squared his shoulders. "Give it up, Fox. You can't do anything for Tessa but ruin her reputation and spoil her chances of finding a decent husband."

"I can make her happy. From what I've seen, she's had little enough of that lately."

Will considered this, then nodded. "You'll make her happy for a little while, and then you'll leave her brokenhearted."

Fox stiffened. "It won't be like that between us. She knows we aren't meant to stay together, but we can enjoy each other for a little while. No strings attached."

Will shook his head. A man could think like that easy enough, but how could a woman? Will had learned a few things in his lifetime, and one of them was that women weren't made of the same stuff as men. When they felt something, they felt it deeper. Their hearts lacked the callousness that allowed men to keep things on a merely physical level. "You're not listening to a word I say," he complained.

Fox nodded and brought the ax down on another chunk of wood. "You're right. And I don't intend to."

Will left then, disappearing on the downstroke of the ax, while Fox was intent on hitting his target. Invisible once more, he looked toward the house again. A single light shone in an upstairs window. Tessa would be getting ready for bed about now. She was a sensible woman. She'd listen to reason.

Most of all, she'd listen to *him*. She always had. A man couldn't have asked for a better wife. She'd trusted him to take care of her, and she went right on trusting him now. He'd have a little talk with her, and she'd see it was time to send Micah Fox packing.

He found her seated on the end of the bed, wearing a long cotton nightgown. Her hair was undone, falling in waves to her waist, like dark water overflowing onto new-fallen snow. As he watched, she picked up a silver-backed brush and began to brush the long locks. *"I always like to watch you comb out your hair,"* he said softly.

She jerked and looked around, one hand pressed to her heart. "Will, you startled me."

"I didn't think I had to knock to come into my own bedroom." He settled onto the bed, the pillows denting with his impression.

She looked away and resumed brushing her hair. "It's my bedroom now, Will. And . . . well, sometimes I need my privacy." She stood and carried the brush to the dresser. "I don't like the thought of you dropping in without warning."

"That doesn't sound like the Tessa I know. What's gotten into you?"

She faced him again, arms folded under her breasts. "Maybe I've changed. Grown up."

"You haven't changed. You're still the same sweet Tessa I married."

"I'm not the same," she insisted softly.

He ignored the remark and put his hands behind his head, getting comfortable. *"I'm glad you're working with Deering on his mission project,"* he said. *"It's a crazy idea, but it will help you get to know each other better. Before long, he'll see what a good wife you'll make him."*

"I don't want to marry Reverend Deering." She sat on the end of the bed.

"Not want to marry Deering? Don't be silly. He's perfect for you."

She looked toward him, or rather at the dented pillows, which would be all she was able to see of him. "I don't love him, Will."

He let out an exasperated breath. *"You'll learn to love him. Plenty of marriages start without love. It'll come with time."*

She shaped her mouth into the stubborn pout he was coming to know too well. "I don't want to settle for that. I married for love the first time, I won't do less the second."

Her mention of her love for him touched him. He was beginning to think she'd forgotten. He leaned forward and reached out his hand. *"Oh, Tessa—"*

She flinched, and he shrank back, cursing the coldness that never left him, the feelings he could no longer feel. One by one, the physical senses were leaving him. But the deeper sensations, like this pain when he saw her saddened, lingered, sharper than ever in the absence of a body to dull them.

"I know what Fox has done to you," he said. *"He's seduced you and made you think about things you never would have before."*

"It's not Micah, it's me. I *want* to feel these things."

"Don't do something you'll regret later. Don't ruin your reputation with a man like him."

"Reputation won't warm this bed at night." She drove her fist into the mattress. "Reputation won't hold me and make me feel alive again."

"Tessa, listen to me—"

"No!" She was crying now, tears streaming down her face. "I can't listen to you. I have to think of myself for a change. I'm not a girl anymore, Will. I'm a woman and I'm tired of being alone all the time.''

"You're not alone. You've got me to look after you."

"You're *dead*, Will. You can't look after me.'' She shook her head. "I'm sorry, but that's the truth. I have to take care of myself.''

"You're making a mistake."

She bowed her head. "Then it's my mistake to make.''

He stared at her for a long while, too stunned to think. He felt numb, light. Like dying all over again.

Micah finished chopping wood and put away the ax. The old hermit's words still burned in his brain. Was he doing the wrong thing? Was he really hurting Tessa?

In his room at the barn, he stripped and washed. He scrubbed hard, until his skin burned from the harsh lye soap. But even that did not dull his desire for Tessa. He dressed in a loose white shirt and jeans and combed out his hair. He started to retie it but decided to leave it loose. After he'd come to live with his aunt and uncle, he'd cut his hair short, in an effort to fit in with everyone around him. But when he'd hired on with the Army, they'd assigned him to work with the trackers. He'd let his hair grow long again, like the Tonkawas, Utes, and Apaches he worked with. He'd never felt the urge to cut it again. His short hair had always felt like a disguise; a disguise that fooled no one.

The moon was up by the time he emerged from the barn, a waning quarter like a Spanish silver piece suspended between the trees. Barefoot, he walked across the yard, the ground cool beneath his feet. He paused near the back porch and gazed up at the single light on the second floor. Tessa's bedroom.

He wondered if he should knock on the back door. After a moment's hesitation, he opened it and went in without announcing his presence. The moonlight shone through the windows onto a room set in order. Dishes waited on the sideboard, ready for breakfast. The fire was banked in the stove, the table freshly scrubbed and smelling of soap and lemon.

He walked into the hallway and started up the stairs, moving slowly, soundlessly. The dim glow from beneath the door to Tessa's room guided him like a beacon. Heart pounding, he stopped outside the door and tried to calm his ragged breathing. He sounded as winded as if he'd run a mile. Now was the time to turn back. To take up his saddle and walk down the road the way he had come. Those were his choices: either go to her now or leave forever.

He put his hand up and knocked, the hard sound echoing in the stillness. No answer came. He tried again. Still only silence. He put his ear to the door and listened. Was she so sound asleep she didn't hear him?

And then he heard it. A low, muffled sobbing, coming from below, someone grieving as if her heart was broken.

He turned and descended the stairs, following the sound to the front porch. She was curled up in the porch swing, weeping almost soundlessly. The sobs shook her, each one tearing at him.

"Tessa, what's wrong?" He stood over her, his hand hovering at her back. He was afraid to touch her, fearful she might shatter beneath his fingers.

She looked up and stared at him through her tears. Her face was red, her eyes puffy from crying, yet to him she was beautiful.

"Hold me," she whispered. "Please hold me."

He sat and gathered her into his arms, as gently as he might have held a child or a newborn colt. He stroked her back, over and over in a soothing rhythm. Her sobs slowed, and the shaking subsided.

"What's wrong?" he asked again.

She shook her head, still unable to speak.

"Is it . . . were you thinking about your husband?" Shame followed close on the heels of the jealousy that pricked him. How could he be jealous of a dead man?

His emotions were as unruly as a wild horse where Tessa was concerned.

"No." She wiped her eyes with the full sleeve of her gown. "Yes." She looked up at him through lashes sparkling with tears. "It doesn't matter. You're here now." Then she startled him by kissing his neck, burying her face in his hair. He savored the feel of her soft lips caressing his skin.

He pulled her face up to his, and his lips found hers. He kissed her gently at first, then with greater urgency as his need for her reawakened.

Her hands twined in his hair, then stroked down his back, drawing him nearer. He coaxed open her mouth and kissed her with his tongue, tasting the remnants of her tears, salty and sweet. She answered the invitation with gentle forays of her own, tasting, teasing, seeking.

They kissed for long minutes, and then suddenly kissing was not enough. A sigh escaped her as his hand slid to her breast. She pressed against his palm, coaxing him to knead the firm softness of it through the thin fabric of her gown, to stroke the sensitive tip until she gasped with pleasure.

Wanting to please her more, he bent and undid the row of round pearl buttons up the front of her gown. She gasped as the cool air rushed over her skin, then sighed as he gathered the tip of her breast into his mouth. With little coaxing, she straddled his thigh and arched against him as he lavished attention on each luscious breast in turn.

Just when the need within him became painful, she drew away and smiled at him, her eyes bright with passion. "Take your shirt off," she ordered, tugging at the fabric.

He removed the shirt and unbuttoned his trousers as well, taking her hand and wrapping it around the length of his desire, gasping at the sharp jolt of pleasure this brought him. He wouldn't wait much longer to take her, to satisfy the longing they'd both endured too long.

He bent to kiss her, then caressed the tip of her ear

with his tongue. "We should go in the house," he murmured.

She nodded and began to unwrap herself from around him. Then she stiffened in his arms, and her eyes widened with fear. "Look out!" she screamed, just as a flowerpot came hurtling through the air toward his head.

He ducked, shielding her with his body, and the pot sailed over them, exploding against the wall in a rain of dirt and pottery fragments. Raising up, he set Tessa gently away from him and stood, scanning the area for whoever had thrown the pot. But the yard and the porch were empty. He stared at the scattered flowers and dirt, trying to make sense of things. "How did that happen?" he asked.

The only answer was a slamming door. He heard Tessa's feet as she raced up the stairs, and the sound of her door opening and closing, then the hollow echo of the bolt being driven home.

Micah didn't have to ponder the question long to know who had thrown the pot of flowers. Only one person had suspected his intentions regarding Tessa, and tried to stop him. "Old man!"

The word echoed in the still air. Micah rose and stared out over the yard. "Hey, you can't hide from me forever!" he shouted. "Come out and face me like a man."

"No need to shout. I'm right behind you."

Micah whirled and saw the old man seated in the swing, arms crossed over his barrel chest. He glared at him. "You threw that flowerpot, didn't you?"

Will shrugged, poker-faced. "If you insist."

"What did you think you were doing? You could have hurt Tessa."

The old man frowned. "I wouldn't have hurt Tessa. *You* were the one I was after."

"Why? Did you really think a bump on the head would keep me away from her?"

"It might make you think twice."

"Old man, I've had enough of your interfering." He stepped forward, intending to jerk Will up by the collar.

Suddenly the swing was empty.

"You're too slow," said a voice behind him.

Micah blinked and turned. Will grinned. "In any case, I stopped things cold tonight."

"Leave Tessa alone!" Micah growled. "And if you know what's good for you, you'll leave me alone, too."

Will's smile changed to a sneer. "Do you really think you worry me?"

"Don't push me—"

The old man took a step forward, until he was practically nose to nose with Micah. "I'm pushing."

All the frustrated passion and pent-up anger at past hurts went into the punch Micah threw. It was a punch that should have sent the old man sprawling. Instead, Micah felt a rush of cold air and then—nothing.

Will stood in front of him, steady on his feet. "You missed," he observed.

"Put up your fists and fight," Micah ordered.

Will shrugged. "Like this?" He struck a boxer's pose.

Micah nodded and drew his fist back once more. He aimed for the old man's jaw, hoping to fell him quickly and avoid hurting him too badly. He'd been in his share of brawls and knew just the force to put behind the blow. Aim true, he leaned forward and connected solidly with—nothing.

He stared at his hand, sunk to the wrist into Will's face. Yet he felt nothing but an icy cold. He blinked, wondering what he had eaten, or drunk, to produce such hallucinations.

"Care to try again?" Will asked.

Micah slowly pulled back his hand, watching it emerge whole from the left side of Will's jaw. "Who . . . who are you?" he choked.

"Ask Tessa."

Then he was gone. Nothing but empty space where he had been, and a lingering chill in the air.

Chapter Thirteen

Tessa paced her bedroom floor, back and forth across the scrubbed floorboards until her legs ached. Every nerve felt rubbed raw. She jumped at the slightest sound and shivered at the merest breath of wind at her window.

A hundred times she started to go to Micah. A hundred times she stopped before she reached her bedroom door. Oh, God, how long had Will been watching them? How much had he seen?

She stuffed the edge of her shawl into her mouth to keep from crying out. The thought that her husband . . . or at least his ghost . . . had watched her make love to another man filled her with shame.

Yet was it so wrong for her to want to be with a man she felt this attraction for . . . a man she had even come to love? She jerked the shawl out of her mouth and hugged her arms under her breasts, shaken by the admission. She'd never meant for this to happen, never *wanted* to love again. But she might as well have tried to run from a tornado. "We can't go on like this, Will!" she cried. "I can't have a normal marriage with a ghost, and you won't let me love anyone else."

She listened, half hoping for his answer, but if he was with her now, he was stubbornly silent.

Exhausted, she sank onto the edge of the bed. What was she going to do? What if Will tried to hurt Micah?

Now, strong on the heels of her shame, came a wild terror. Would Will go so far as to try to kill Micah, in the mistaken belief that he was saving her?

She had to talk to him, to convince him not to make that mistake. But how did you argue with a ghost? Especially a ghost who was so sure he knew what was right?

A knock on the door startled her. "Tessa, are you all right?" The concern she heard in Micah's voice brought fresh tears to her eyes. She stared at the door, unanswering, words knotting in her throat.

"Open the door," he said. "Please."

She wanted to see him, but fear paralyzed her. What if Will was still watching? If he saw them together again, would he do more than throw a pot of flowers this time? "I don't think you should come in," she said, her voice trembling.

"I just want to talk." He sounded tired, as tired as she felt. "We need to talk."

The truth of his words won out over fear. If they didn't discuss this now, it would loom even larger before them tomorrow, and the next day, and the next. "All right." She started to unlock the door, then thought better of it. "I'll meet you downstairs."

"All right."

She waited until she heard his footsteps retreat, then she dressed. As if a few extra layers of clothing could change what she and Micah felt for each other. But maybe the clothes would be a signal for Will, a way to let him know that this was an innocent visit, nothing more.

Micah had put on the kettle and was measuring tea into two cups when she walked into the kitchen. He glanced at her buttoned-up dress and pinned-up hair but made no comment. He looked the same as when she'd left him, shirt unbuttoned, hair tangled where she'd twined her fingers in it. A streak of dirt across his forehead reminded her again of the danger he was in. "Are you hurt?" she lifted her hand as if to brush away the dirt, but stopped short of touching him.

He felt his forehead, then wiped away the dirt himself. "No. I ducked in time."

The kettle began to steam. She moved past him and added water to the cups, then carried them to the table. He held out a chair for her, then took his usual place across from her. Everyday actions, charged with meaning by what had taken place between them only a little while before. "We need to talk," he said again. "About the hermit."

She stirred sugar into her tea, avoiding his gaze. "What about him?"

"He was the one who threw the flowerpot at me, wasn't he?"

"What makes you think that?"

"He came to me this afternoon and told me to keep away from you."

She wrapped her hands around her cup, hiding the trembling in her fingers. "Yes. I think he threw the flowerpot. He's . . . very protective."

Micah leaned over the table and grabbed her hands. "Tessa, who *is* he? *What* is he?"

His face was pale, his eyes wide, as if he'd seen . . . a ghost. "Wh-what do you mean?" she stammered. "He . . . he's just a friend. An old hermit. Maybe he's a little crazy."

Micah fell back into his chair. "Maybe *I'm* the one who's crazy."

"What happened? Did you see the old hermit just now? Did he say something to you?"

He let out a groan. "I challenged him to a fight."

"Micah! He's an old man."

"He's an old man who interfered one too many times." He shook his head. "Maybe I shouldn't have done that, but I was so furious I couldn't think straight.

I wanted to teach him a lesson. To make him leave us alone.''

She took a deep breath. ''What happened?''

He stared out across the kitchen. ''He just stood there and let me hit him.'' His voice dropped to a whisper. ''I swear, my fist went right through him.''

She tried to take a drink of tea, but her hands shook so badly it sloshed out of the cup, down the front of her dress.

Micah turned to her. ''Tell me I'm not losing my mind.''

She set the cup down and pushed it away. ''You're not losing your mind.''

He rubbed his hand across his face and slumped forward, elbows resting on his knees. ''Tell me.''

Where should she begin? It was all so unreal, and she had had trouble believing it herself at first. She would go back to the beginning. ''The hermit was my husband.''

''Your husband.'' He sounded numb. ''I thought . . .'' He stared at her. ''You told me you were a widow.''

''I am.''

''But . . . how . . . ?''

''The man you saw . . . he . . . he's a ghost.''

''A ghost?''

She spread her hands flat on the table in front of her. ''I don't know why or how it happened, but a few days after Will died I had what I thought was a very vivid dream. He came to me and told me he didn't intend to leave me alone, that he would look after me.''

Her eyes filled with tears at the memory. She'd been so grateful then, so glad to know that a part of him would be with her forever. But now . . . it seemed wrong that he should be suspended in time like that, not truly dead and yet not truly alive.

''But it wasn't a dream?''

She shook her head. ''He came to me again a few months later, while I was wide awake. I was afraid at first that I was losing my mind. But gradually he convinced me he was real—or as real as a ghost could be. I know it sounds strange, but after a while I just . . . accepted it.''

''I've never believed in things like ghosts.''

''Neither have I, until Will. Haven't you noticed how cold he always is when you're near him?''

He rubbed his wrist. ''Like ice.'' His eyes widened. ''The first day I met him, when I thought the barn was cold—?''

She nodded. ''You should be flattered. He seldom appears to anyone. Even me. He says it takes too much effort.''

He looked thoughtful. ''So he was much older than you?''

''Almost twenty years older.''

''And you were how old?''

Young. So very young. ''Eighteen. Seventeen when we met.'' She smiled, remembering. ''He was the blacksmith in our town. He bought my box at a school box supper, and we were together ever since.'' He'd been so strong and handsome. And a little exotic. A little dangerous. She'd been dazzled by him.

Micah studied her over the rim of his cup, as if he were trying to picture her as that fresh-faced girl. ''What did your family think?'' he asked.

Her smile faded. ''They were furious.'' Those were the memories she shied away from—her mother's tears and pleading, her father's angry words. ''They told me if I married him, I should forget that I was their daughter.''

Micah winced. ''But you married him anyway? In spite of that?''

She shrugged. ''I loved him.'' At eighteen, her choice had been that pure and simple, untarnished by logic or experience. ''I was so young. I didn't know what it would mean to isolate myself from everyone that way.''

Micah bowed his head, his gaze focused on his teacup, as if he could divine the future there. Or maybe he was just struggling to understand the past that had brought them to this point.

"That's why he's so protective," she said softly. "He married a girl and now he doesn't know how to deal with the woman I've become. He's not used to letting me make my own decisions."

Micah didn't say anything for a long time, and she had no words left. She wondered if he would leave her now. Would he rise from that chair and walk away from a woman crazy enough to attract the protection of a ghost?

"So what are we going to do now?" He raised his head and looked her in the eye. The determination she saw there made her weak with relief.

"I don't know. I've tried to talk to him, but he won't listen." She paused, then added, "He really means well."

Micah's expression hardened. "Not for me, he doesn't."

"Only because he's trying to protect me."

He looked at her intently. "Do *you* think I mean you harm?"

The question stunned her. "I know you don't."

"And yet I could harm you."

She leaned forward and touched his shoulder. "No! Don't say that."

"It's true." He looked away. "Old Will was right. You're starting to make friends in town, to be a part of the community. I could ruin it all."

She wanted to protest that none of that mattered. But the lie died bitter on her tongue. Micah had never promised her more than a few nights' pleasure. How could she trade that for a return to the isolation she'd grown to dread? He had never claimed to love her, only to want her. The difference between those words weighed heavy in her mind.

She started to pull away from him, but he reached out and covered her hand with his own. They sat like that for a long moment, their bodies touching, their thoughts traveling the same path. Desire still hummed between them, tempered by a blanket of regret. Cold logic had moved in where blind passion had once held sway. Never again could they act on their feelings without weighing the consequences.

Micah was the first to break the silence between them. He stood, releasing her hand, pushing it gently away. "We'd both better get some sleep," he said softly.

Without so much as a glance back at her, he left the house. The door clicked shut behind him, a heavy, final sound that sent a shiver up her spine.

Micah lay on his bunk, nerves too stretched to sleep. He stared at the underside of the barn roof and absently rubbed his wrist, which still ached from the burning cold of Will Bright's touch. He squeezed his eyes shut and opened them again, half hoping that this time he would wake up with the knowledge that this was all a horrible nightmare, like the sweetgrass dreams of the Indian shaman.

But, no, it was all horribly real: Tessa and Micah and the ghost of her husband, who had not been content to die and go on to his reward but insisted on staying on to take care of a wife who no longer needed looking after.

He sat up and swung his legs over the side of the bunk. Tessa didn't need Will; she didn't need him either. He saw everything so clearly now, as if the minute his hand sank into Will's face, a veil had dropped from his eyes. He'd been foolish to believe he could do anything but bring trouble to this place. The sooner he left, the better off Tessa would be. Her arm was almost healed. In the meantime, she could hire someone else to work for her. Someone more respectable. Someone with a wife, perhaps, who wouldn't fall in love with her.

He couldn't bring himself to say those words out loud. Just the thought of them stung like a whip. He'd heard it preached that the truth was an avenging sword. In this case he felt its blade pierce him to the heart. He'd fallen in love with Tessa, a woman who could never love him in return. How could she, when loving him meant losing everything else—her friends, her place in the community she'd fought so hard to reclaim?

He'd heard the regret in her voice when she spoke of being rejected by her family, as if now, older and wiser, she might have made a different choice.

Quickly, before emotion could change his mind, he stood and began gathering his belongings. A new shirt, a winter coat, a wooden chain he was carving. Spreading his saddle blanket out on the bed, he tossed these into it. He picked up the bison-horn cup Sun Bear had given him. The smooth horn fit perfectly in his hand. He remembered the night they'd spent with the Indians—was it really less than a week ago?

Sun Bear had invited him to stay, to come and live as an Indian again. Could he find a place there? Could he go back to a life he hadn't known since childhood?

He put the cup in the blanket and began rolling it into a bundle. He didn't yet know what he would do, where he would go. He only knew he couldn't stay here, loving a woman who could never love him in return.

At first light he was ready to go, his saddle at his feet, blanket strapped across his back. He could have taken a horse. He had enough pay saved up to buy one. But he thought it best to leave the way he had come, on foot, taking nothing to tie him to this place.

He paused at the end of the drive to look at the ornamented gate one last time. How could the man who had attacked him with the flowerpot last night be the same person who made this work of art? The Will Bright he knew as a grumpy old hermit was also a gifted artist, who loved his wife enough to scorn death and return to her.

How could Micah Fox, half-breed wanderer, stand a chance against a man like that? As he pulled the gate shut behind him, his hand brushed the welded antlers of the deer. He recognized the scene now—it was the first man and the first woman in the Garden. Only Will had depicted Eden as right here, on the Texas plains. Now that he knew Tessa, Micah couldn't argue with that vision of paradise.

The steady cadence of a horse approaching at a fast clip made him turn around. As the rider neared, he recognized Reverend Deering. "Good morning, Mr. Fox," Deering said, reining the bay in beside him. "You're up and about early."

"I could say the same for you, Reverend."

"I confess I couldn't sleep. I'm anxious to get started."

"Started?"

The preacher rested his hands on the saddle horn and grinned. "On the mission. I've managed to raise funds to buy lumber. I thought today we could select a building site."

Micah nodded. "I'm sure Tessa will be glad to help you."

"Yes, but you're the man I wanted to talk to this morning." He glanced at the saddle on the ground, as if seeing it for the first time. "Am I interrupting you? Are you going somewhere?"

"Just into town," Micah lied. "What did you want to see me about?"

"I need someone who can help oversee construction. Someone to keep an eye on things when I'm away."

Micah avoided the preacher's sincere gaze. "Why don't you ask Tessa?"

"Oh, I intend to. But I'm sure she'll be able to spare you for a few hours every day. Besides, I need a translator for services."

"Tessa can do that for you, too."

"Tessa doesn't know Comanche. You do."

Micah shook his head. "I'm sorry, but I won't be able to help you."

Deering leaned forward, scrutinizing him. "Why not? Of course I intend to pay you."

"It's not that." He fixed his gaze on the saddle at his feet. "I won't be around here much longer."

Deering looked alarmed. "Has something happened? Has Mrs. Bright fired you?"

"No. It's just time to move on."

Deering looked at the saddle again. "You're leaving today, is that it?"

Micah said nothing.

Deering dismounted and came to stand in front of him. Worry lines creased the preacher's brow. Up close, he looked older, more careworn. *Less like an avenging angel and more like a shepherd,* Micah thought.

"I think you're making a serious mistake," Deering said.

"I don't see that it's really any of your concern, preacher."

"Mrs. Bright has come to depend on you. Her arm is still in a cast, isn't it?"

"Yes." Guilt pinched at him. "She's managing fine with it. It comes off in a week or so."

The preacher's voice was gentle, coaxing. "Where are you going in such a hurry that it can't wait a few more days? Especially when you're needed here?"

Would it hurt so much to wait until he'd fulfilled his promise to Tessa? Wasn't he man enough to stay here a few more days? Reluctantly he nodded. "All right."

Deering smiled. "Ride with me over to the creek. I'm thinking that's where I should build my chapel."

Micah opened the gate and waited for Deering to mount up, then shouldered the saddle and followed the preacher down the drive. The thought came to him that a more religious man might have believed God had sent the preacher to stop him from leaving. As it was, Micah still wasn't sure why he'd let Deering persuade him to stay. Perhaps it was only that he'd had little enough experience in his life with being needed. He couldn't afford to pass up the opportunity to savor the feeling a while longer.

Deering led the way past the house, back to the barn. "We won't bother disturbing Mrs. Bright this early," he said. "Soon as you saddle up, we'll ride out and have a look. We can tell her about it later."

Micah unfurled his saddle blanket and dumped its contents on his bunk, then went out to the corral to catch up the roan mare. He was just as glad not to see Tessa. He wouldn't know how to explain what he'd been doing at the end of her drive with his saddle, or how or why Reverend Deering had changed his mind.

Tessa woke to bright sunshine and ringing silence, a silence that was out of place at this late hour. Micah must have overslept too. After the night they'd had, it was no wonder they were exhausted. She still felt drained, and the question of what they would do about Will, and about their relationship to each other, weighed heavy.

She dressed and pinned up her hair, then went downstairs to start coffee and biscuits. As she worked, she listened for the sounds of Micah awakening—the creak of the barn door opening, the splash of the pump as he washed his face, his steps on the back porch. But only birdsong and the occasional restless whinny of a horse disturbed the morning stillness.

When she could stand the emptiness no longer, she poured a cup of coffee and carried it to the barn. Her hands shook as she worked the latch on the door, and she hesitated outside the tackroom. This was his bedroom, and the very act of coming here seemed to suggest so much. Would he think she had come here to finish what they had begun last night? If he pulled her to him, there on his bed, would she be able to deny herself again, even in broad daylight?

Taking a deep breath, she knocked on the door and waited for him. No answer came, no sound of movement on the other side. "Micah?" she called, and knocked again, but only the shuffling of a horse in the box behind her disturbed the stillness.

Heart thudding in her chest, she grasped the latch and tugged it, pulling the door toward her.

A single window, high in the wall, cast a pale light upon the solitary bunk and a tumble of blankets and belongings. She stepped inside and remembered the last time she had been here, the night of the major's party, when she feared Micah had left her.

She frowned at the heap of belongings on the bed. Of course, he hadn't left her yet. He had promised he would stay until her cast came off. She rubbed the graying plaster and frowned. Only another week, the doctor said. Too little time.

She plucked the horn drinking cup from among the folds of blanket, souvenir of their visit to Sun Bear's camp. Micah had said he could never live with the Indians again, but did he really mean that?

A sudden chill swept up her spine and the door slammed behind her. She whirled around, anger rising. "Will!" she shouted. "Answer me. I know you're here."

Suddenly, he was before her, a faint image hovering against the door, growing more solid as she stared. *"Looking for your lover?"* he asked.

"If you've done something with Micah, so help me, I'll—"

He scowled. *"I don't know where he is. I don't care."*

"Promise me you'll leave him alone," she said. "That you'll leave *us* alone."

"Nothing is settled yet." Will moved closer, enveloping her in a chill. *"You still need a husband. A man to run the ranch. Fox isn't that man."*

She bowed her head. "I know."

He pulled a blanket from the bed and swept it around her shoulders. *"You're shivering."* His voice softened. *"I lost my temper last night. Something I didn't think I had anymore. I'm sorry."*

His tenderness touched her. She pulled the blanket closer about her and looked up at him. "I know you mean well, but it's just—"

"You want to make your own decisions. I know." He sighed. *"Until things are settled with you, I can't rest*

easy. But I will promise to honor your privacy. With Fox, or Deering, or whoever you choose. Whatever . . . physical that might happen between you, I promise not to interfere.''

''Or to watch.''

He faded, then grew brighter again, so that she could clearly see the offended expression on his face. *''Of course not.''*

''That's all I want.'' She smiled and stood to kiss his cheek, but before her lips could touch his icy flesh, he'd vanished.

The two men rode eastward, toward the narrow ribbon of water that divided Tessa's ranch from the Clear Fork reservation. This time of year the creek was little more than a trickle, reduced to an expanse of damp sand in places. Deering rode up a small rise and faced the reservation. ''I like this spot. We'll erect a small white building with a large wooden cross. They'll be able to see it for a long way off as they approach.''

Micah thought of the Indian camp, with its cluster of tepees in the bend of the river. ''Sun Bear and his people would probably feel more at home in a simple brush arbor,'' he said.

Deering shook his head. ''No, I want a building. Something permanent. A sign of our faith.''

Micah wondered if anyone but Deering had faith in this scheme, but he kept silent. He dismounted and picked up a large rock. ''Show me where you want it, and I'll mark the corners.''

Deering followed him around as he stepped off the boundaries for a building some thirty feet square. ''I believe you're right that we should have some accoutrements to make the Indians feel more at home,'' the preacher said after a while. ''Are there any elements of their beliefs we might incorporate?''

''Every tribe believes different things.'' Micah stopped and considered. ''Each Comanche usually has his own guardian spirit, so to speak, where he gets his power. It's usually some kind of animal. But they don't go in much for organized religion.''

''What about your people? What do they believe?''

Micah hesitated. For years he'd been discouraged from even thinking about his father's people and their beliefs. But like his mother's memory of the books of the Bible, which survived sixteen years of captivity, there were some things he could never forget. ''Kiowas believe in a lot of different gods,'' he said after a moment. ''The sun is the most powerful.''

In Micah's tenth summer, his father had taken part in the sun dance. It was considered a sacred honor to be one of the dancers, fasting and dancing nearly round the clock for four days in the medicine lodge constructed for the festivities. Micah had watched with other spectators and had been filled with pride at his father's performance.

''That will never do.'' Deering's words pulled him back to the present. ''Obviously Christians don't believe in more than one God, or more than one Spirit either,'' the preacher said. ''We'll have to find something else.''

''What about ghosts?''

Deering paused. ''Do Indians believe in ghosts?''

''Some do.'' Micah hefted the rock in his hand and thought of Will and the flowerpot. ''I've met white people who believe in them, too.''

Deering looked disapproving. ''The church does not sanction belief in ghosts.''

''What about exorcism? Isn't that what they do when a house is haunted, to drive out the ghosts?''

''I believe that's for evil spirits. In any case, it's not a Prostestant ritual.'' Deering added a rock to a corner marker. ''What about pews? Would the Indians be more comfortable seated on the ground?''

After an hour they had four stone cairns marking the corners of the future chapel and lines in the dirt designating a future bell tower and well. Deering smiled approvingly. ''In my mind's eye, I can see it already.'' He turned to Micah. ''Let's go tell Mrs. Bright.''

As they rode, Micah only half listened to Deering's plans and instructions for building the chapel. Thoughts of Tessa, and what he'd say when he saw her again, filled his head. He began to wish he hadn't let the preacher talk him into staying.

Tessa met them at the door, her smile doing little to mask the anxiety in her eyes. "I was wondering where you'd gone off to so early," she said, ushering them inside.

"We've been out marking the site for my new chapel." Deering removed his hat and took a seat at the table. "Mr. Fox has agreed to oversee construction for me."

Tessa glanced at him. "I'm glad to hear that."

"Then you won't mind sparing him for a few hours every day?" Deering said. "I know it's a lot to ask—"

She shook her head. "No. That's all right."

"I thought maybe you could manage without me," Micah said. She would have to learn to eventually, anyway. Perhaps a physical separation would help him sort out the conflicting feelings that wrestled within him.

Chapter
Fourteen

Work on the chapel progressed slowly at first, largely
due to the difficulty Reverend Deering had in recruiting
workers. The majority of his congregation expressed little interest in his project to minister to the heathens on
the reservation. The few that did show up to work refused to take orders from a half-breed.

Reverend Deering sent them back and recruited help
from an unlikely source. Emmett Hardy persuaded half
a dozen of his clientele to work for the preacher as a
way of paying off their bar tabs. Gabe Emerson was the
first to show up. Micah supposed that, owing to his pre-
dilection for breaking mirrors, he had the largest tab.
Like the others before him, he adamantly refused to la-
bor at the direction of Micah. "I'll be damned if I take
orders from the likes of him," he declared, folding his
arms across his chest.

"Now, Mr. Emerson, think of it as working for the
church, not Mr. Fox." Reverend Deering tried to smooth
things over.

"Either he goes, or I go," Emerson said.

"Fine, I'll just quit." Micah turned to leave.

"Now, gentlemen, this arguing isn't accomplishing

anything." Reverend Deering gave Micah a stern look. "You agreed to oversee this project, Mr. Fox. Do you intend to keep your word?"

Micah nodded grudgingly. "I won't go back on my word."

"And you agreed to work as well, Mr. Emerson." He turned to the older man.

Emerson grunted. "But I never said I'd work with *him*."

What do you have to be so proud of? Micah thought as he stared at the older man. *Besides the color of your skin?* But then, that pride was the only thing some men had to cling to. Perhaps he could use Emerson's vanity to his own benefit. "Maybe *you* ought to be the one in charge, then," he said. "Why don't we just let the preacher here decide who's the better carpenter? You can pay off your debt and have the chance to get the better of me in public."

Emerson eyed him warily, like an animal who knows he's been trapped but can't figure out how. "I don't have anything to prove to you," he growled.

Micah shrugged. "Then our little competition should be easy for you."

"I don't know—" Deering began.

"I'll do it!" Emerson snatched up a hammer and a sack of nails. "I'll run this redskin into the ground if he tries to keep up with me."

After that, recruiting workers was easy. Jackie Babcock took time off from his forge to help. Woody Monroe lent a hand, along with Bryan Ritter. Even old man Thornton and Milo Adamson deserted the whittler's bench in favor of a front row seat at the competition between Micah Fox and Gabe Emerson.

The women did their part by providing a midday meal for the workers. Two volunteered each day to bring food to the work site. As luck would have it, Tessa was assigned the same day as Trudy Babcock. Trudy arrived first, the scent of Jasmine Nights heralding her arrival. She bore a plate of deviled eggs and cheese and crackers and greeted each worker with a thin smile that never quite reached her eyes. The men were polite to her, deferential even. But as soon as Tessa rolled up in her wagon, the workers deserted both Trudy and her deviled eggs, in favor of beans and potatoes simmered with fat bacon, and Tessa's genuine friendliness.

The doctor had cut the cast from her arm the day before, and she moved with more grace than ever. She no longer needed Micah to hitch up the wagon for her or to saddle a horse. His promise to stay until she'd healed no longer bound him, though he lingered. He told himself he stayed to fulfill his agreement with Reverend Deering, but that was only half the truth.

He watched the two women move around the work site and hoped Tessa couldn't see the looks Trudy directed her way. Even Jackie Babcock had left his wife standing alone while he feasted on Tessa's cooking. "Now there's a woman who knows how to feed a working man," Jackie declared as Tessa ladled dinner onto his plate.

Micah waited until the other men had been served before he approached Tessa. "Any left?" he asked casually.

A warm look flashed briefly into her eyes before she demurely looked away. "I made plenty," she said, reaching for a plate to serve him.

"That's good." He helped himself to cornbread from a basket on the wagon's tailgate. "Some of the women always seem to run out before they get to me."

Her expression clouded, and she looked directly at him, eyes filled with sympathy. "Oh, Micah."

"Shhh. It's all right." He took the plate and hesitated. He wanted to eat with her, to sit and get his fill of looking at her. He didn't dare with so many unfriendly eyes watching them, but he couldn't resist the urge to linger and talk with her a moment. "What do you have planned this afternoon?" he asked.

"Margery is coming over to help make pies for the Library Society bake sale." She put the lid on the kettle and shoved it back into the wagon. "What about you?"

"I'm working on the roof today. We ought to be ready to start putting on the shingles by tomorrow."

She folded her arms under her breasts and studied the almost completed framing of the chapel. "It's coming along well, isn't it?"

"Everyone is working hard."

"How's your competition with Mr. Emerson going?"

He followed her gaze to where the older man sat slumped against a corner post. Emerson's face sagged with weariness. "He hasn't slowed down for a minute. He won't risk being bested by the likes of me."

Tessa nodded. "Did you know Indians killed his wife?"

"I'd heard. Who were they?"

"Comanche raiders. He was away from home at the time. His sister moved in to look after his children, but he was never the same afterward. I don't think he drank nearly as much before then."

"He isn't drinking here." Micah scooped potatoes and beans onto cornbread and shoveled it into his mouth. "At least, I don't think so," he added when he'd swallowed.

She hesitated, then said, "I think what you've done, proposing this absurd contest in order to prevent a fight . . . well, I just think it's very wise. And generous. You didn't have to . . . to humble yourself that way."

He shrugged off her praise. "Maybe this hard work, doing something constructive for a change, will do him some good." He shook his head. "Then again, he might sweat the alcohol out of his system here, but I doubt he'll let go of a grudge that easily."

"I think I'll go talk to him." She picked up a water pail and carried it to Emerson. Micah leaned against the wagon and ate the rest of his dinner, watching Tessa. Emerson greeted her with a look of suspicion, but he accepted the cup of water she offered. Micah had to admit that, except for a look of weariness, Emerson did appear to be in better health. The pastiness was gone from his skin, and he'd lost some of the flab around his waist.

Micah had expected more trouble from the man—sabotage perhaps, or general mischief. But despite a definite animosity toward Micah, Emerson had caused no problems. Micah had to admit the work he'd done was some of the best on the job.

He wiped the bacon-flavored juice from the bottom of his plate with the last of the cornbread and popped it into his mouth. Jackie Babcock was right; Tessa knew how to satisfy a man's appetite. In more ways than one.

He stretched lazily and indulged himself with watching her now as she knelt and talked to Gabe Emerson. The posture emphasized her smoothly rounded backside, shaped just right for a man's hand to cup . . .

A woman's scream jerked him out of his fantasies. Knife in hand, he scanned the area for some sign of danger. Gabe Emerson had shot to his feet and stood with his pistol drawn and aimed out across the prairie. Micah followed his gaze to a pair of Indians riding toward them.

"Put your weapons away," Reverend Deering ordered. "They mean no harm."

As they rode closer, Micah recognized Sun Bear and Drinking Wolf. He relaxed and slid the knife back into its scabbard. Emerson was slower to comply, and he kept his hand on the butt of the pistol, his eyes trained on the two Comanches.

"Hello." Deering raised his hand in greeting. "It's good to see you again."

Micah could feel the stares of everyone around them. Even Trudy Babcock, half hidden behind her husband, had her attention riveted on the visitors. Deering motioned to Micah, and he walked over to translate.

"We came to see what you are building," Sun Bear said. He nodded toward the chapel frame.

"This will be our chapel," Deering said, beaming. "The house of the Great Spirit."

The chief looked doubtful. "If the Great Spirit lived in a house, I think he'd choose a better one than that," he said. "It doesn't look very strong. Big wind, knock it down." He pantomimed the fragile structure blowing over. "Fire, burn it up." He eyed the frame of the church critically. "It looks like the bones of the house vultures have picked clean of the skin."

Micah admitted the chapel did not look very sturdy right now. "Once the walls and roof are on, it'll be sound enough," he said.

Reverend Deering was more effusive in his praise. "Isn't it grand?" he declared.

Sun Bear and Micah exchanged doubtful glances.

"I'm so glad you came out to see it, Chief," Deering said. "I hope you'll come to services when it's completed."

The chief nodded. "You said there would be food and presents. We will come."

"Of course. And food for your souls, too. Bring everyone. I plan to hold a joint service with my congregation from town to dedicate the chapel."

Sun Bear looked over the assembled workers. "What is everybody eating?" He spied Trudy, who was still holding a plate of deviled eggs, and started toward her. Trudy's eyes widened, and she looked ready to let loose another scream.

"Don't be such a ninny." Tessa snatched the plate from Trudy's trembling hands and turned to Sun Bear with a smile.

Sun Bear returned the look. "How is my favorite white woman today?"

No one said anything while Tessa served the Indians the rest of the food, though Micah thought some of the men looked impressed with her calm handling of the situation. When there was nothing left to eat, Sun Bear and Drinking Wolf said good-bye and rode away. The women packed up their belongings and prepared to depart also, although Trudy insisted Jackie come with her. "I'm not riding all that way by myself when there are savages running around loose,'' she protested.

Micah breathed a sigh of relief when she was gone. Even Reverend Deering didn't seem disappointed. Tessa left soon after. Micah knew his weren't the only admiring eyes that followed her slight figure as she guided the wagon across the prairie. He had no doubt that once he was gone, she'd have no shortage of suitors. In fact, the sooner he left her, the better off she'd be. Suddenly the dinner he'd eaten felt like a rock in his stomach.

"How much longer do you think it will be before we're ready?" Reverend Deering interrupted his musings.

Micah studied the growing structure. "Maybe a couple of weeks.''

Deering looked dejected. "I never realized it would take so long.''

"We'll get it finished soon enough, Reverend. Don't you worry.'' He walked over and picked up his hammer once more. He climbed a ladder and crawled out onto the rafters and began to hammer in the crosspieces. It was awkward work, straddling the ridge beam and stretching out to drive in the nails. One wrong move, and a man would fall a long way down.

Micah didn't mind. He wasn't afraid of heights and he was just as glad to spend all his spare time working on the chapel. It kept him occupied and away from Tessa. As it was, his feelings for her were stronger than ever. He woke at night, half-remembered dreams of her filling his mind, torturing his body.

He scooted down to the next crosspiece, indulging himself with the memory of how she'd looked sitting across the supper table from him last night. He hadn't been able to stop watching her mouth, remembering how it felt to kiss her.

When she'd leaned forward to pass the potatoes, the swell of her breast had caught his eye. He'd had to clench his hands into fists, fighting the urge to reach for her. It was a sickness, really, this longing for something he could never have. But a sickness he was reluctant to seek a cure for.

Tessa added another stick of wood to the stove and slammed the door shut. She leaned back, red-faced and panting in the heat. "Why didn't the Library Society decide to hold an ice cream social instead of a bake sale?" Margery asked, looking up from the basket of peaches she was peeling.

Tessa glanced at the row of pie shells lined up on the table in front of her, waiting to be filled. "Where would we get ice in the middle of summer?" She took a seat at the table and picked up a knife and a peach. She still felt awkward, now that Doc Richards had cut the cast off her arm, though it was good to have use of both hands again.

"If I had the money, I'd freight in a whole lake full of ice." Margery fanned herself furiously.

"If you had that kind of money, you could just donate it to the Library Society, and we wouldn't have to be holding an event like this at all."

Margery laughed and held up the peach she was peeling. "Think I've scalped this one enough?"

Tessa considered the wounded fruit with a critical eye. "I'd say you've taken off more peach than peel."

Margery added the peach to the bowl in front of her. "I told you I couldn't cook. We always had a striker to do the cooking when I was growing up. Besides, I knew a man would never marry me for my cooking."

Tessa smiled. "No, I don't imagine most men who see you care whether you can make a nice cream gravy or not."

"Maybe it's time I learned, though. They say the way to a man's heart is through his stomach, after all." Her voice caught on the last words.

"Alan hasn't softened up any?"

She looked dejected. "No. The only thing that gives me hope is that he looks as miserable as I am." She shook her head. "Never hurt a man's pride, Tessa. They can't bear it."

Tessa thought of Will. Had she hurt his pride when she rejected his attempts to look after her? She hadn't seen or heard from him since that morning in Micah's room. He'd never been so quiet for so long. Was he plotting some revenge? Or had he merely left for good?

The thought grieved her. Surely after all this time, he wouldn't leave without saying good-bye.

"What about you and Micah?"

She looked up at her friend, startled by the question. "What about us?"

"Neither of you looks very happy these days."

Tessa assumed a blank expression. "I don't know what you're referring to."

Margery shook her head. "I'm not blind, you know. I've seen you making calf eyes at each other." She dropped another peach in the bowl and wiped her hands on a cup towel. "Why don't you admit you love him?"

"I can't do that." She concentrated on carving an even curl of peel from the peach, avoiding her friend's gaze.

"Why not?"

"People will talk."

Margery dismissed this excuse with a wave of her hand. "People will always talk, honey. You just learn to ignore them."

Tessa sighed and laid aside the peach. "That's easy for you to say. You're the center of attention wherever you go. You don't know what it's like to be the outcast."

Margery leaned forward. "Don't you believe it. There's no bigger caste system in the world than in the military. Rank and money are the only things that matter. That and conforming to the rules the person at the top of the pecking order sets down. I never conformed." She sat back. "The only reason anyone will have anything to do with me now is because I'm married to Alan.

Don't let somebody else decide your happiness for you. Tell 'them' to go to hell."

Margery's words both thrilled and frightened her. "I'm not like you, Margery. I'm not that brave. Maybe when I was younger . . ."

"Liar!" The word exploded from Margery's mouth. "You run a ranch in the middle of nowhere, practically by yourself. You make friends with Indian chiefs. You volunteer to make six peach pies for the high and mighty Pony Springs Library Society and have the gumption to ask me to help you. Don't tell me you're not brave."

Tessa had been close to tears, but now she found herself laughing. "Oh, Margery, I'm so glad I met you."

"I'm glad I met you, too, hon." She leaned forward and patted her hand. "Now, I've got to get out of this kitchen for a minute. It's hot enough in here to peel paint. I think I'll catch my breath out on the porch."

Tessa picked up the bowl of peeled peaches. "I'll just finish slicing these. Then we'll be ready to make the pie filling."

Margery glanced into the bowl. "Maybe I'd just better watch you. I'd probably do something awful like put in salt instead of sugar."

Tessa laughed again and sent her friend onto the porch while she pitted and sliced the peaches.

Only a few minutes passed before Margery called to her. "Tessa, you'd better come out here a minute."

The note of caution in her voice made Tessa hurry outside. Margery nodded toward the horizon. "Who do you think is headed this way in such a hurry?"

The wagon bounced toward them across the east pasture, dust boiling up around its wheels. Gabe Emerson sat in the driver's seat, shouting oaths and cracking a whip over the horses, who were white-eyed and flecked with foam. Another man huddled in the wagon box, hanging on for dear life. Tessa and Margery ran to meet them.

"Mr. Emerson, what's wrong?" Tessa asked, as he stood and hauled back on the reins.

"It's that damn half-breed," Emerson growled. "He about got hisself killed."

"Micah?" Tessa's steps faltered, and she grabbed Margery's arm to steady herself. As Emerson's words echoed around her, the edges of her vision went gray, and she swayed.

"What happened?" Margery asked, clinging to Tessa, patting her shoulder.

"He f-fell off the r-ridge beam, ma'am." Bryan Ritter scrambled out of the wagon and jerked off his hat, nodding to the two women. "S-some b-bushes broke his f-fall, but he hit his . . . his head on a r-rock."

Tessa's head cleared, and she pushed forward, hardly feeling Mr. Ritter's hands as he helped her into the wagon. Micah lay on his back, his head cushioned on a folded burlap sack, the brown sacking stained dark red with blood. "He bled like a stuck pig," Emerson observed. "It was a mighty long fall."

"Did he fall or was he pushed?" Tessa whispered. A memory of Micah up on the roof of the house, Will seated beside him, flashed through her mind. How easy it would be for an invisible Will to make a fall look like an accident . . .

"Now wait just a minute." Emerson squared his shoulders like an angry bull. "Fox was up on that ridge beam by hisself. None of us would have pushed him."

"Oh, really, Mr. Emerson." Margery gave him a cutting look. "I understand you threatened to shoot Mr. Fox one night in the saloon."

Emerson's face reddened. "Aw, that was the whiskey talkin'." He glanced over his shoulder into the wagon bed. "He's one hardworkin' bastard, I'll give you that."

"We'd better get him into the house," Tessa said. "Margery, fetch a blanket from my bed. We'll make a sling to carry him."

Within minutes, the men had transferred Micah's still form to the blanket and carried him up the stairs. Tessa followed, fighting the dizzying sensation that she had gone back in time, to the horrible day when Will had been thrown from a horse and landed wrong.

A man and his son had stopped by that day to buy a horse. They had carried an unconscious Will up these same stairs, to the same bed, then gone to fetch the doctor. "One of you, ride into town and fetch Dr. Richards," she said, the very words she had used that day. "You can take a fresh horse from the corral."

"I'll go," Emerson said, and headed from the room.

"I-I-I'll go with you." Ritter followed him down the stairs."

"Cowards." Margery cast a scornful look after them, then turned back to Micah. He hadn't made a sound all the way up the stairs, and his face was the color of undercooked biscuit dough. She put out a hand, as if to stroke his forehead, then drew it back. "What can I do to help?" she asked.

Tessa forced herself to think, to act. "Fetch some hot water from the stove boiler. And some clean towels."

Margery left the room, and Tessa eased onto the side of the bed. With trembling hands, she stroked the hair back from Micah's forehead. The black locks were damp and sticky with blood. It soaked into the blanket beneath him, the metallic smell of it sharp in the air.

Sick with fear, she forced herself to probe his scalp, until she located the sharp jagged cut, a few inches back on the left side of his part.

"The water's good and hot, at least." Margery appeared in the doorway, a stack of towels over one shoulder, a basin of steaming water in her hands.

Tessa pulled a chair out from the wall and arranged it by the bed. "I'll need the scissors from my sewing kit," she said. "It's over there by the window."

Margery fetched the scissors and watched as Tessa cut through the thong that tied Micah's hair. "You aren't going to cut his hair, are you?" she asked.

"I have to cut it away from the wound." She clenched her teeth, concentrating on keeping her hands steady, and snipped the first lock of hair, close to the scalp. When the cut was laid bare, she sat back, exhausted. But her work had only begun.

"Where is that doctor?" Margery wrung her hands and peered out the window.

Tessa soaked a cloth in water and began to clean around the wound. Blood still seeped from the cut, but she thought it flowed more slowly now. Because it was finally clotting, or because there was less in him to bleed? Gently she washed his forehead, passing the damp cloth over his eyes, sunken above the taut skin of his cheekbones. Her hand trembled as she brushed his lips, remembering the kisses they'd shared.

"Why won't he wake up?" Margery stood at her shoulder, staring down at the bed with tear-filled eyes.

"He will," Tessa said. *Surely he will.*

Micah dreamed he was falling. A long, long way down. He kept reaching for the crossbeam of the roof, but it wasn't there. Then he was lying on his back, eyes open, a gray haze closing in. Gabe Emerson was leaning down in his face, shouting words he could barely hear. Something about not giving up that easy.

Then Emerson was picking him up, carrying him. And the grayness was closing in.

Horses' hooves clattered on the hard dirt of the drive. "Finally!" Margery exclaimed and ran to the window. Moments later, Dr. Richards and Reverend Deering raced up the stairs.

The doctor glanced over his patient and opened his bag. "The wound's ready to suture. I'll take care of that first."

Tessa retreated to the end of the bed. Reverend Deering came and took her hand. "We must pray," he said.

She nodded, but words failed her. Only an inexpressible sorrow in her heart cried out for relief. She had watched one man she loved die in this very bed, in this very way. How could she bear to lose another?

While the doctor worked, Reverend Deering per-

suaded Tessa and Margery to come downstairs to the
kitchen, where he made tea and offered words of comfort. At last they heard the doctor's footsteps on the
stairs.

"Now all we can do is wait," he said.

"I'll send word to the fort that I'm spending the night
here," Margery said as the doctor prepared to go.

"I'll stay also," Reverend Deering said.

"No." Tessa fended off their concerned looks with a
flood of words. "It'll be all right, really. You've been
so much help already. Go home and rest. You can come
back in the morning."

They offered up protests, but in the end they agreed
to go, promising to return at dawn.

When they had departed and the house was empty
once more, Tessa climbed the stairs to watch and wait
at Micah's bedside. She moved a chair close beside the
bed and stared at his still form, unconsciously matching
the rhythm of her breathing to his own shallow respi-
rations. The whole scene had the surreal quality of a bad
dream. Only an hour before, her main concern had been
preparing pies for the Library Society bake sale. Her
world had been full of people and activity, all of it seem-
ingly important. In an instant, her vision had narrowed
to this one room, this one man. Nothing else, large or
small, mattered to her anymore.

She reached for Micah's hand and squeezed it, trying
to summon up a prayer. But the only words she could
speak were more threat than plea: "Dammit, Micah Fox,
don't you dare die on me!"

A pounding reverberated inside Micah's skull, as if
someone were beating a drum close to his ear. He shuddered and tried to move away from the painful noise,
but his limbs felt as if they were encased in sand.

Opening his eyes, he stared into unfamiliar dimness.
As he strained to see, his surroundings swam into focus:
an embroidered sampler on the wall, rows of alphabet
letters picked out in blue cross-stitching; a square of

light framed with lace-edged curtains; a bowl of beaded flowers atop a dresser. Where had he seen these things before?

The fog began to recede from his brain. He concentrated, trying to remember. Last he knew, he'd been atop the ridge beam of the chapel, nailing crosspieces to the rafters. How had he gotten here, flat on his back in a bed?

Something soft brushed his arm. He turned his head, though his skull throbbed with the effort, and saw a woman's brown hair spread out on the mattress beside him. Tessa sat in a chair next to the bed, slumped forward in sleep.

He raised his hand to touch the downy softness of her hair. She stirred, then drew back with a start. "Micah." The word came out as a sigh, and she closed her eyes, as if in silent prayer. "How are you feeling?" she asked when she looked at him once more.

"Like someone took a hammer to my head." He gingerly touched the place from where the pain seemed to radiate and felt a lump of bandages. "What happened?"

"They said you fell off the roof of the chapel." She smoothed the blankets along the side of the bed. "I wondered if you were pushed."

"Pushed? Who would have pushed me?"

She looked down. "I thought maybe . . . Will."

He frowned, trying to think. But he had no recollection of anything after climbing to the ridge beam and reaching for a hammer. "I don't remember." He felt the knot of bandages again. "Who cut my hair?"

"I did. I had to." She smoothed the remaining hair away from his forehead. "It will grow back."

He captured her hand in his and kissed her fingers, feeling them tremble beneath his lips. "Thank you." Then he pushed himself up on his elbows, wincing with the effort.

"You should lie down and rest." She stood and leaned over him, alarmed.

He shook his head. "I won't lie here like an invalid. Help me sit up."

The worried look did not leave her face, but she helped him to sit, propping pillows at his back. He fought dizziness and gave her a weak smile. "That's better." He looked toward the window, at the gray light outside. "How long was I out?"

"Most of the night. Are you hungry?"

He shook his head. Food did not interest him at the moment. "Sit down and keep me company."

She settled in the chair again and took the hand he held out to her. He thought of her, sitting through the night, unsure that he would wake again. "I'm sorry to put you through this," he said softly.

"Shhh. It doesn't matter now." She squeezed his hand.

He wished he had the strength to gather her in his arms and comfort her, to hold her until the haunted look left her eyes. "You said you thought Will pushed me. Why?"

She looked away. "Because he doesn't want us to be together."

"He was your husband. Do you really think he'd resort to murder?"

"I don't know." Her voice was anguished. "Wouldn't you kill to protect the woman you loved?"

He nodded. "But . . . I don't think he would do something like this." He said the words to comfort her, but instinct told him they were true after all. Will Bright was not the sort of man—or ghost—to ambush his enemy. He had thrown a flowerpot in a moment of anger, but even that had been an act of passion, not premeditation, not like throwing a man from a rooftop. Still, they couldn't be certain Will was not behind this.

"Promise me you'll be careful," she said.

"I promise." The tenderness he saw in her eyes made his stomach twist. The time had come to speak the truth. "You know I still want you," he said.

"I still want *you*," she whispered.

He slipped his hand from beneath hers and looked away. "But we can't always have what we want, can we?"

He waited for some protest and prayed she wouldn't make this more difficult than it already was. But after a moment of silence, she stood and walked out of the room.

He turned his face to the wall, knowing the wound to his heart would take far longer to heal than the one to his head.

Chapter
Fifteen

Reverend Deering designated the second Sunday in August as the date to consecrate the new chapel. "We'll hold a joint service, with our congregation and the Indians from the reservation," he announced from the pulpit the last Sunday in July. "I expect to see all of you there."

"I don't see how we're expected to worship in the presence of half-naked savages," Mrs. Tucker complained to Tessa and the other women as they visited after services.

"It *is* rather difficult to concentrate sometimes with all those handsome bodies on display." Margery winked at Tessa from behind her fan.

Mamie Tucker flushed deep red. "I certainly don't intend to *look*!"

"No?" Margery hid her smile. "What a shame."

Mrs. Drake frowned at Margery. "Did you hear we're expected to *feed* all these Indians? I have no idea what they eat—and no interest in finding out."

"Bake some of your delicious cookies," Tessa said. "No one would fail to enjoy them."

"Why are you wasting your time planning a menu?"

Trudy asked irritably. "The real concern here is our safety. What's to keep the redskins from murdering us all?"

"My husband and a detail from Fort Belknap will be there to preserve order," Margery assured her.

"I can assure you, my Jackie will be armed," Trudy said. "We won't stand for any trouble from those savages."

"It sounds to me as if the Indians have a lot more to worry about from us," Tessa snapped.

"Yes, well, not everyone is so *friendly* with Indians as you are, dear."

Tessa didn't miss the snide tone in Trudy's voice. She started to fire back an angry answer, but Margery took her arm. "We have to be going." Margery waved to the other women. "See you next Sunday."

"Thanks for stopping me before I said something I might regret later," Tessa said as she took her place beside Margery in the Army ambulance. Margery was giving her a ride back to the ranch.

"I told you, you just have to learn to ignore people like that."

"I guess I haven't had enough practice."

Margery worked the ostrich fan back and forth in front of her face. "How's Micah?"

Tessa smiled. "Back at work. Except for the missing hair and a scar, you'd never suspect he'd been hurt."

"I'm glad." She turned toward Tessa. "Do you really think Gabe Emerson or one of the others pushed him?"

Tessa hesitated. She couldn't very well tell Margery that Mr. Emerson was not her first suspect. "I don't know what to think," she said finally.

"At least Micah knows how you feel about him now."

She looked away. "I . . . I never really told him."

Margery patted her hand. "I imagine when he first opened his eyes and saw you there, watching over him, he knew. It's been two weeks since your cast came off, and he's still here, isn't he?"

She shrugged. She couldn't risk putting more meaning into Micah's presence here than was warranted. After all, since their conversation in the bedroom the other morning, he'd kept his distance. If he really wanted her as much as he said, wouldn't he try harder to win her? "I expect after the chapel consecration, he'll go."

Margery sighed and looked away. "I plan to leave then, too."

The words stunned her. She stared at her friend. "Why?"

"Not with Micah," Margery hastened to reassure her. "I don't want you thinking that. No, I'm going back east."

Tessa felt like crying. "Things aren't as bad as all that, are they?"

Margery folded her fan in her lap. "Maybe it would be better for Alan and me to live apart for a while."

The words pained Tessa. If she had to lose Micah, did she have to lose Margery as well? "I wish you wouldn't go."

"I wish I didn't have to. But Alan seems determined to maintain this . . . this distance between us."

Tessa took her hand, and the two friends rode in silence. She wondered how love, which was meant as a good thing, could end up causing so much pain.

"Now, gentlemen, if you'll move the pulpit a little to the left, please. That's it. No, no, those pews go on the right. The other side is for the Indians. Mr. Fox tells me they'll prefer to sit on the floor."

From the vantage point of the rafters, Will watched Reverend Deering giving orders to the crew moving furnishings into the new chapel. Even with half of the windows lacking glass, the preacher had decided to go ahead and hold his dedication service. Now he was running around like a hen trying to herd ducklings. Even the Lord would have had a hard time harnessing his attention, much less Will's poor imitation of Him.

Will sighed. He didn't have much heart for the old

game anymore. Ever since the morning Tessa had told him off, he just felt . . . tired. As if he'd like nothing better than a weeks'-long nap.

You've got a job to do, man, he reminded himself. *Best get with it.* He floated to the floor and drifted up behind the preacher. *"Deering, I'd like a word with you,"* he whispered in his ear.

"I'm busy at the moment. If you could just wai—" The preacher turned and gaped at the empty space behind him. "Who is it?" he demanded, hugging his arms to himself as if to ward off a chill.

"Perhaps now would be a good time to go somewhere private," Will continued in a low voice.

Wide-eyed, Deering jerked his head in a nod. "Yes, Lord," he rasped. He searched the sanctuary. Throughout the building, workers hammered siding or shifted pews. "Perhaps . . . outside?"

"Just someplace where we can get away from all this racket."

Deering hurried outside, to a cluster of scrub oak some distance from the chapel. Once there, he dropped to his knees. "Are you there, Lord?" he asked.

Will ignored the question. *"I have a favor to ask,"* he said.

Deering's eyes widened. "Anything, Lord."

"I want you to have Tessa translate your message into sign for the Indians tomorrow."

"But I thought I'd get Micah Fox to do that, Lord. He knows Comanche and—"

"Use Tessa instead."

Deering blanched. "Yes, Lord."

"And I want you to pay extra attention to Tessa tomorrow. She's a very pretty woman, sweet and devoted. The kind of woman a man would be proud to claim as his wife." Will swallowed past the knot in his throat. Maybe he hadn't done right by Tessa in the past few weeks, but he'd make up for it now. Deering would make her a good husband. He was an honorable man who would look after her and give her standing in the

community—something Will had not been able to do.

Deering looked puzzled, but nodded. "All right, Lord. Whatever you say."

Will frowned. Had he made himself clear enough? Maybe he'd better try again. He opened his mouth to elaborate, but another voice interrupted.

"Reverend Deering?"

Will looked up and saw Micah Fox headed toward them. He swore to himself. He'd have to leave now. He still felt bad about the flowerpot incident—not for Fox's sake, but for Tessa's—and the bad opinion it had given her of him. He wouldn't give her an opportunity to see that side of him again. *"Remember what I told you,"* he whispered to Deering, then floated away, in search of a warm place to take a nap.

By nine-thirty Sunday morning, Tessa was wishing she'd never been foolish enough to allow Reverend Deering to build his chapel on her land. At least twenty buggies had stopped by the house to ask directions to the chapel, and she'd burned two batches of cookies while she was talking to them. Every man she'd seen this morning had been bristling with weapons, and she had waking nightmares of a gun battle breaking out in the middle of Reverend Deering's message. Margery was leaving on the afternoon stage, Micah was nowhere to be found, and her hair absolutely refused to curl properly.

A knock on her door resounded through the house. "Not again!" She gingerly unwrapped her hair from the curling iron and surveyed the frizzed ringlet. The knocking continued. "Just a minute!" she shouted, shoving the iron back into its holder on the stove and heading for the door. Why wasn't Micah seeing to all these lost people?

"Mrs. Bright, good morning." Reverend Deering swept off his hat, then added, "Uh . . . you're looking very lovely this morning."

Tessa looked down at the stained apron she'd tied on

to protect her Sunday dress and put a hand to her half-curled hair. Obviously the poor man was too distracted by concerns for the morning's service to know what he was saying. "Thank you, Reverend. What can I do for you?"

"Ah. Well, I need you to translate my sermon this morning. For the Indians."

"But I thought you were going to have Micah do that."

Deering flushed and fidgeted with the hat in his hand. "Yes, well, there's been a change in plans. You'll just, uh, stand up at the front, off to one side, and translate what I say into sign."

She shook her head. "Oh, no. I really don't know the language that well. Micah knows Comanche. You'd better ask him."

"No. It really needs to be you." He nodded firmly and put his hat back on his head. "Don't be nervous. I'm sure you can handle it."

She was still fumbling for words to explain to him all the reasons she *couldn't* do this when he turned and walked away. "Reverend Deering!" she called after him.

"See you at the chapel," he said as he mounted the bay and rode off.

Frowning, she returned to the kitchen. The poor man was downright addled. As soon as she was able, she'd find Micah and explain the situation to him. He'd make things work out.

Micah shoved the last of his belongings into the bedroll and tied it tightly. There'd be no turning back this time. He counted out ten gold coins and arranged them in a neat stack on the bunk. That was a good price for the roan mare; Tessa wouldn't be able to say he'd taken advantage. The horse would allow him to be far away before she discovered he'd left. As soon as the service ended and he could slip away, he'd ride out. He hadn't wanted it to end this way, but he could see it was for the best.

As he emerged from the barn, he heard his name, and looked up to see Tessa hurrying toward him. His throat felt tight at the sight of her. She wore one of her new dresses and she'd fixed her hair up differently, but if she'd appeared to him in rags and pigtails he knew he would have felt the same. Tessa would always be beautiful to him. She had captured a part of his heart he'd never be able to reclaim.

"Micah, you've got to help me," she said, sounding desperate.

"What is it?" He forced himself to concentrate on the here and now, surface things that didn't have to involve his tortured emotions.

"Reverend Deering insists that *I* be the one to translate his sermon for the Indians." She twisted her hands. "I don't know nearly enough sign language to do that."

Leave it to the preacher to throw a new wrench in the works. "Did he say why he changed his mind?"

She shook her head. "He just insisted I do it instead. You've got to talk some sense into him."

He looked doubtful. "The preacher isn't likely to listen to anyone this morning."

"What am I going to do? I can't make a fool of myself in front of all those people. Not to mention it won't do the Indians much good if they don't have any idea what Reverend Deering is saying."

He wanted to gather her close and soothe her fraying nerves, to assure her he would take care of everything. But he was leaving. He couldn't let her think he was someone to rely on. "What if I sit beside you and tell you what to do?" he suggested. "If we both sit on the floor, directly in front of the Indians, we won't be very noticeable to the congregation."

She nodded. "All right. Anything. I can't believe he's changing his mind at the last minute. What has gotten into the man?" She laughed. "I showed up at the door in a dirty apron with my hair half done and he actually told me I was looking lovely! I think the strain is getting to him.''

You always look lovely to me, Micah thought, but he dared not say so. ''I'll bring the wagon around now if you're ready to ride over to the chapel.''

''I'm as ready as I'll ever be, I suppose.'' She gave him a grateful look. ''I feel better now that you're with me.''

The words stung like a whip. *Coward,* a voice in his head whispered. He should tell her he was leaving, but he didn't want to see the hurt in her eyes when she found out.

Or worse, what if she would be relieved to be rid of him?

They rode to the chapel in silence, Micah grateful for a reprieve from the effort of making conversation when all he really wanted was to hold her close, without speaking.

The area around the chapel teemed with horses and wagons and people. A detail of soldiers from Fort Belknap, in dress blues and bristling with polished sabers, occupied the south approach to the hill. Major Alan Finch was at their head, mounted on a sorrel gelding, casting a worried eye on the band of Indians on the opposite side of the chapel.

Sun Bear and his people had come in force, lured more by curiosity and the promise of food and gifts, Micah was sure, than any real interest in the white man's religion. The Indians wore their finest beaded buckskin and buffalo robes. Sun Bear was resplendent in a bead and bone vest over his buckskin tunic. Eagle Feather stood by his side, Tessa's camisole and petticoat proudly displayed on top of an intricately beaded deerskin tunic and leggings. The old chief raised a hand to salute Micah and Tessa as they rode past, and Eagle Feather smiled in greeting.

Trudy Babcock was holding court in the shade with a group of town women. She cast a disdainful look at Tessa as she and Micah rode past. Tessa pretended not to notice. Micah admired her determination not to acknowledge Trudy's hateful attitude.

"There's Margery," she called, waving to her friend, who stood under a blue parasol near the chapel door. Margery didn't return the greeting, however, her attention riveted on something else.

Micah followed the path of her gaze and saw Alan Finch, his face resolutely turned away from his wife. "I wish we could do something to bring them back together," Tessa said. "I can't believe he'd fall out of love with her so easily. When I saw him that first day, he was positively besotted."

Micah shook his head. "I don't see how there's anything anyone can do," he said. "It's a private matter."

"If you saw a friend about to walk off a cliff, wouldn't you stop him?" she countered. "I can't just sit here and watch them both make this huge mistake."

He shook his head. "Better to stay out of it."

His words made no impression. She continued to stare after her friends, brow furrowed in thought. "If only I could think of something."

He parked the wagon in a row of other vehicles and helped her down. For one precious moment, she was suspended in his arms, her hands on his shoulders, the fullness of her breasts brushing his sleeves. The urge to pull her close and cover her lips with his own was as strong as the urge to breathe, and when he set her down and released her, he could feel the pain tearing at him.

Reverend Deering mounted the steps of the chapel and rang a handbell, the signal for everyone to begin filing in. Indians and whites entered through separate doors. Deering directed Sun Bear and his people to one side of the sanctuary, where they arranged themselves on blankets and buffalo robes, while the people of Pony Springs filled pews on the opposite side.

Micah and Tessa made their way to the front. Once there, he belatedly remembered Tessa had nothing to protect her skirts from the floor. He removed his jacket and spread it for her. The smile she offered in thanks would have made a man want to bring her the moon. Fighting a mounting sadness, he settled himself beside her.

The service began smoothly enough. Tessa translated the prayer without difficulty, her hands and arms tracing the signs with eloquent grace. He heard the murmur of voices among the Indians as those in front passed the words back to those at the rear. The quiet reverence of the moment infected them all, and even the usually boisterous children and young braves were quiet and attentive.

The congregation rose to sing "Love Divine, All Loves Excelling." The Indians shuffled to their feet also, but after an abortive attempt to translate the words, Tessa gave up. The Indians didn't seem to mind. Some kept time to the music with their feet. Others contented themselves with looking across the room at their white neighbors, most of whom were trying to pretend they didn't see the Indians, while watching them out of the corner of their eyes. Micah saw more than one white woman studying the Indian men in their breechclouts and beaded vests, though Mamie Tucker blushed the shade of ripe strawberries and looked as if at any moment she might faint.

Everyone settled into their seats again, and Reverend Deering approached the pulpit to begin his sermon. Micah sensed trouble right away. Indian sign didn't have words for vague theological concepts. When Deering spoke of God's grace, Tessa looked at him blankly.

Micah leaned closer to her. "Try the sign for 'gift,' " he whispered.

She shook her head. "I don't know that one."

"How about generosity?"

She thought a moment, then made a series of gestures whose literal translation was "big-hearted great mystery."

In the end, the phrase translated to, "a most generous gift from the Great Spirit."

The rest of the message proceeded in similar fashion.

Micah moved closer as he and Tessa conferred on each phrase. He put one hand behind her back to brace himself, and she settled naturally into the curve of his body. The soft scent of her hair filled his nostrils, and the delicate shell of her ear tempted him to trace it with his tongue. He looked away, only to have his eyes rest on the swell of her breasts showing through the lace at the top of her dress. His fingers twitched as he thought of tracing that line of plump flesh.

He rolled his eyes heavenward. Of all the places to be having such lascivious thoughts!

"Micah, what is the word I'm looking for now?" Tessa prodded him. "How in the world do I translate 'parable'?"

"Try 'story,' " he suggested, dropping his gaze to the soft skin at the back of her neck. He shifted his leg to hide his growing arousal. Was this his punishment for trying to do the right thing?

Tessa could hardly think, she was so aware of Micah beside her. The heat of him warmed her back, and every time she traced a sign across her body, her sleeve brushed his chest. She drew a deep breath and forced her mind back to the task at hand. It was obvious the Indians didn't understand half of what Reverend Deering was saying, though the gist of his sermon was about brotherly love, and that was the message she'd settled on conveying. If only he would stop talking! She had to get out of here, and away from Micah, before she did something drastic and probably sinful!

"You just told them if their neighbor gives them a horse, they should take two," Micah whispered in her ear.

"I did?" She stared at her hands, as if they were not part of her body. Then she looked out at the Indians. Some of them were laughing, translating her message down the line.

She rolled her eyes. "That's not exactly what I meant."

"It's all right. They enjoy a good joke."

Somehow she got through the rest of the service. When it was over, she excused herself quickly and ran outside for some fresh air. She retreated to the area by the buggies, where she could be alone for a moment, to gather her thoughts.

But she had not been standing there long when she saw Alan Finch emerge from a grove of trees, adjusting his cavalry saber at his side. Apparently he'd been answering the "call of nature." Tessa started toward him. Here was her chance to talk to him alone, to convince him to patch up his differences with Margery.

"Major Finch! Might I speak with you a moment?"

He turned toward her. "Hello, Mrs. Bright. Is something wrong?"

She fell into step beside him, walking back toward the chapel. "I was just remembering the day we met, when you went to meet Margery at the stage station. You were so happy to see her."

A pained look came into his eyes. "Yes, I was."

Tessa touched his arm, forcing him to look at her. "Then how can you let her go now?"

He looked away. "Mrs. Bright, this is really none of your concern."

"It *is* my concern. Margery is my best friend. How can you still be angry with her? She admitted she was wrong to run away that day."

"You couldn't possibly understand."

She crossed her arms under her breasts and faced him. "I might. I'd like to try."

He stared at the toes of his polished boots. After a tense moment, he spoke, the words coming slowly, as if dredged from deep inside. "That day, when I thought she was in danger, I went numb. I couldn't think. I couldn't act. I was unfit for command. The thought of any harm coming to her—" He turned his gaze to her, burning into her. "It's too dangerous out here. Too many things could happen. I knew I had to make her leave."

Tessa stared at him in disbelief. "That's absurd! You've gone all this time letting her think you've stopped loving her."

"My wife is a very stubborn woman. She would never go just because I asked or because I ordered it. When she's safely back east, I'll write and tell her the truth." He looked away. "It's best this way."

"Why are men so arrogant?" The angry words exploded from her. "How can you presume to know what's best for a woman, when you haven't bothered to ask what *she's* thinking, what *she's* feeling? This isn't the only place on earth that's dangerous. What if she's off in some eastern city and needs you?"

"Then I shall do my best to go to her, of course," he said stiffly. He touched a hand to his forage cap. "Now if you'll excuse me, I must return to my duties."

She stared after him, knotting her hands at her sides in frustration. He wouldn't listen to reason. He thought he was protecting Margery, when all he was doing was breaking her heart. Suddenly an idea came to her like a word whispered from an angel—or a devil, depending on the theology you subscribed to.

She hurried through the crowd, searching for Micah. She had a plan to teach the good major a lesson and maybe bring him and Margery together again in the process.

Chapter Sixteen

The ladies of the church had arranged for dinner on the ground after the service. After some discussion over what to feed the Indians, they'd decided that even a savage wouldn't say no to fried chicken and biscuits, with assorted vegetables and desserts on the side. From the looks of the heaping platters of food being passed around, Micah suspected half the chickens in the county had been sacrificed for the feast.

Midway through the meal, Sun Bear stood up and declared he wanted to make a speech. Everyone looked up from their chicken and eyed him curiously. "Of course, of course." Reverend Deering rose, beaming. "By all means, let our guest speak."

Micah didn't bother to tell him the chief intended to talk whether he had permission or not. He set aside his chicken leg and told Sun Bear he was ready to bring his words to his white hosts.

It was a good speech, in the Indian way. Sun Bear complimented the food, saying that for such a skinny, sickly looking bunch, the paleface women knew how to put on a feed. With a straight face, Micah translated this into suitably flowery praise.

Sun Bear said Crow-Man's speech had been interesting, and it seemed they all had some things in common. This custom of giving each other horses was a new one for them, but never let it be said his people couldn't learn new customs, especially when they involved free livestock.

Reverend Deering had a confused look on his face. The chief's interpretation of the sermon was probably not quite what he'd intended to get across.

Sun Bear wound up by asking the whites to be guests at his camp next full moon. The women would cook up some buffalo and prairie dog stew, and they'd pass around the pipe and trade stories.

Micah relayed the invitation, leaving out specifics about the menu. The men and women of Pony Springs traded uncomfortable expressions. Inviting the Indians onto their territory was one thing, but visiting the reservation was something else altogether. It would be interesting to see how Reverend Deering would smooth over this one.

But Micah wouldn't be around to find out about that, would he?

Sun Bear sat down to a smattering of polite applause. Micah looked at his chicken. He'd lost his appetite. Maybe he should go ahead and leave now, while everyone was occupied. No one would notice.

He circled around the chapel, intending to cross the pasture and work his way back to the barn. But he hadn't gone far before Tessa hurried up to meet him. "I need your help, quickly," she said.

"What is it?" Her face was flushed, and she looked as if she'd been running. Alarmed, he grabbed her by the shoulders. "Is something wrong?"

She shook her head. "I need you to kidnap Margery."

"You need me to *what?*" He dropped his hands and stepped back.

"I know how we can get Alan to see what a mistake he's making. You just need to keep her from getting on that stage this afternoon and take her someplace secluded. I'll take care of the major."

Micah stared at her. "Isn't that what started them fighting in the first place?"

"This is different. I just want to get them together so they can talk things over."

"Do you know what the major will do when he sees Margery with me? Are you trying to get me shot?"

"That's even better." Her smile alarmed him. "Oh, I don't mean your getting shot. It won't come to that, I promise. But it won't hurt the major to have jealousy working on him as well as fear."

He folded his arms over his chest. "I won't do it."

"Micah, please!"

"Why not get someone else, then? One of the men from town?"

"Because I can trust you. And because I know Margery will go with you."

"What are you going to do while I'm kidnapping Margery?"

She grinned. "I'm going to be kidnapping the major."

Will sidled up to Deering, who was working his way among the Indians, smiling and shaking hands and prattling along in English they couldn't understand. As if sensing Will's presence, the Indians began to give the preacher a wide berth. Or maybe it was just the good reverend's overly eager expression that drove them away.

"You're supposed to be paying attention to Tessa," Will said abruptly.

Deering jumped, and put a hand to his heart. "Tessa? Oh, Mrs. Bright. Yes. Um, I was just getting to that, Lord."

"She'll make a fine wife, Deering. A real helpmate." That was a nice biblical word that ought to appeal to the preacher.

"Where is she, Lord?" Deering looked around the crowded gathering.

"Last I saw, she was headed into the trees over behind the horses."

Deering straightened his shoulders and brushed off his coat. He wore a determined look, as if he were preparing to deliver a sermon, or testify to a cranky unbeliever. Not exactly the face of a courting man, but perhaps Tessa could soften him up.

Will followed at a distance. He'd leave the couple alone as soon as he saw they were headed in the right direction. After all, he'd promised Tessa her privacy.

Deering found Tessa next to her wagon, which was backed up to the edge of the trees. "Oh, Reverend Deering!" She looked across the wagon bed at him, startled. Then she bent over and tugged at something on the ground.

"What are you doing back there?" Deering craned his head to see around the wagon. "Are you all right?"

"Just fine. Um, as long as you're here, could you help me with something?"

"Of course." He walked around the wagon toward her. About that time, Will spotted the man on the ground. An Army officer, judging by his blue coat and polished boots. He was bound and gagged and sending Tessa murderous looks.

"Major Finch!" Deering gasped. "What happened?" He bent and started to release the gag.

"Don't do that, Reverend." Tessa put a restraining hand on the preacher's arm. "It took me a quarter hour to get him trussed up properly. Could you just help me get him into the wagon?"

Deering stared at her, his mouth working, but no sound came out. "Mrs. Bright, I don't understand. Has the major done something wrong? Has he harmed you in some way?"

"Not exactly." She bent and took hold of the major's arm. "Now, if you'll just get his other arm, we'll settle him on those blankets in the back of the wagon."

Protesting all the while, Deering bent and helped her. Finch didn't make it easy on them. He dug in his heels and refused to budge.

"Can you get his legs, Reverend?" Tessa asked. "He's not cooperating."

"Mrs. Bright, you cannot be serious. We must untie him at once."

Holding back his laughter, Will moved forward and clamped his hands around Finch's ankles. The major's eyes widened, but he ceased his struggles.

"That's better." Tessa climbed into the back of the wagon. "Now, Reverend, if you'll just slide him forward. That's it. I'll put these blankets under his head. Is that comfortable, Major?"

The major's look would have singed a lesser woman. Tessa ignored him, climbed forward, and took the reins. "Thank you for your help, Reverend. I promise I'll explain it all later."

"Better go with her," Will whispered.

"I'm coming with you." Deering climbed onto the wagon seat beside her, while Will settled himself on the major's legs, just to make sure he didn't escape.

"Ask her how she managed to tie and gag a man twice her size," Will whispered as the wagon started forward.

"Mrs. Bright, how did you manage to overcome a man of the major's size and experience?" Deering asked.

She blushed. "I confess I waited until he went into the woods to—well, you know. And while his back was to me, I sort of lassoed him."

"Lassoed him?" Deering's own face was quite red by now.

"I tossed a rope over his shoulders and pulled it tight." She glanced back at her prone passenger. "Then I stuffed the gag in his mouth and tied his hands. Oh, and of course I buttoned his pants."

Deering made a choking noise. Will looked down. Sure enough, the major's trousers were neatly buttoned.

He shook with silent laughter. When had this wild streak grown in his demure little Tessa? He smiled. He guessed it was true; she had grown up and somehow he hadn't realized it.

"Where are we going?" Deering asked as the wagon bounced along a faint trail across the prairie.

"Somewhere private."

Will looked around, trying to get his bearings. They were following the creek, roughly to the west. They crossed an old buffalo wallow and headed for a low line of hills. Ah. He knew where he was now. A place he hadn't thought of for years.

He leaned forward to address Deering. *"Don't forget what I told you,"* he whispered.

The preacher cleared his throat and looked at Tessa. "That was very impressive back there, the way you dispatched the major," he said. "I mean, it's not something just anyone could have done . . . not, of course, that they would want to . . ." His voice trailed off, and he looked dismayed.

"Are you all right, Reverend?" Tessa glanced at him. "You look ill."

"I . . . I'm fine." He took a deep breath and squared his shoulders. "Dinner was delicious. I've always been partial to fried chicken."

"I'm glad you liked it. But I didn't make the chicken."

"Oh. Well, whatever you did make, I'm sure it was delicious as well."

Will sighed. Didn't the man know anything about women?

Tessa stopped the wagon in front of a log-fronted dugout half hidden in a hillside. "What is this?" Deering asked. "Why are we stopping?"

Tessa set the wagon brake and climbed down. "This is the dugout where my husband and I lived when we first married. We built the house closer to the road, so this has been abandoned for a while now. No one will bother us out here."

Will smiled. He had happy memories of those days, when he and Tessa were newlyweds. She'd made him feel like a young man then. He tapped Deering on the shoulder. *"Tessa needs a new husband to look after her,"* he said.

Deering nodded and scrambled down from the wagon.

Tessa knocked on the door to the dugout. It opened, and Micah Fox emerged. His shirt was torn and his hair had come undone. "What happened?" Tessa gasped.

"She didn't want to come with me at first. She finally calmed down when I told her this was all your idea."

"Who are you talking about?" Reverend Deering asked.

"What's he doing here?" Micah asked.

"I needed someone to help me with the major."

"Who else is with you?" Deering asked again.

"Margery is in there," Tessa said.

A strangled cry came from the back of the wagon, and the major began kicking at the wagon boards. Tessa and Micah rushed over and hauled him to the ground. "Calm down, Major, she's perfectly all right," Tessa said. "Reverend Deering, will you open the door, please?"

Deering held the door open, and Tessa and Micah shoved the major inside. "You can untie him after we're gone, Margery," Tessa called as she and Micah wedged a tree trunk against the door. "Now, you two talk things over. We'll be back in the morning."

Micah fitted a large rock against one end of the tree trunk. "This is crazy," he said.

"They've been avoiding each other for weeks," Tessa said. "All they really need is time to sit down and talk. They love each other, after all. They're intelligent people. I'm convinced they can work this out."

"And if they don't?" Micah asked.

She shrugged. "We'll come back in the morning and let them out. The major won't speak to me, but I doubt if he'll tell anyone what happened."

Micah nodded. "He'll be too embarrassed." He

helped Tessa into the wagon and climbed up beside her. Deering took a seat in the back. "What about his men?" Micah asked. "Won't they wonder about him?"

"I left a note for Lieutenant Hamilton. It says he's taken a day of personal leave to work things out with his wife."

Deering had been silent, a dazed look on his face as he listened to them. Will nudged him. *"Remember what you're supposed to do."*

"Oh. Yes." Deering cleared his throat. "All this talk of marriage has made me think."

Micah and Tessa both turned, questioning looks on their faces. "About what?" Tessa asked.

"A woman like you, Mrs. Bright, young, beautiful, with a ranch to run. Well, you need a husband."

Tessa stared at him. Micah glowered, knotting the reins in his hands.

"This concern has been on my mind for ... for a while now," Deering continued. "And after much prayer it has come to me that the solution is ..."

"Yes?" Tessa asked.

"What?" Micah growled.

"Well, for you and Mr. Fox to marry, of course." Deering smiled, clearly pleased with himself. "It's obvious you're fond of one another and you work well together. I'd say it's a match made in Heaven."

Will couldn't believe it. Of all the men he could have chosen for Tessa, he'd selected an idiot! He groaned and left in disgust.

Tessa stared at Reverend Deering. She couldn't have heard him right. Marry Micah? The words made her heart race, though whether from elation or panic, she couldn't be certain. She risked glancing at Micah. He looked as stunned as she felt.

"You think about it," the preacher said. "I'll be happy to perform the ceremony whenever you're ready. Now if you'll drop me off back at the chapel, I need to help with the cleanup."

They left him at the chapel and rode back to the ranch house in silence. More than once, Tessa opened her mouth to speak, but she could find no words to express her feelings. Maybe Micah didn't want to marry her. Maybe he was trying to find a way to tell her so. Maybe he was being sensible, realizing it could never work out.

Ahead of them, the setting sun painted the sky with streaks of pink and umber. Was Reverend Deering right? Were she and Micah a match made in Heaven?

If only she knew how Micah felt about all this! Out of the corner of her eye, she watched his impassive face. He stared straight ahead, as if the wheel horse's hind end was suddenly the most fascinating sight he'd ever come across.

Why didn't he say anything?

He halted the wagon by the barn, and she leapt to the ground before he could come around to help her down. If he didn't want to talk about it, she wasn't going to make him. She wasn't going to beg a marriage proposal out of him. Not daring to glance his way, she raced to the house and up the stairs.

Fumbling with the hooks on her dress, she thought of what a long time had passed since she'd put it on this morning. Not so much physical time, but she felt as if she'd lived years in the space of a day. What had possessed her to tell wild tales to Indians one moment and to kidnap an Army major the next?

She folded her dress over a chair, then sat on the side of the bed. What were Margery and Major Finch doing right now? She knew what she'd be up to if she and Micah were alone in that dugout.

She stood and walked to the dresser and began to remove the pins in her hair. A sad-eyed woman stared back at her from the mirror, a woman in the prime of her life who today had decided to stop waiting for others to act and instead had taken action herself.

She glanced out the window, at the last pink light of sunset. The time for action wasn't over yet. Maybe Reverend Deering was right. Maybe she and Micah were meant to be together, but like Margery and the major, they were both too stubborn to admit it.

She laid the brush aside, then went to the washbasin and filled it with water from the pitcher. Tonight, before it was too late, she would go to Micah and find out once and for all if they had a chance together.

Micah parked the buggy and fed and watered the horses. Then he spread his bedroll out on his bunk. It was too late to set out now. He'd have to wait for first light and leave then.

He stripped off his shirt and lay back against the blankets. It was too early for sleep, but the tension of the day had drained him. He smiled, remembering Sun Bear's speech, Reverend Deering's sermon, and the look on Margery's face when he told her he intended to abduct her. But he couldn't keep his thoughts away from Tessa for long. He'd waited for her to say what she thought of Deering's advice, but she'd ignored it, as if it was too far from possible to deserve her consideration.

Well, he knew that, didn't he? A respectable woman couldn't marry a half-breed, any more than a half-breed could ever be accepted by people in a town like Pony Springs. That was the way of the world, and there was nothing he could do about it.

On this bitter thought he fell asleep, though his dreams were filled with images of Tessa, all of them pleasant.

He opened his eyes and saw Tessa standing before him. Silver moonlight flooded the room, silhouetting her figure and making her gown but a diaphanous veil caressing her feminine curves.

He smiled at this dream and reached for her, determined to enjoy in sleep what he could not have in real life. Her hand touched his, trembling. He raised the fluttering fingers to his lips and caressed each one, soothing her as he would soothe a nervous colt.

Her skin was soft, even the calluses from hard work seeming delicate in his large hand. He kissed the tip of her forefinger, then drew it into his mouth, savoring the taste of her, the delicate scent of her skin.

A breathy moan escaped her lips, and he raised his eyes to hers. "Micah," she whispered. With a jolt, he realized he was not dreaming.

Slowly, reluctantly, he drew away from her. "What are you doing here?" he asked.

"I came because I feared you wouldn't come to me." Her voice strengthened, and her expression grew more determined. "I want to be with you, Micah. Tonight. All night."

The words stopped his heart. He would not insult her by asking if she was sure. Her eyes told him she had never been more sure. He took her hand again and drew her to him, pressing her against the length of him, savoring the feel of her in his arms, never wanting to let her go.

But holding was not enough for her. She dipped her head and kissed his shoulder, feathering moist kisses all along his collarbone, down his chest to suckle at the erect nub of his nipple. He buried his hands in her hair and held her there, until the force of his pleasure was close to pain. Then he swept her into his arms and carried her to his bed.

He sat her down on the side of the bunk and began to unfasten the buttons at the top of her gown. She put her hands up to help, but he pushed them away. "I've wanted to do this for too long to be denied the pleasure," he said as he peeled the fabric away from one full breast.

Moonlight blanched her skin to silvery cream. He weighed the fullness of her in his palm, then traced his thumb across the taut pink tip. She jerked, a spasm that shook the bed, and he smiled. "I've not forgotten how sweet these are," he murmured and began to kiss and suckle each breast in turn.

The gown in a puddle around her waist, he lavished attention on her breasts until she moaned and writhed in his arms. Still holding her close, he pushed the gown up over her thighs and curled her legs around him, so that the damp curls at the juncture of her thighs brushed against his stomach. "When you first came in, I thought I was dreaming," he said. "But no dream could be this sweet." He kissed her, long and deep, as if their tongues could say in this way everything that couldn't be expressed within the limitations of spoken words.

Breathless, they broke apart. "Take your clothes off," she whispered. "Please."

The plea was almost his undoing. He moved out of her arms and stripped his trousers off in one swift motion. He stood in the beam of moonlight, letting her look at him, his arousal straining toward her.

Her laughter was joy distilled, and he felt an answering laughter bubbling within him. He bent, tugged at the gown bunched around her waist, and sent it sailing over his shoulder. Then she held out her arms, and he fell onto the bed beside her, rolling her over on top of him.

Her eyes widened in surprise as he hugged her close. "What are you doing?" she whispered.

"The bed's so narrow and I'm so much bigger than you, I think it'll be more comfortable this way." He put his hands on her hips and adjusted her so that she straddled his thighs, his arousal straining against her. The pleasure was near pain, but he struggled to restrain himself, wanting to love her slowly—to make her half mad with passion, forgetting every other time she had ever made love, wanting her to think only of him.

"I . . . I've never done it this way," she admitted.

He grinned. "Good." He raised his head and took the tip of her breast in his mouth once more, eliciting a gasp of pleasure.

He used every skill he possessed to arouse her to the fullest, and watched her face as he worked, reveling in the emotions he saw there—love and wonder and a desperate longing he wanted more than anything to satisfy. She moaned and strained against him, until he feared he might lose control altogether. Only then did he grasp her hips and nudge her away from him.

Chapter Seventeen

Tessa started to protest his pushing her away, but Micah calmed her with a smile and pulled her close once more. She knew what he wanted now and adjusted her position so that he glided easily inside her. A sigh escaped her as he filled her. She had craved this closeness, this physical and spiritual oneness, for far too long.

She looked down into his eyes, letting her hair fall like drapery around them, and hugged him tightly with her thighs. This unfamiliar feeling of being in control of their loving both thrilled and disturbed her. "Now what do I do?" she whispered.

"You ride." He rocked beneath her, sinking deeper within her. The movement sent shock waves of sensation through her, calling forth an instinct to move with him in a slow, seductive dance that gained speed as passion and need increased. She braced herself against his chest, fanning her fingers across hard, sweat-slicked muscles.

She could feel the pressure building within her, near to overflowing. If only she could make this ecstasy linger. Raising up on her knees, she experimented with pulling away from him. His hands gripped her hips to draw her back down, his eyes mirroring the pleasure she felt.

"You're a fast learner," he said. "Now I'll teach you something else." He moved his hand from one hip and slid it across her thigh to cover her crisp brown curls. She gasped as his thumb delved there, sending spasms of pleasure through her, spasms that rocked them both.

They rode in earnest then, from walk to lope to gallop.

Her release shook her like a jolt of thunder, reverberating through her in waves. She saw her own joy reflected in his face, and then he bucked beneath her, the sensation rocketing through her, leaving them both empty and fulfilled, too spent to move or speak.

Tessa dozed with her head on Micah's shoulder, his strong arms encircling her, forestalling all danger of her slipping off the narrow bunk. Even in sleep, she knew she smiled. Happiness filled her like the scent of a sweet perfume, seeping out of every pore.

Then she heard it, the sound that had pulled her from her slumber: a noise like a gunshot, somewhere nearby. She raised her head, straining her ears to listen. There they were again. Three shots, close together. A distress signal. "Micah, wake up!" She shook him.

Something in her voice must have alerted him. He sat up beside her, still holding her close. "What is it?"

"Gunfire. Someone's trying to summon help." She reached for her gown, which lay in a tangle on the floor beside the bunk. "I'll go get dressed. You saddle two horses. We'll travel faster on horseback."

She raced to the house and wasted no time pulling on clothes and shoes. By the time she returned to the barn, he had saddled two horses and lit a lantern. The gunshots still sounded at regular intervals.

Soon they no longer needed the gunfire to guide them. The acrid scent of smoke blew from the east, a burning tar and wood smell that sent a wave of fear through her. She urged her horse into a jarring trot.

They saw the first flames long before they reached the

chapel. Set on the rise as it was, it was visible from a long distance away. Tongues of fire licked the roof beams and engulfed the wooden cross just outside the door. Half a dozen people had formed a bucket chain from the creek. Micah and Tessa raced to join them.

"What happened?" Tessa asked the woman in front of her in line. "Who found it?"

"The preacher was asleep inside," she said. "Luckily the smoke woke him. We were on the way home from visitin' my sister when we heard his cries for help."

Tessa passed the full bucket and paused to stare up at the outline of the church against the night sky. The tar-paper roof had already burned away, leaving the roof beams sticking out like ribs from atop the charring walls.

A boy of about ten came over, a pistol in his hand. "I'm out of bullets, Papa," he said.

"That's all right, son," a tall, bearded man said. "I think we've done about all we can here."

"Go watch your little brothers," a woman admonished. "See that they don't get too close to the fire."

"Yes, Mama." The boy turned away.

"It's gettin' away from us," another man agreed.

"We'd better see to keeping it from spreading," one of the women said.

The men stripped blankets from the horses and wet them in the creek, then dragged the sodden wool around and around the burning building. The heat was more intense now, as the whole chapel glowed with flame, and the smell of cinders brought tears to Tessa's eyes.

She found Reverend Deering on his knees under a tree, staring at the collapsing building. She knelt in front of him, hoping to distract him from that horrible vision. "How do you think it started?" she asked.

He shook his head. "I walked around the yard myself before I retired, to make sure all the campfires were doused."

"It wasn't a campfire," Tessa said. "That would have started outside the chapel. There's nothing burnt but the building." She reached out and clasped his arm. "Thank God you woke in time to save yourself."

He shook his head. "I was sound asleep when I heard knocking and someone yelling for me to leave."

"But the woman back there told me you found the fire—and that you shouted for help."

"I did. When I woke up, I could smell the smoke. I searched, but there was no one there." He nodded. "I believe the Lord saved me."

Tessa thought of Will. Had he been the one to save Reverend Deering?

A cry went up from the crowd. She turned in time to see one of the walls collapse in a shower of sparks. She shuddered and brushed ash from her hair. Who would have wanted to burn this place—and why? She turned back to the preacher. "Did you see anything else, hear anything else, that might point to who did this?"

He shook his head. "It was such a pleasant night out. We had a little bit of a breeze after the heat of the day, and I could even smell flowers."

She sighed and patted his hand. The poor man had obviously been caught up in fantasy. The flowers that bloomed at this dry time of year had little fragrance.

Will watched the fire from a distance. He'd come upon it just as the first smoke was curling up from the roof and rushed to wake the preacher before he smothered to death. Then he'd taken off after the rider he'd seen fleeing the scene, but he'd lost him in the darkness.

Tessa was kneeling in the dirt over there by the preacher. A few hours ago he might have tried to use that scene to his advantage, to bring the two of them together. But now he knew it was no use. Tessa had made her choice. He had no control over her anymore. As much as he regretted it, he was man enough to see that it was time to let her go.

The first wall collapsed in a great shower of sparks. The others would follow soon. In a few more hours, Deering's Indian chapel would be reduced to a pile of ashes. *He should build the next one of something more durable,* Will mused. *Stone and iron, the kind of things that lasted.*

A woman's scream rent the night, pulling Will away from his musings. He looked up to see one of the traveling women, the mother of the boy who had fired the gun, being restrained by two men. She was gesturing toward the fire and moaning about her baby.

Quick as lightning, another man shot out of the crowd. Will recognized Fox, his long hair streaming down his back. His shirt pulled up over his nose, Fox fought his way through smoke and cinders, searching for the child.

If Will had had breath in him anymore, he would have held it, as he was sure everyone else did, watching the man run over coals and through smoke, toward the child, who sat screaming amid a rain of sparks. Fox reached the boy and jerked him up into his arms, then started for the clearing.

The second wall of the chapel swayed, creaked, and began to fall, its collapse heralded by a gasp from the crowd, and a single woman's scream. "Micah!"

The coals felt hot even to Will, who had thought he would never feel warm again. Flames licked out at him, and he wondered if this was what it was like in hell. He tried to move faster, knowing he had only seconds to reach the man and the boy in his arms.

He slammed into Fox, knocking him to the ground. The wall collapsed around them, cinders sizzling as they hit Will's ghostly form, with a sound like bacon frying. Will draped himself over Fox and the boy, shielding them from the brunt of the flames. Fox tried to squirm free beneath them, and Will hit him hard with the flat of his hand. *"Lie still,"* he hissed.

He could feel the pounding of Fox's heart, that sign of life that held man and spirit together in one frail form. Oh, Fox was not frail by human standards. His corded muscles radiated the strength of a young man accustomed to hard work. But Will knew too well how fleeting such strength could be. Will had only to move back, and the fire would melt away all Fox's strength. A man Will had regarded as his enemy would be done away with, or at least badly injured.

The prospect held little temptation for him. Instead of moving back, he held himself more closely over Fox and the boy, as if he might merge his own restless spirit with the younger man and reclaim the vitality that had been denied him. He could almost feel what it would be like to be Micah Fox; he could feel it because he himself had once been not so very different from the man he sheltered now. He knew what it was like to struggle for acceptance in a place where you were different. He had not forgotten the healing to be found in the arms of a woman you loved, who loved you in return.

They lay together for a long while, until the worst of the flames subsided. The boy began to wail, and at last Will moved back. The air reeked of smoked earth and burnt cloth, and he saw that Fox's pants had been burned away below the knee, his flesh saved only by the tough leather of his boots.

Slowly Fox rose to his feet, the boy in his arms. He looked around, dazed, then walked out across the ashes, toward the boy's waiting mother, and Tessa's waiting arms.

Will turned away, weary. The ghostly body that had seemed so light before now sagged like lead. He needed rest, and quiet, and time alone.

Tessa did not try to speak to Micah right away. She merely wiped the soot from his face with a damp rag and brushed the ashes from his hair with her fingers. When everyone agreed they had done all they could, they mounted their horses and rode back to the ranch.

Reverend Deering had refused her offer to spend the night at the house. "I'm wide awake now," he said. "I'd rather ride into town and try to think."

Micah followed her into the house, to the kitchen, where she heated water and made tea, strong and full of sugar. The stench of smoke still stung her nose, and she wondered if it would ever leave her—the smell or the memory of seeing that wall fall to engulf Micah and the boy. How long had they lain there, surrounded by fire but not burning?

"Did you see what happened?" he asked after a long while.

She nodded. "I couldn't bear to watch, yet I couldn't keep from watching."

"Will was there—with me," he said.

Some part of her had known this. Perhaps in staring through the flames, she had glimpsed his form, sheltering Micah and the boy. "I think he saved the preacher, too," she whispered. She stared into her cup. "I guess this means he didn't push you off the roof that day."

"I don't think so." He paused, then added, "There's something else."

"What is that?"

"When we first arrived, before the whole building had started to burn, I noticed glass around the base of one corner, as if someone had bashed a lantern against the side to start the fire."

"Who would do something like that?" she asked.

"Someone who hates Deering. Or more likely, someone who hates Indians."

She reached for his hand. "I don't want to think about that tonight. I just want to go to bed."

"All right." He rose and moved toward the door.

She went to him and laid her head on his shoulder. "Don't leave me alone tonight. Please."

Wordlessly he took her hand and led her up the stairs. In her room, she lit the lamp, then turned and began to unbutton his scorched shirt.

When they had both stripped, she wrapped herself in a robe and took their clothes down to the back porch. She'd have to soak them in vinegar water to get the smell out. She was turning to go back inside when she spotted the zinc hip bath, hanging in its place on the wall. A bath would be wonderful.

She took the tub from its hook and ladled a bucket of

warm water from the boiler. Micah met her halfway down the stairs. The sight of him, standing naked on the landing, made her blush, even though she couldn't stop herself from looking at him. "I thought we might take a bath," she said, holding up the bucket.

He took the full bucket from her, and the tub as well. "That's the best idea I've heard in a while."

She went back to the kitchen for more water, then retrieved a pair of towels from the pantry shelf, along with the bar of lavender soap she'd left there to scent her linens.

When she returned to the bedroom, she found that Micah had lit a second lamp and filled the tub with the steaming water. She bent to arrange the towels and soap on a chair, and he slipped up behind her and began to unfasten her robe.

"Wait, my hair—" She reached up and fumbled with the pins.

"Your hair is beautiful." He deftly plucked the pins from the tangled locks and combed his fingers through the strands. "The bath's ready," he whispered, feathering a kiss alongside her temple.

He led her to the tub and lowered himself in first, then held up his arms to guide her to a seat between his knees. "Ahh, this feels good." He sighed, wrapping his arms beneath her breasts and pulling her closer.

She leaned back against him, reveling in the feel of his hard body pressed against her, the evidence of his desire straining between them. She ran her hands down his legs, delighting in the sensation of the wet, silky hairs against her palm.

His hands did not stay still for long either. They moved to cup her breasts, his thumbs idly brushing her nipples until she squirmed against him and gasped. "Micah, we're supposed to be taking a bath," she scolded, laughing.

"Of course."

His hands moved away, and at once she wanted them back, but he returned quickly with the pitcher from the washstand and the bar of soap. "Bend forward, and I'll wash your hair," he said.

She obediently bowed her head, and he sent a cascade of water over her. She closed her eyes and gave herself up to the luxury of his fingers massaging her scalp, enveloping her in a cloud of lavender-scented lather. He poured more pitchers of water until no trace of soap remained, and her hair lay against her skin like satin.

"That was wonderful," she said with a sigh.

"I don't intend to let the rest of you feel neglected." He took up the soap once more and coasted it along her shoulders, down her arms, and across her belly. Once more he gathered her breasts in his palms, kneading and massaging, until they were slick and soapy, the nipples extended and aching.

"Do you think they're clean enough?" she said, gasping.

"Maybe. But what about the rest of you?" He slid his hands down her belly, ripples of arousal following in his wake. He moved down, soaping her thighs, lavishing attention on the nest of curls between her legs. She writhed against him, sending water sloshing out of the tub.

He loosened his hold on her for a moment as he reached for the pitcher again. As more water cascaded over the side of the tub, she rolled over on her stomach to face him.

"My turn," she said, with a wicked grin.

His eyes sparked with desire, and he threw up his hands in surrender. "I'm all yours."

She took her time with the soap, lathering every inch of him, beginning at the toes. She reveled in the taut slickness of his wet skin beneath her caressing fingers and acquainted herself with every curve and bump of his body. The muscles of his thigh jumped as she skated her palms over them. When she began to lather his erection, he groaned and sank further into the water, eyes half closed.

Kneeling between his legs now, she soaped the flat

plains of his stomach and traced the muscles of his chest. His flat brown nipples pebbled beneath her palm, and she squeezed her thighs together tightly against the growing ache within her.

When he reached out and pulled her near, she did not protest, pressing herself full-length against him, enjoying the easy slip and slide of their wet bodies together. He captured her mouth in a devouring kiss and continued to kiss her as he lay back and ducked his head under, causing her to jerk away, squealing and laughing.

He raised up and smoothed back his wet hair, water streaming off of him, drops glittering in the lamplight. "You still have some soap right . . . there." Grinning, he flicked his fingers at her nipple. "Better make sure it's well rinsed," he said, just before he leaned forward and took it into his mouth.

On her knees in the tub, Tessa scarcely felt the hard tin bottom or the now cool water, or anything but Micah's warm mouth on her, caressing each breast in turn, with dizzying effect. She arched her body toward him, eager to be even closer.

He obliged by pulling her tightly against him. "Wrap your legs around my waist," he murmured.

She did as he instructed, his erection captured between her thighs, rubbing against her with each movement of his body. Still holding her close, he stood and stepped out of the tub, trailing water over to the bed, where he set her bottom on the edge of the high mattress.

Drawing back a little, he smoothly entered her. His hands clasped her buttocks and drew her tightly against him once more.

She twined her fingers in his hair and pressed her forehead against his chest, lost in the trembling waves that coursed through her body with each thrusting movement. A low cry rose up somewhere from deep inside her, an animal sound that both frightened and thrilled her. Micah had unleashed this other side of her, a primitive, passionate nature she never knew existed. With each jarring thrust, she felt closer to some elemental core of her being, some secret rapture never before revealed.

Their thrusting grew more rapid, almost violent. Her release shook her as sensation burst forth in one shattering moment. Her senses slowly returned to normal, and she discovered she was sobbing, clinging to Micah and crying like a child.

Tessa swore she was crying for delight, but as he held her, listening to her sobs subside, Micah wondered if some part of her didn't sense that he had meant this last time together as a way to say good-bye.

He could still smell smoke, a scent of death and hatred. Hate had set the fire that burned the chapel, the kind of hate that couldn't be ignored or avoided. He'd seen that brand of evil before, in the eyes of white men who saw the Indians as vermin to be destroyed.

Men like that didn't differentiate between Indians on reservations or in the wild, or between a half-breed living as a white man and a full-blood warrior. They had burned Deering's chapel this time; what if next time they burned Tessa's home?

He shuddered, remembering the feel of the flames licking all around him, and the icy sensation of Will at his back. Tessa's husband had saved his life; now Micah had to make a sacrifice of his own. No matter how much he loved Tessa, he wouldn't stay here and expose her to the gossip and maliciousness of her neighbors.

She'd spent too many years alone already, without family or friends, with only Will for company. In the end, even he had to leave her. Micah wouldn't see her punished that way for loving him.

He smoothed his hand over her drying hair and inhaled deeply the lavender scent of it. He wanted to fix the memory of this moment in his mind, like Tessa's perfect summer day she'd wanted to bottle. In years to come, when times were hard, he would have this moment to take out and relive. He'd remember what it was like to be loved this much.

Chapter
Eighteen

Tessa had heard people talk of women glowing. Brides supposedly glowed, as did expectant mothers. She'd never been sure what the expression meant until the next morning when she woke. She felt warm and filled with light, as if a candle burned somewhere within her. She woke smiling and felt as if she couldn't wipe the expression from her lips if she tried.

She rolled over, reaching for Micah, but found only the empty pillow, still warm from his head. The unexpected emptiness startled her, but reassurance came quickly. He'd probably just gone down to feed the horses, leaving her to sleep in, undisturbed.

Wanting to repay this thoughtfulness with some kindness of her own, she dressed quickly and went downstairs to make coffee. When it was done, she poured two cups and carried them out to the barn.

The Morgan gelding leaned over its stall and neighed in greeting, then kicked the boards as if impatient for breakfast. Surprised, Tessa glanced over into the hayrack. Empty. Fear flickered up her spine, but she quickly stamped it out. Perhaps Micah planned to turn the horses out to pasture shortly.

Her gaze automatically moved to the place where he kept his saddle. The sight of the empty rack took her breath. *He's just out for a morning ride,* she told herself. *Maybe he even rode out to check on the fire.*

Determined to believe this, she found herself nonetheless headed toward the tackroom, seeking the reassurance of the sight of his possessions arranged around the room.

The neatly made bunk looked no different. An old harness rested beside the bunk, ready for repair. The books she'd loaned him were stacked on a crate, along with an old oil lamp and a neat tower of gold coins.

When she saw the money, she gasped and began to shake so violently the coffee sloshed onto the floor, splattering her boots. Setting the cup aside, she rushed forward and gathered up the coins, counting and recounting them. A hundred dollars. Twice the price she could expect to get for one of her horses.

She turned and stumbled toward the stalls. Racing past each open door, she counted, then ran to the corral. She didn't have to do more than glance at the horses milling there to know that Pigeon, Micah's favorite, was missing.

She clenched the coins in her hand, the money burning into her skin. The pain stabbed her as she closed her eyes, and images of last night rose to taunt her: Micah's hand, dark against the paleness of her breast; his hair falling like a thick curtain around her; his face, flushed with passion at the moment of climax. He had loved her so completely and yet left her without so much as a note of explanation.

"Nooo!" The keening wail tore from her throat as she hurled the coins over the fence, into the dust and straw and manure of the corral. She started back toward the barn, intending to saddle a horse and ride after him, but she stopped before she even pulled open the door. She wouldn't stoop to go after a man who didn't want her.

She wouldn't risk seeing rejection in his eyes or hearing from his own lips that their time together had meant nothing.

Blindly she set about feeding and watering the horses. She would go on. The daily chores of looking after the animals, cooking and cleaning, sewing and harvesting, did not wait for grief to heal or pain to dull.

As she worked, she made a list of things to do, tasks to fill the time before she had to face her empty bed again. If she had a choice, she would work through the night, anything to avoid those dark hours when she knew from experience the pain would cut the deepest.

She emptied a feed bucket and pulled her mind back to her mental list. The Library Society meeting was this morning. She'd need to arrange her hair and dress to drive into town. Perhaps Margery would come to visit this afternoon . . .

The feed bucket clanged and bounced across the dirt when she dropped it. Margery! She and Major Finch were no doubt cursing her soundly for failing to retrieve them from their prison as promised.

She hurried to the house and collected the makings of a cold breakfast—bread and cheese and jam—as well as the coffeepot, which she wrapped in a towel to keep warm and stuck in the basket with the food. She stowed this in the wagon, then hitched the horses and set out, driving as fast as she dared toward the old dugout.

The log was still in place in front of the door. Tessa reined the horses to a halt and listened, expecting angry cries, but the cabin sat silent. Setting the brake, she climbed down and listened at the door. At first she heard nothing, then she detected the low murmur of a man's voice and a woman's answering giggle.

She dragged the log away from the door, then knocked. "Margery? Major Finch? It's me, Tessa."

She was about to knock again when the door opened slightly. Major Finch stood before her, dressed only in trousers, his hair disheveled. "We're not, um, ready just yet." He glanced over his shoulder. In the dim light,

Tessa thought she saw Margery sitting up in bed, swathed in a sheet.

"Tell her to leave the food and come back tomorrow," Margery called, laughing.

"I've brought breakfast." Tessa forced a smile, relieved to see that at least someone's love affair was going well.

Major Finch returned the smile. "I confess I have worked up an appetite. Give us a minute." He shut the door gently, and Tessa retreated to the wagon to wait.

She studied the dugout, which each year seemed to melt further into the hillside. When she'd first seen it, she'd been dismayed at the thought of living in little better than a hole in the ground. But with the resilience of youth, she'd made the hovel a home. She'd fought off loneliness and despair with the reminder that she had Will; that was all that mattered. In those halcyon days, she'd never imagined she would end up alone.

She looked up as the door to the cabin opened. Major Finch and Margery emerged, fully dressed, faces wreathed in smiles. "I'm glad to see you both looking so well," Tessa said.

The major glanced at Margery. "We ought to be angry with you for tricking us this way."

"But we aren't," Margery said, shaking her head.

Tessa took the basket of food from the front of the wagon and unpacked it on the tailgate. She served cheese sandwiches and coffee, while the lovers exchanged long glances and smiles. She felt she could have driven off, and neither of them would have noticed until some time later. "I'm glad to see you've worked out your differences," she said.

Margery nodded. "We've had a long talk, and I understand now that Alan was really just afraid of losing me." She reached up and caressed his shoulder while a red flush crept up his neck. "And he knows now that I just want to feel important to him."

He took her hand and kissed the knuckles, tenderness

filling his eyes. "We've agreed to take time for each other every day from now on."

Tessa looked down, fighting tears. Her friends' happiness made her own misery that much sharper, as if she were seeing acted out before her all that might have been, if only—

"Tessa? Is something wrong?"

She shook her head, even as tears rolled down her cheeks. "I . . . I'm fine," she stammered, even though everything about her betrayed her lie.

"What is it?" Margery's voice rose in alarm. "Where's Micah?" She looked around. "Why isn't he with you?"

"He . . . he left." She had to squeeze the words past a knot in her throat. Just saying them was like facing the reality of his leaving for the first time all over again.

"Oh, honey!" Margery gathered her close, wrapping her arms around her like a mother comforting a small child. It took all of Tessa's self-control not to dissolve into sobs.

The major looked on, his face bearing the tortured expression of a strong man faced with a situation he could not handle. "Do you want me to go after him? I'd be happy to give him a taste of his own medicine, so to speak. After all, I feel I owe you both for bringing Margery and me back together."

Tessa tried to stem the tide of tears with her fingers pressed against her eyes. "No, thank you." She attempted a smile and failed. "It's kind of you to offer, though."

Margery patted her shoulder. "Let Alan drive you back to the ranch so you can rest."

"I don't need rest," she said, though she suddenly felt as if she were dragging the weight of a whole building behind her. But the thought of climbing into bed again terrified her. It would be too easy to pull up the covers and never come out to face the world again.

She allowed Alan to help her into the wagon. Margery climbed up to sit between her and the major. "The Library Society meeting is today," Tessa said once they were on their way.

"I'd forgotten all about it." Margery gave the major a sly smile. "I suppose I've had other things on my mind."

"They're going to finalize the plans today." Tessa sniffed and her skirt. "For the board and the building."

"Are you going to go?" Margery asked.

She nodded. "Yes. I think it would be good . . . to get out of the house."

Margery patted her hand. "Of course. I'll come with you."

"You don't have to do that," Tessa said. "Stay with the major. I know it's what you really want."

"Yes, it's what I want. But I also want to help Alan with his career. If that means smiling and making small talk with the town dames, so be it."

"You'll have them all eating out of the palm of your hand." The major patted her knee. She leaned across and kissed him on the cheek.

Tessa felt her heart pinch. Would she ever know that kind of comfortable, familiar love again—the kind that comes from knowing a person for years, knowing him inside and out, through shared experiences and goals?

"If you'll lend me a horse to ride to the fort, I'll return for Margery this afternoon," the major said.

"Of course."

He saddled a gray gelding and departed with a kiss for Margery and a tip of his hat to Tessa. When he was out of sight, Margery turned to Tessa again. "Out with the whole story. You don't have to be strong with me. Heaven knows, I've cried on your shoulder enough. It's time for me to return the favor."

Somehow the tears came easier now, providing an unexpected release. When she could find words, she told Margery about waking alone after a wonderful night with Micah and finding the stack of gold coins in the barn. "Why couldn't he at least have left me a note?" she asked.

Margery shook her head. "He probably did this out of some noble, misplaced idea of love. He wanted to protect you from something, or save you the trouble of something else. Just like Alan thought he could protect me by sending me away. Men can be so foolish."

"And yet we still love them," Tessa said through a fresh flood of tears.

Margery gathered her close again, rocking her back and forth. "Yes, we do love them," she whispered. "Yes, we do."

Tessa's tears were like salt in a wound to Will, stinging him with every drop. He circled around her, searching his mind for some way to distract her. To comfort her.

But in the end, he knew he didn't have that power in him. It was Micah Fox she wanted. Fox she needed.

Last night, lying there with Fox as the fire raged over them, he'd realized a new respect for the man. They had more in common than he'd wanted to admit at first. They were both stubborn, refusing to back down. And they'd both won Tessa's love, in spite of their flaws.

He stared at her, feeling a tightness in his throat—an urge to cry and rage at God for bringing them to this impasse. In all the time since his death, he'd been accepting of his fate, grateful that at least he'd been allowed this in-between state of being, so that he had not left the life he loved, and the woman he loved, entirely.

Now he only cursed his helplessness. If only he could help Tessa. But he was tired. So tired.

The Library Society assembled in the home of Trudy Babcock. Tessa and Margery joined the others in the parlor, balancing china cups of tea and plates of delicate petit fours, exchanging small talk with the other women in a ritual Tessa suddenly found unbearably boring.

Reverend Deering entered the room shortly before the meeting was to begin. He wore the same rumpled suit he'd had on the day before, the smell of smoke still lingering about him. He'd combed his hair, but haphazardly, as if he'd managed without a mirror. Despite this carelessness and the weariness he must have felt, his eyes were alive with purpose.

He walked to the front of the room and cleared his throat. "I'd like to address this group for a moment, if I may," he said.

"By all means, Reverend," Trudy said. She settled into a chair nearby and gave him an encouraging nod.

He looked out over them and folded his hands behind his back as if about to give his Sunday sermon. "As most of you know by now, the chapel I built for the Indians burned last night."

A murmur rose up among the women. Some of them had not yet heard the news, and they were filled with questions.

Deering waited for silence. "There has been some discussion that it may have been burned by vandals," he continued. "Whatever hand set the fire, I see it now as a message from God."

More discussion among the ladies. Tessa smiled in spite of her grief. Only Deering would see this awful thing as a sign of direction.

"I came here because I felt a call to work as a missionary to the Indians." He captured their attention once more. "I realize now that I was attempting to wade into the river without getting my feet wet, so to speak. I expected the Indians to come to me to hear the message in the way I wanted to present it. I now know that a missionary is charged to go into the world, in this case the world of the Indians, and to bring the message to them in a way that will be meaningful to them.

"Therefore, as of today, I am resigning my position as pastor of the Pony Springs church. I've already spoken to Robert Neighbors, who oversees the Indian reservations, about working as chaplain there. I hope you will understand why I have done this."

The women raised their voices in protest and confusion. Tessa remained silent, nodding to herself. Despite everything that had happened, she couldn't help but feel that this was right. Reverend Deering had made some mistakes, but he was committed to his work. He would help the Indians all he could. They, in turn, would teach him.

"I'm sorry I can't stay and visit longer, ladies, but I must be going. I have much to do to prepare for my new work." He bid them farewell and departed, leaving much lively discussion in his wake.

Mrs. Drake rose and raised her hands for their attention. "I believe we should get started," she directed. "Mrs. Tucker, would you present the treasurer's report?"

Mamie Tucker stood and read from the sheet of paper in her hand. "As of August tenth, we had collected four hundred and sixteen dollars in cash and a number of books donated from citizens' personal collections."

Applause greeted this news. Mrs. Tucker smiled and sat down.

"Now we'll have a report from the building committee," Mrs. Drake said. "Mrs. Babcock?"

Trudy perched a pair of half glasses on her nose and reviewed her notes. "In preparation for building, we have decided to appoint a board to oversee operation of the library," she said. "Various citizens, including our most generous donor, Mr. Hardy, have agreed to serve." With a stern look, she quelled the murmurs that greeted this news. "But we'll also need two members from this group," she concluded.

Margery's hand shot up. "I nominate Tessa Bright to serve on the new library board."

Trudy looked as if she'd just swallowed half a bottle of Hostetter's Stomach Bitters. "I don't believe that would be appropriate."

Ammie Smith raised her hand. "I second the nomination."

Tessa looked around, flustered. "I really don't—"

"Hush." Margery took her hand and squeezed it. "You'd be perfect for the job."

Trudy raised her head and regarded Tessa as if she were a particularly disagreeable child. "Board members must set a fine example for the community," she lectured. "They should be of exceptional moral character, unquestionable loyalty, and impeccable reputation."

Margery rose, her gaze pinning Trudy with a frightening intensity. "Are you saying Mr. Hardy meets those qualifications and Tessa doesn't?"

Trudy frowned. "Mrs. Bright is a single woman. She must naturally be held to a higher standard."

"In the time I've known her, she has been one of the most giving, hardworking, caring people I've ever met," Margery declared.

The lines etched on Trudy's forehead deepened. "I'm not surprised someone like you would be taken in by such a shallow thing as appearances. Even Reverend Deering has apparently mistaken youth and beauty for character. *I* know better, however." Face dark with ill-concealed hatred, she turned to Tessa once more. "Ever since you came to town, you've been pulling the wool over people's eyes. I won't allow it to go on any longer. You are carrying on an illicit relationship with that half-breed who works for you."

A gasp rose up from the assembled women, followed by a buzz of conversation.

"If you are referring to Mr. Fox—" Margery began.

"I don't care to know his name," Trudy said softly. "He is a half-breed vagrant from the lowest level of society. I could never condone—"

Tessa rose, her heart pounding, and faced the older woman. Her knees shook beneath her skirts from a mixture of fear and sheer rage. "Are you saying if I discontinued my relationship with Mr. Fox, I'd be welcome to serve on your board?" she asked.

Trudy's expression did not waver. "That would be one condition before we could give serious consideration to your nomination."

Tessa nodded. She turned and looked out over the room. Margery still stood, her eyes full of sympathy for her friend. Ammie Smith clenched her hands in her lap, her cheeks bright pink with feeling. Some of the women looked away, ashamed, while others met her gaze with looks of righteous indignation.

''When I was first invited to join this group, I was flattered.'' Tessa's voice shook, but she made herself go on. ''I wanted to be just like all of you, involved, part of the community, with friends all around me.'' She swallowed hard and continued. ''For years I felt excluded because of things I'd done or who I was. So I was grateful to have another chance.'' Her gaze settled on Margery. Dear Margery, who nodded encouragingly and gave her the strength to continue. ''Now that you've let me in, now that you've made me one of you, I can't imagine what the attraction was.''

She gathered her skirts and walked out of the room, head high, tears blurring her vision. It didn't matter. She didn't care to see in their eyes what they thought of her now. She had lost Will. She had lost Micah. She had lost everything that mattered to her. The opinion of these women was the least of her concerns.

Chapter
Nineteen

Will had never been to Jackie Babcock's house, but he had no trouble finding it now. The four-room frame structure sat in a grove of trees behind the blacksmith's shop, a white gravel path leading up to the door.

Will waited until the last of the women had left the Library Society meeting, then went around back to a yard littered with scrap iron and broken pots and half a dozen unfinished projects. Babcock's attempt at an ornamental gate was there, its animals resembling primitive pictographs, thick and awkward. He smiled as he passed it. Poor Jackie. He should stick to making plow blades.

The wash pots were back here, too, bubbling over a split oak fire. His smile broadened, and he concentrated on making himself appear. Then, whistling under his breath, he followed the scent of Jasmine Nights up the steps and into the kitchen.

Trudy Babcock stood with her back to the door, bent over a scrub board and a wooden tub. "Trudy Babcock," Will said in his most forbidding tone, "I want a word with you."

She squeaked and whirled to face him, flinging soapsuds from her hands. She wore a stained gray wrapper, her hair covered with a black kerchief. "Who are you?" she demanded. "What are you doing in my house?"

Will ignored the question. He walked to the washtub and fished out a pair of trousers. "Isn't this an odd time to be doing the wash?" he asked.

"I was busy earlier today, hosting the Library Society meeting." She straightened. "It's no business of yours, anyway. Get out of here before I call my husband."

"Perhaps I was drawn here by the scent of your perfume. What is it called again?"

She looked confused. "Jasmine Nights." She raised her chin. "It's imported. Very expensive."

"Is that so? The way you wear it, you must spend a fortune." He brought the dripping trousers up to his nose and made a face. They reeked of kerosene and smoke. "Smells like something burning," he observed.

Her face paled, but she quickly regained her indignant expression. "My husband is a blacksmith. His clothes always smell of the forge."

"That's right. Your husband is a blacksmith, isn't he?" He let the wet trousers slide back into the tub. "Or what passes for one, in any case."

"How dare you come into my home and insult me!" she shouted.

Will struck a casual pose against a kitchen chair. He hadn't anticipated how much fun this would be. "I hear Will Bright was a much better smithy than your husband."

The remark had a spectacular effect on Trudy. Her face blanched white, then bloomed bright red. She clenched her fists at her sides and seemed ready to lift off the ground with the force of her rage. "Will Bright was a fraud!" she shouted. "He made all those fancy things people had no use for. My husband is a proper blacksmith. He makes good, serviceable—"

Will studied his nails. "Will Bright made that gate, didn't he?"

For a moment, he worried he had sent her into apoplexy. She shook her fists at him. "That gate! All I've heard about for the past month is that gate! Every time people drive out to Tessa Bright's ranch to work on that worthless Indian chapel, they come back talking about that gate." Her voice rose to a mocking simper. " 'Oh, isn't that a beautiful gate. It's a work of art. Too bad there'll never be another like it.' "

"Yes. It is too bad, isn't it? And too bad about the chapel, too."

Her expression grew guarded. "What do you mean?"

"I mean, too bad it burned. Now Reverend Deering will have to start over."

"That chapel was never Reverend Deering's idea, anyway. Tessa Bright wanted it, so she could be close to her friends, the Indians, and close to the preacher, too."

"Oh?" The idea amused him. "And how do you figure that?"

"She wants the handsome preacher all to herself and everyone's attention focused on her." She nodded knowingly. "She was that way when her husband was alive, too. Always throwing it up in my face that I didn't have the fancy things she did, like that gate."

As far as Will knew, Tessa had never exchanged more than two words at a time with Trudy Babcock over the years. The woman was clearly addled. It was time to put an end to this conversation, he decided. He straightened and took a step toward Trudy. "If you know what's good for you, you'll leave Tessa Bright alone," he growled.

"And what if I don't?" She tried to look fierce, but he could feel her fear.

"I'll tell everyone the truth—that you set fire to the Indian chapel." He didn't give her time to think on that, or to come up with some clever denial. He merely nodded in dismissal and disappeared.

Trudy Babcock collapsed in a dead faint on the kitchen floor.

• • •

Micah wondered if traveling for him would always involve leaving someplace behind. He was always leaving, never making his way toward a place where someone waited to welcome him. In every place he left—the Kiowa village, his aunt's home, the Army forts, and now Tessa Bright's ranch—some small part of him stayed behind. Would he soon be wandering the earth as only half a man, with a soul as empty and drained as the walking dead?

Tessa had taken the biggest part of him yet, a part of him he wondered if he would ever learn to do without. He gripped the reins tighter and marshaled his will against the dark thoughts. He just had to keep riding. Today and tomorrow and the next day, just riding.

He glanced down at the roan mare. Taking her had been a mistake. He couldn't look at her without remembering Tessa. This was the horse who had always wanted to head back to the ranch, the way his own spirit still wanted to. He'd have to sell her, in the first town he came to. He leaned over and smoothed the dark red mane, tangling his fingers in the horsehair the way he'd twined them in Tessa's long locks. If only he could trade his memories as easily as the horse.

Without warning, the mare shied. Her front feet came off the ground as she reared back, then came down hard, her back legs kicking out. Micah clamped his legs tight and searched the ground for signs of a snake or cactus or some other reason for the docile mare's sudden excitement. She twirled and bucked, frantic now, eyes rolled back in her head. Micah's head snapped back, then forward. He left the saddle and slammed down into it again with bone-jarring force. The mare shot up again, bowing her back in the middle, then straightening out, sending him flying.

He landed with a thud, all the breath knocked out of him, the world a gray haze around him. He blinked, struggling to inhale, and things gradually swam back into focus. But the sight he saw made him groan and close his eyes again.

"I reckon you'll live."

He opened his eyes again. Yes, that was Will Bright standing over him. "Haven't you plagued me enough?" Micah asked.

"Not nearly enough." Will folded his arms over his chest. *"Get up."*

Micah shoved himself to his feet, ignoring his protesting head. He avoided Will's gaze, instead looking at the mare, who stood grazing a hundred yards away.

"Afraid she'll run away again?" Will said. *"Didn't you train her well enough?"*

Micah kept silent. He didn't have anything to say to the old man—ghost—whatever he was.

"I trained Tessa well." Will walked around to stand in front of him, his feet making no sound, leaving no tracks in the dust of the road. *"I didn't realize it at the time, but I trained her to stand on her own two feet, so when the time came for her to be alone, she didn't really need me anymore."* He paused a moment. In the silence, Micah could hear the mare's teeth tearing at the grass. *"What she did need was a young man by her side, to work with her, not over her."* Will sighed, a sound like wind in the trees. *"It took me a while to see it, but now I know she needed you."*

Micah looked up, into old eyes that looked as if they'd seen everything. "You were right the first time. I'm the last thing she needs."

"She needed you last night, didn't she?"

Micah flushed. "How—"

"I wasn't there to see, but I know Tessa well enough by now." He nodded. *"Even better now. All those earthly passions get in the way of knowledge sometimes. It took me a while to let go of a lot of that, but I'm learning."*

The rage Micah had refused to give in to before now rose up inside him. "You haven't learned anything if you can't see what living with me would do to Tessa. Those people in town, the ones whose opinions matter so much, would hate her because of me."

To his amazement, the old man smiled. *"Maybe some would. The kind of people whose good opinion she doesn't need."*

"She thinks she needs it."

"You don't give her enough credit."

"I didn't ask your opinion." He started toward the mare. The sooner he got back on the road, the better. The old ghost couldn't follow him clear across the country, could he?

Will watched him, frowning. When he'd decided to come after Fox, he'd thought it would be easy to persuade him to return. All he saw when he looked in the man's eyes was pain and love for Tessa. The vision had jolted him at first, made him angry even. But he'd been handed an extra measure of wisdom these past few days, and he knew now what he had to do.

"Fine, go on," he said. *"Leave Tessa to face things on her own."*

Fox's steps faltered. "She's a strong woman. People will forget me soon enough."

"Tell that to the mob headed to the ranch."

Fox whirled to face him again. "What mob?"

Will shook his head. *"You waited too late to leave. The townspeople have already made up their minds. They're marching out there right now. But what do you care?"* He made a motion like shooing chickens. *"Go on."*

Will turned away, but he heard Micah close the distance between them in three long strides. "How big a mob? What do they intend to do?"

"I didn't stop to count heads and I didn't bother to ask their intentions. I thought you'd want to help her, but I guess I was wrong."

"You're wrong about a lot of things, but not this one."

Will turned in time to see Micah vault into the saddle. *I always wanted to be able to do that,* he thought.

Micah spurred the horse and took off. Will had to hurry to catch up with him. They left the road and raced cross-country. Will began to regret telling Fox the lie. He was liable to ruin a good horse in his haste.

Little more than two hours later, they reached the ranch gate. Stunned, Will stared at the cloud of dust approaching. A mob of buggies, wagons, and horses crowded the road to the ranch. Men and women filled the vehicles, armed with shovels and axes and hammers. The mob he'd predicted had indeed arrived!

Fox rode up to block the gate. He turned to the mob, his face set as if stone. Any one of the group might have shot him, but the terrifying anger in his eyes stilled them. "What's this about?" he demanded.

A woman worked her way to the front. Margery Finch, looking as beautiful as ever in a brown-and-black riding habit, announced, "We've come to rebuild the chapel."

"We're not going to let one hateful person ruin the reputation of our whole town." Ammie Smith stepped up beside Margery.

The sound of an approaching rider echoed down the drive. Will and Micah turned to watch Tessa ride toward them. The look of joy in Fox's eyes made Will sick with envy. But as Tessa neared, the joy faded, replaced by sharp pain.

"What's happening?" She reined in on the opposite side of the gate and looked at the townspeople, confused. "What is going on? Why are you all here?"

"After you left the meeting, Mrs. Finch made everyone see the error of their ways," Miss Smith said.

Tessa turned to Margery. "What did you say?"

"I simply pointed out that most of us aren't in any position to cast stones when it comes to the question of character." She looked at old man Thornton and Jackie Babcock. Most of the men had the grace to look sheepish.

Gabe Emerson pushed his way to the front of the crowd. "We worked hard building that chapel. We can't let some criminal destroy it."

Tessa raised one eyebrow. "Even if it's for the Indians?" she asked.

He flushed, but gave a curt nod. "I reckon church might do 'em some good."

"Come on, everyone. We have work to do." Ammie Smith unfastened the gate. Fox helped her swing it wide. The crowd streamed through, Margery riding in last, pausing and bending down to draw Tessa close in a hug.

At last, Tessa and Fox were alone, facing each other, one on either side of the entrance. They were both silent for so long, Will wondered if he'd have to step in. But at last, Tessa found her voice. "Why did you leave?" she asked.

"I couldn't stay. I'll only bring you trouble."

"I've had my share of trouble, and it hasn't killed me yet."

"Don't even joke about that." He looked down the drive, toward the retreating crowd. "Maybe burning the chapel was only the beginning. Maybe next time whoever did that will burn your house."

"And maybe tomorrow I'll discover gold in the creek and be a millionaire." She sighed. "We can't live our lives on maybes, dreading what might be."

He shook his head. "It's too much to ask."

She bowed her head a moment, as if considering or praying. "Come to the house with me," she said at last. "I want to show you something."

Without waiting for an answer, she turned and rode up the drive. Fox looked after her for a long moment, then followed, pausing to close the gate behind him. Will trailed along last.

They left their horses in the yard and went into the house and up the stairs, neither speaking, though Fox never stopped looking at Tessa. The set of her shoulders told Will she knew he was watching her; she knew and she wanted him to keep watching.

She scarcely paused in the doorway to her bedroom, but walked straight to the trunk at the end of the bed and opened it. Quilts, blankets, dresses, and bundles of old letters collected on the bed as she searched for the one thing she needed. Fox waited in the doorway, but Will watched over Tessa's shoulder, though her actions puzzled him. When she finally withdrew a small silver case, he didn't recognize it at first.

"Look inside," she instructed, handing the case to Fox.

Carefully, like a man approaching a caged rattlesnake, Fox opened the case and stared at its contents, a single daguerreotype of a man and woman in Sunday clothes. The woman, scarcely a girl really, stared at the camera, wide-eyed and nervous in a ruffled dress of some stiff dark fabric. The man struck a proud pose, decked out in a three-piece suit and silver-topped cane, his long, dark braids and coppery skin the only incongruity in the image.

Fox stared. He put one finger out to touch the girl's face. "This is you?" he asked.

She nodded. "It was taken on my wedding day."

Fox turned his attention to the man in the photo. "Then Will is—was—Indian?"

Tessa came to stand behind him, sharing his view of the photo. "He was full-blooded Choctaw. Their village was near ours, and many of their people worked in town. Even though he was Indian, and so much older than me, I fell in love with him." The tenderness in her voice moved Will. So after all this time, Tessa still believed she'd made the right choice.

"And you became an outcast when you married him?"

"Maybe." She raised her eyes to meet his. "But I think I let my pride hurt me almost as much as other people's prejudice. One person snubbed me in a place, and I would never go back there to give anyone else another chance. My family threw me out, and I never contacted them again. Maybe they wouldn't have forgiven me, but maybe they would. People say things in the heat of anger they don't mean in their hearts." She took the picture and folded it closed again. "I'm not saying we can make prejudice go away by ignoring it. But we shouldn't magnify it larger than it is."

Micah shook his head. "I can't do anything that might endanger you."

She laid the picture inside the trunk and lowered the lid. "If you're still worried about the fire, I don't think the fire had anything to do with the Indians," she said.

Fox looked puzzled. "Why do you say that?"

"I think Trudy Babcock set that fire. Not because she hates Indians, but because she can't stand for me to have any attention. The chapel is on my land, so naturally it draws attention to me."

Fox nodded, slowly. "I remember she was there the day Sun Bear talked about how fire could burn up the chapel."

"She's always been jealous of me. She wanted that gate the first day she set eyes on it, and everyone had to pass through it to get to the chapel."

"What will you do about her?"

She shrugged. "She's a coward at heart. I'll casually let her know that I know she set fire to the chapel, and that will be it."

He frowned. "That won't stop her hating you."

She reached out and took his hands. "Micah, what other people think and do doesn't matter to me anymore. It took me a long time, but I've finally learned that I can only worry about me and what I do. I have to live my life the way I feel called to live it. And that's with you."

"Reverend Deering said whatever your calling is, you can't *not* do it. Every path you take leads you right back to it." He squeezed her hands. "No matter how many times I set out to leave, I always end up back here, just like that runaway horse."

She smiled. "Maybe somebody's trying to tell you something."

He pulled her close, cradling her head on his shoulder. "I love you, Tessa Bright."

"I love you, Micah Fox." She smiled into his shoulder. "I can't seem to help myself."

He stroked her hair, over and over, as if he couldn't quite believe the softness of it. "Would you give me another chance?" he asked. "Will you take me as your husband?"

Eyes shining, she raised her head to look at him. "I'll take you. And I'll keep you. Forever."

Will left them as they joined in a kiss. Contentment filled his soul. He could rest well now, knowing he'd done this one thing right in his life.

Epilogue

Tessa frowned at her reflection in the mirror and adjusted her veil. "Do I look all right?" she asked.

"For the hundredth time, you look lovely." Margery smiled and patted her shoulder. "Everything will be perfect."

There was a knock on the door. "Is the bride ready?" Alan Finch asked.

"I'm ready." Tessa picked up her bouquet from the dresser, fighting butterflies in her stomach. Why was she so nervous? After all, she'd done this before.

Alan smiled and took her arm. He looked handsome in his dress blue uniform. Together, he and Margery made a stunning, and stunningly happy, couple. Margery collected her own bouquet and led the way out the bedroom door and down the stairs.

As they approached the first landing, Tessa could see the crowd gathered below. Ammie Smith smiled up at her, while Ada Drake nodded approvingly. Gabe Emerson, who'd recently taken a job as a cabinetmaker, looked uncomfortable in a shiny blue suit, but Emmett

Hardy was quite dapper in his black coat. Mamie Tucker fussed with her two youngest children. Everywhere she looked, Tessa saw familiar faces, people she knew as neighbors and friends.

Then Alan led her around the corner, and she had her first look at Micah and Reverend Deering, waiting in front of the parlor stove. She caught her breath at the sight of the man who a few minutes from now would be her husband. He wore his hair down, as she'd asked him to, and a new dark suit enlivened by a beaded belt, a gift from Sun Bear. But even his everyday work clothes would have been made special by the smile with which he greeted her, a smile that spoke of all the love he had for her, and the love they would share in the future.

Reverend Deering greeted her with a smile, too. Already he had grown tan from so much work out-of-doors. Instead of rebuilding the chapel, he had persuaded the townspeople to use their resources to construct the new library. He said he intended to conduct his services in the open, or in tepees, or wherever the Indians needed him to be.

Alan handed Tessa over to Micah, then Reverend Deering began speaking. She scarcely heard the words of the ceremony. All her attention was focused on the man beside her, the man she would cherish for the rest of their lives. She hoped they'd grow old together.

"I now pronounce you man and wife," Reverend Deering said. "You may kiss the bride."

Micah bent and gave her a chaste peck on the cheek. "You'll have to do better than that," Gabe Emerson crowed.

Smiling, he pulled her close and kissed her soundly, his lips lingering over hers long enough to draw cheers and catcalls from the guests. When he finally released her, she was flushed and smiling, a secret smile that told him she was looking forward to the time when they would be alone once more.

Later, after the guests had toasted the happy couple

over cake and coffee, Micah and Tessa walked up the hill behind the house. Already the trees were beginning to brown, and the afternoon breeze hinted at autumn soon to come.

With Micah at her side, Tessa knelt and placed her bouquet on Will's grave. She stepped back and surveyed the grave, filled with thankfulness that things had turned out the way they had—not that Will had died, but that they'd all been allowed this second chance at happiness.

Micah took her hand. "Do you think he's really resting in peace now?" he asked.

She smiled up at her husband. "Yes."

"How can you be sure?"

She put her hand over her heart. "I feel it. His work here is done." She glanced back at the grave, at the flowers and the simple stone. The marker was new. Reverend Deering had helped her select the words carved there, words that filled her with contentment: *Here lies a man who followed his calling with a cheerful heart and a willing spirit.*

"Amen," she whispered, and turned to walk back down the hill with Micah, to begin their new life together.

Presenting all-new romances—featuring ghostly
heroes and heroines and the passions they inspire.

Haunting Hearts

__*A SPIRITED SEDUCTION*
by Casey Claybourne   0-515-12066-9/$5.99

__*STARDUST OF YESTERDAY*
by Lynn Kurland   0-515-11839-7/$6.50

__*A GHOST OF A CHANCE*
by Casey Claybourne   0-515-11857-5/$5.99

__*ETERNAL VOWS*
by Alice Alfonsi   0-515-12002-2/$5.99

__*ETERNAL LOVE*
by Alice Alfonsi   0-515-12207-6/$5.99

__*ARRANGED IN HEAVEN*
by Sara Jarrod   0-515-12275-0/$5.99

Prices slightly higher in Canada

TIME PASSAGES